MW00626796

Windy

Book Three of The Weather Girls

Jennifer Lynn Cary

Tandem Services Press

44

What Readers Are Saying

The Crockett Chronicles

"I love historical novels and this one did not disappoint. I was caught up from the first sentence and completely in love with the Crocketts by the end. Can't wait to follow along their next journey. Well done!" –Virginia Denise

"This is an amazing story of families that went through the wars - fighting against Catholics & Protestants and the problems the Protestants had. There is danger but more of life mainly about 1 family but with others also.Their faith in Jesus Christ keeps them strong when things happen. While at the same time, Joseph keeps having doubts - but he is not the only one."—bets29

"I love this book! The story is soooooo engaging! I can hardly put it down!"—DeNage

Tales of the Hob Nob Annex Café

"This is a well written book that hooks you on the first page. It's a very enjoyable read that makes you forget about all your troubles and step back in time. I loved this book and look forward to what this author writes next." –Ann Ferri

"Cute story of a young woman who goes to visit her grandmother in an assisted living home. She gets lost in the halls and meets a sweet couple who tells her stories of their cafe, The Hob Nob Annex Cafe. Can the stories all be true? Will her editor like them? Clean Christian read. Novella length." –Nana698

"I loved reading this book! It had me intrigued from the first page, and as the stories began, I could hardly wait to turn the page to see what happened next! Love the mix of true facts mixed with some good, clean, fun fiction! Easy, quick read. I highly recommend this book!" –CatSmit

The Relentless Series

"I lost my heart in this book, caught up in the lives of each character. I remember these times, which made it more real to me. I had tears of joy, tears of sorrow, grief, and smiles in the unexpected. Great story and hard to put down. Keep reading.... You won't regret it."—Novabelle

"I enjoyed another book by Jennifer Cary! As with all her books the story held your attention from the beginning to the end and I look forward to reading all her future books!"—Mary Rima

"I live in Indiana so I know of the places this book talks about. I so absolutely LOVED this story. It's the first one in this series I've read. I'm glad because I feel it should be the first book as it tells of the 2 families & how they connect. It so touched my heart that at times I cried. I couldn't put it down after starting it so anxious to know how things would turn out with all the difficulties Val & Jimmy had. I'm sure the other books in this series are equally as great."—Pat

"This book will make you laugh and will make you cry it is beautifully written and the last of the Relentless series Jennifer lynn Cary covers all the characters in the series and I hated for the series to end but I am sure Jenny will write more good books for us to read." –Peggy Baldwin

The Traveling Prayer Shawl

"When her sister's inheritance depends on it, Cami must do the thing she resolved she'd never do, the thing which will break her heart as well as add one more tough task to her already overstuffed calendar. She must fulfill her grandmother's last request - and what's more, there's a deadline that puts in jeopardy her major project at work. As she begins working on the request, she finds even more complications. The inheritance may raise a conflict of interests. How Cami negotiates these and other potential pitfalls made for an interesting and warmhearted story.Although I read more historical fiction than contemporary, I loved this gentle novel. It left me with a strong desire for a prayer shawl of my own. If you find yourself longing for such a garment, crochet instructions are included in the book.Recommended to those who enjoy Christian Women's Fiction and readers who enjoy Debbie Macomber's stories."—Dana McNeely

"I loved this book so much I hated for it to end!"—Cindy

Also by Jennifer Lynn Cary

The Crockett Chronicles Series:
The Patriarch: Book 1
The Sojourners: Book 2
The Prodigal: Book 3
Tales of the Hob Nob Annex Café
The Relentless Series:
Relentless Heart
Wedding Bell Blues
Relentless Joy
Silver Bell Christmas
The Traveling Prayer Shawl
The Weather Girls Trilogy:
Sunny: Book 1
Stormy: Book 2
Windy: Book 3
Nonfiction:
When God Holds Your Hand (a devotional)

Copyright © 2021 by Jennifer Lynn Cary

Published by Tandem Services Press

Post Office Box 220

Yucaipa, California

www.TandemServicesInk.com

All rights reserved. No portion of this book may be reproduced in any form without written permission from the publisher or author, except as permitted by U.S. copyright law.

Print ISBN 978-1-954986-61-9
Ebook ISBN 978-1-954986-64-0

Scripture quotations marked MSG are taken from THE MESSAGE, copyright ©

1993, 2002, 2018 by Eugene H. Peterson. Used by permission of NavPress. All rights reserved. Represented by Tyndale House Publishers, Inc. THE HOLY BIBLE, NEW INTERNATIONAL VERSION®, NIV® Copyright © 1973, 1978, 1984, 2011 by Biblica, Inc.® Used by permission. All rights reserved worldwide.

This book is a work of fiction. Names, characters, places, and incidents are either products of the author's imagination or used fictitiously. Any similarity to actual people, organizations, and/or events is purely coincidental.

Cover design by London Montgomery Covers

Dedicated to my three beautiful, strong, and brilliant daughters,
Jaime, Alyssa and Meg.
You each are a delight, and I couldn't be prouder of you.
I love you dearly. Thank you for making me a mom.

And in memory of Dino Volikas
who kindly laughed at my joke.

... and to comfort all who mourn,
To care for the needs of all who mourn in Zion,
give them bouquets of roses instead of ashes,
Messages of joy instead of news of doom,
a praising heart instead of a languid spirit...
Isaiah 61:3a MSG

Contents

1. Prologue   1

2. Chapter 1   3

3. Chapter 2   17

4. Chapter 3   33

5. Chapter 4   47

6. Chapter 5   61

7. Chapter 6   75

8. Chapter 7   89

9. Chapter 8   103

10. Chapter 9   117

11. Chapter 10   131

12. Chapter 11   145

13. Chapter 12   161

14. Chapter 13   177

15. Chapter 14   193

16. Chapter 15   207

17. Epilogue   219

Acknowledgements: 225

Author's Note   227

About the Author   231

Sneak Peak of Relentless Heart   233

Sneak Preview of Cheryl's Going Home   247

Prologue

A aron Day drew the pink blanket aside from the tiny, scrunched face. His third daughter. As beautiful as her sisters, she tried to take in her entire surroundings through her large eyes. This little girl would be the curious one, he could tell already. Her stare drank in his features as if she memorized every wrinkle. All the while her tiny fist gripped his pinkie, conquering his heart. Funny how her hair was so much darker than Sunny's and Stormy's. She had a look all her own.

He strode to the window, staring out at the June gloom, the marine cloud layer that the westerly breezes brought about when they mixed with the moist air over the ocean. The winds pulled it in and then blew it out, the ocean's breath playing through the sky.

Wind. Windy. That was it. "Cheryl, I've got her name."

His wife lay with her eyes closed, though he knew she was still awake. "I'm afraid to ask."

"Windy June."

Her lids opened wide, like her daughter's. "Oh, Aaron, why must you do this to your girls? If she'd been a boy, I could've named her something normal."

"Hey, we agreed. Besides, they're special California girls and need unique names." He raised his pinkie. Windy continued to grab hold, never breaking eye contact.

"You're a good father, but they're going to resent you one of these days." She put her forearm over her eyes. "I never should have agreed to let you name our daughters."

"Cheryl, watch her. She's in a staring contest with me, her tiny fist is tight on my finger."

"I'm hurting here, Aaron. Can't you find the nurse to give me something? This gets harder each time." She rolled to her side.

"Sure, hon. Be right back. Here, hold the baby." He set Windy in Cheryl's arms. Maybe then she'd become excited about their newest family addition.

But his wife didn't snuggle in like he expected. Perhaps she was in too much pain. He needed to find the nurse, get her some help. Then he'd enjoy this precious little bundle as long as they let him.

His mother had flown out to care for their other girls, two-year-old Sunny May and one-year-old Stormy April (who started running at nine months to keep up with her older sister). Three daughters, two years of age and younger. That'll be a handful, no doubt about it. But what an amazing blessing.

After locating the charge nurse, Aaron returned to his wife's room and gathered baby Windy, settling in a chair to continue the staring match.

He could only imagine what flashed through her little brain.

Chapter 1
Saturday, October 31, 1970, Kokomo, Indiana

W indy pulled her shawl closer. It was more for fashion than function anyway. The Hoosier evening on the balcony had chilled.

Kris stood close, his arm snaking around her.

That was kind of strange. They were just friends, or she thought they were until Heather was born. Then she began to notice stuff. Little things. Protective in nature. Still, he never pushed for more in their relationship. So maybe she read something he didn't intend. The bottom line? Kris Norman was a nice guy.

Proved by his gentle side-embrace against the chill.

"Look, the first star of the evening. Make a wish." He pointed while his breath tickled her ear.

Windy obediently closed her eyes, wishing the one thing she hadn't confided to a soul. She didn't risk a prayer about it. As if God couldn't figure out what went on in her brain. Even so, the idea was remote. She wasn't about to share it with anyone.

She relaxed against Kris's secure frame—well over six-feet tall. Sturdy and muscular. "Did you make your wish?"

He nodded. "Don't ask."

"I won't. Some things aren't meant for sharing."

She heard a giggle behind her and glanced over her shoulder.

Her sisters were giving brother-in-law Rob what for. Stormy and Rob renewed their wedding vows this evening, so the ensuing party was in their honor. Still, Windy was only two weeks out from having given birth to baby Heather. She'd returned to her job as the creative partner at *The Weather Girls Wedding Shoppe and Venue*, without allowing herself much recovery time. Didn't Pearl S. Buck say the Chinese women returned to the fields mere hours after delivery?

Windy was healthy. She could jump back in. Why not?

Ever since they'd opened their company, she'd lived with her sisters above their business in one bedroom. One cramped bedroom.

Tonight, though, Stormy'd go home with Rob to live across the street in their new Tudor-style, three-bedroom-two-bath.

Sunny was officially engaged to Pat. By next May, they would be married and setting their household up in Ferguson House, the old mansion that housed their company.

That left her with a deadline to move elsewhere.

But where does a single mother go with her baby? Fortunately, she'd been planning with Gramma.

"I'd better get Heather. Feels like it's time to feed her." Windy was still becoming used to the nursing routine, though it had improved from when she started. If only her tiny one would sleep longer than four hours at a stretch so she could rest too. That would be wonderful.

Kris escorted her inside to where Gramma cooed over her great grandchild.

"How's she doing?" Windy leaned in, stroking the infant's hair that was lightening from the nearly black it had been at birth. Dad said she'd started off with the same dark tufts only to have it turn auburn before falling out, leaving her basically bald until she was almost two. When it grew in, it was white blonde and stayed that way. He bet her Heather's baby fuzz would do the same. She passed on that. Dad was too sure of himself.

"She's a sweet little angel. Oh, she's waking." Gramma kissed Heather's forehead.

"I had a notion." Windy's arm scrunched next to her breast noting she was full. "Time to feed her again. I'll take her to our room. See you in a bit."

"If you have to, I guess." Gramma handed the bundle over. "Nothing like baby warmth to make you relax."

"Maybe I need to check her diaper too?" Windy winked drawing Heather close.

"Oh, you." Gramma swatted the air. "You know what I meant."

"I do. We'll be back." Windy carried the baby from the third-floor ballroom, down the stairs to her bedroom on the second floor. The room appeared like a tornado had hit, but with everything happening to get ready for Stormy and Rob's service and party, cleaning private quarters was a low priority.

Windy got comfortable on her bed, Sunny's cat Frazier joining her at the foot to stand guard. She undid her blouse and nursing bra and got Heather started. Curling up with her daughter while she fed her helped her relax, which allowed her milk to come down, which encouraged her baby to feed enough to grow. She'd already regained what she lost those first few days, surpassing her birth weight. Dr. Schwartz said they were both doing fine.

However, as she glanced about the room, it grew obvious. This season of the *Weather Girls* living together must end. Sunny would be stressed at this mess. Stormy had packed most of her belongings in the suitcases and boxes scattered about the floor. She'd return tomorrow after church to walk them to her new place.

Then it'd just be Windy and Sunny in here—and Heather. Who liked to make sure everyone woke when she did. Sunny and Stormy never complained, at least not to her face. Yet they all dealt with the strain of not sleeping straight through to morning.

"Sweet girl, do you think you might give your old mom a break tonight? Mommy and Aunt Sunny are pretty tired from getting Aunt Stormy's shindig together. I'd really appreciate it, lovey."

Heather pulled away, her mouth sheened a milky white, her eyes capturing her mother's gaze. Then she closed her lids and latched back on.

Windy couldn't tell if her daughter agreed to the request or merely asked, "Are you kidding?" with her stare.

Sleep was what she craved. She hadn't had a restful night since she came home from the hospital. Maybe she should've held off a few days getting back to work, but her sisters needed her. Plus, she must prove she's responsible enough to do this single parent thing.

Someone touched her shoulder. Her eyes flew open.

Sunny stood over her. "Didn't mean to wake you, hon. Sorry." She leaned across Windy to stroke Heather's cheek.

"Hadn't planned to doze. What time is it?" The baby lay snoozing against her, no longer attached. Windy fixed her clothes.

"It's eight. You weren't out long. About half an hour. Kris said you were down here."

"If you lift her, I can get up. My arm's fallen asleep."

Sunny scooped up the little one who slept right through. "She's so warm and snuggly."

"I know. She didn't take the other breast. I'm going to feel lopsided. Think anyone will notice?" She shook her arm to gain sensation, not waiting for Sunny's answer. "I almost want to wake her now, so she'll sleep better tonight."

"Nah, there's plenty of people upstairs who'll hold her and pass her around. She'll wake on her own with all that." She pulled Heather close. "Makes me want to get married immediately and start working on a family."

"Seriously?"

"Not enough to change my wedding date, but the thought has crossed my mind." Sunny grinned at her.

"Maybe I should let you take care of her tonight. Then I could catch some sleep." Windy yawned. The nap only made her more aware of her exhaustion.

"I'd do it in a heartbeat if I had working equipment. This nursing only thing is convenient, but it means you're the only one who can supply her diet. Want me to take her back up and give you a minute?" Sunny swayed side to side while she spoke.

No need to supply a reason for them to figure she couldn't do this. "I'm ready. Let's go." She made one last glance in the mirror to make sure she'd buttoned correctly and didn't have milk stains on her bodice. That's when she glimpsed her face. Or what purported to be her face. A stranger with purple rings beneath her eyes and a sleep scar running the side of her jaw stared back. Lovely.

Another hour and the party began to break up. Everyone followed Stormy and Rob as they descended the staircase to the first floor, exited through the front, and crossed the street to the sweet Tudor Rob bought for Stormy. The family filled the porch, watching as he carried his wife over the threshold. Their cue to disperse for their homes.

All but Sunny, Pat, and Kris kissed Windy's cheek and Heather's forehead before climbing into cars. Kris hung back, waiting for the others to clear before giving Windy a quick hug and letting the now awake Heather grab his index finger.

"She gets stronger each day." He gazed at the baby, a soft smile teasing his lips.

"Yeah. You'll be at church tomorrow?" Kris started attending in the summer, though he never spoke about God or his thoughts on religion. Windy didn't even know if he was a believer. He was just a nice guy.

"Sure." He slipped his finger from Heather's grasp. "I'll see you then." With his hands shoved in his pockets, Kris headed around the side of the house to the rear parking lot where he always left his truck.

"I think he's smitten."

Windy turned to Sunny, who'd stepped beside her. "Kris? I doubt it. We're just good friends."

"Perhaps. Hey, I'm going to sit out here with Pat for a while. I promise to be quiet when I come in."

Windy nodded. Maybe Heather'd nurse her other side and fall back asleep. If she slipped her daughter into the cradle, she might catch enough sleep to chase away that stranger in the mirror.

Morning came early. Especially when she'd been awakened twice in the night by her hungry daughter. Now it was time for church. Windy used extra Max Factor concealer under her eyes to hide what seemed like bruises at this point. No need to attract attention.

Sunny drove, the car seat Gramma picked up at a yard sale attached in the back. Windy chose to sit with Heather in case she needed something.

Everyone else had filed into their pew. Gramma saved a seat next to her, so she had an easy time capturing the baby. Windy was on to her tricks. Fine. Let her cuddle with her first great grandchild.

After the service, Gramma held Windy aside to talk a moment. "I can see you've tried to cover with makeup, but I'm afraid you're overdoing. I've an idea. Let's go to *K-Mart* and buy a breast pump. That'll not only allow someone else to feed Heather, but it'll also help your milk stay strong. Then I'll watch my sweet great granddaughter while you work. I'm happy to come get her in the morning since you don't have a car, hon. It's getting chilly out and you shouldn't be walking her over as it gets colder. Want to try that?"

Would they think she was passing off her responsibility by accepting Gramma's offer? It'd help knowing Heather was safe so she could concentrate on her job. "Okay. I can't have you feeling like I'm dumping on you though."

"I don't feel that at all. We'll go right after dinner."

Sunday dinner. Not that she'd forgotten, but she'd forgotten. So much for a nap. "Sounds good. Thank you, Gramma."

Pat stayed in Gramma's spare bedroom, like he always did when he came up for the weekend. It was the normal state of affairs until he stopped working for his father in Indianapolis and opened his own law practice in Kokomo next summer. But Windy's old room, once shared with her sisters, was still available. Maybe if she claimed the baby needed feeding, which was true, she could slip up there and catch a nap while Sunny and Stormy helped Gramma in the kitchen. Not her most responsible idea. Yet, it was that or fall asleep with her head in her mashed potatoes.

"I'll be back. Time to feed you-know-who." She tried to sound as nonchalant as possible, hoping they wouldn't catch on to her cat-nap plan.

"No problem, sweetie. Someone will get you when dinner is ready." Gramma threw her a wink as she peeled a spud.

Windy never could get anything past her.

Sunday, November 1, 1970

KRIS PARKED IN FRONT of Hazel and Gramps's.

When they'd married last spring, his grandfather moved into Hazel's house and left his to Kris to live in rent free. Said it'd give him a chance to get his life moving in the right direction. It helped.

Also made it hard to say no to Gramps's one request—attend church and join them for Sunday dinner each week. Considering the whole family attended the service and meal, he wasn't stuck out on a limb with a solo jump. Everyone dove into that pool. He just didn't get what all the splashing was about. However, if Gramps was happy, fine by him.

Guess everyone else had arrived. Might as well put in his appearance.

As he mounted the front steps, his brain flipped through all the personalities he'd find inside. Why was Windy the only person he could hold a conversation with? A couple weeks ago when he and Rob fixed that broken water heater, they worked together for several hours, even shopped for the new one, and he still didn't feel like they were more than a couple guys doing the same job. Rob was okay, but real brainy. Guess if you're a school principal, that's what you have to be. Kris was sure brainiacs were the secret cause of hives.

He opened the front door. It was time to face the intellectuals.

"Hey, Kris is here. Come on in the den. We've got the pregame on. Vikings verses the Lions." At least Gramps was glad to see him.

One seat was left, on the couch next to Pat. Great.

Not that Pat wasn't cool. He was so brainy Kris wondered if they belonged to the same species. The dude was more than a lawyer. He was a high powered one in Indianapolis, working corporate law for his father's multi-billion-dollar conglomerate, Whitcomb Enterprises.

And he was walking away come May. For the woman he loved.

Money wasn't everything. Still, perhaps he wasn't so smart after all.

Aaron, Hazel's son, slipped him a bowl of chips. "Don't let Mom catch you with these before dinner. I'm too hungry to wait, but she'll have a conniption." He winked.

He might like Aaron. If the guy stuck around long enough. He seemed mellow, not professor smart but way talented. Kris respected talent. Maybe that's why he and Windy hit it off. She probably got it from her musician dad. He shook his head. Mind blowing—to work with the likes of Brian Wilson and Sergio Mendez. Bet he had stories.

Bet he didn't go to college to learn to do that either.

Hazel wandered in, giving Gramps a kiss on top of his crown before he pulled her onto his lap. They acted like newlyweds. Okay, so they were. It was just sorta funny at their age.

Oops. Kris tried setting the chip bowl on the floor to the side of the sofa, but she spotted him.

"I've got a lovely meal nearly done for you fellas and you're sneaking snacks?"

Kris thought his head might blow like the top of a too hot thermometer. Even his cheeks wanted to throb. Had Aaron set him up?

"Mom, your meals are wonderful, but we could starve waiting here. Besides, chips go with the kick-off. Right, guys?" Aaron motioned for the rest of the males to join him.

His mother changed her tune. How did sons and mothers do that? True, he'd done it with his own. Guess it never stopped.

Unless you were hundreds of miles apart.

"Well, Kris, don't let them corrupt you. I wonder about these fellas." Hazel winked, kissed Gramps again, and left the testosterone-filled room.

The game didn't officially start until one and the pregame stuff was filler. Kris figured this was the male method for keeping out of trouble and not getting roped into anything uncomfortable.

Pat turned from the TV commercial where Sammy Davis, Jr. sang about plopping and fizzing with an orchestra background. "Hey, did you catch that new comic strip this week? I think it's called Doomsbury, or something like that. It's about these guys in college, they call it Walden, but I noticed a lot of similarities to Yale."

"Yeah, I saw it too." Rob sat up. "That one about the computerized roommate picker cracked me up. Everything at my campus is going the way of technology." He held out his hand. "Hey, pass the chips down here."

Kris glanced where he'd set the bowl. There weren't many left, and he realized he'd been stuffing his face while his mind ran amok. He handed over the snacks but refused to meet Rob's gaze.

Pat continued. "I went to college with that writer, Garry Trudeau. He started a strip back then in the student news. Sorta like this, only it was called *Bull Tales*. Don't always agree with him, but he's got a knack for pointing things out. Bet this strip's gonna take off. Did you see it, Kris?"

He shook his head. "Been busy." No need to expand on that.

Sunny, Windy's sister, peeked around the door. "Dinner is served, gentlemen." She grinned.

The men all stood, Aaron stretched, and then they filed to the dining room.

Here was the best part of the whole deal, Hazel's cooking. And as long as he shoveled the food, he didn't have to talk. Because that's what happened at Hazel's table. A *lot* of talking.

He took his seat and noticed no Windy. He glanced at Gramps. "Is she here?"

Gramps nodded. Soon she appeared, yawning behind Stormy who brought a carry-chair-doohickey for the baby.

Hazel slipped Heather from Windy's arms and set her in the contraption. The little thing never opened her eyes. Just kept snoozing. Wonder what she dreamed about?

Gramps said the prayer and then they started passing dishes and heaping plates. This was one place where his appetite wasn't mentioned. The food was outstanding, everyone wanted some.

He glanced at Windy. She seemed more tired than she did this morning at church. Did she feel okay? Hope she's not getting sick or something.

"Kris?"

He jumped at the mention of his name. "Yes?"

"The corn, please?" Hazel nodded toward the bowl that sat on his left.

"Oh sure." He passed the dish to her as his neck sent heat waves racing to his brain. It was way too easy to get lost in one's thoughts when one didn't belong.

The chatter clamored around him. He continued to fork bite after bite to look busy. Another hour and he should be able to escape with no complaints.

That hour ticked by slower than slow. But once over, he made his proper goodbyes to Gramps and Hazel. Then found Windy stretched out on the living room sofa, Heather on her chest. They were having a staring contest.

"Who's winning?"

Windy grinned without breaking eye contact. "I don't know. I used to be the family champ, but I think this one might have me beat. Or maybe..."

He dropped in the nearby chair. "You could just be tired."

Her grin turned lopsided. "Yeah, probably." She broke off the competition. "Will you hold her while I sit back up?"

He reached over, lifting the tiny bundle, and snuggled her at his neck. Even if she'd grown the last two weeks, Heather still was an itty-bitty slip of weightlessness. He'd held sandwiches that weighed more.

"What are your plans?" Though she appeared sincere, he couldn't imagine why she had an interest. But she often asked and listened when he answered.

"I'm building a frame for some beach artwork for Mr. Hingst. For his office. He likes my wood and wrought iron stuff."

"What's not to like? That's wonderful. Maybe others will see it and ask about the artist." How'd she always know the perfect words to say?

"Hope that happens. What are you doing?"

"Gramma and I are going shopping. She has an idea and at this point I'm willing to try it." She rolled her lips over her teeth, and he knew she wasn't sold on the scheme.

"What's the problem?"

"She wants me to leave Heather with her while I work. That's why we're going shopping, for stuff so I can. But would she be doing this if I were married and working? I don't want special favors. I can do this." She cracked a small smile. "If I could catch enough sleep."

"If you were married and working, you'd have taken more time off. Can I help?" He hadn't meant to ask. But he was willing. Windy touched his heart like no other. And Heather? If that baby ever learned that she had him wrapped around her pinkie, he was a goner.

"Thanks. Not sure how right now. But don't be surprised if I ask." She reached for Heather.

He laid the baby in her arms, at once missing her warmth. "Any time. I'm heading out. Later."

In under ten minutes he was home, changed into grubbies, and in his garage working on the frame. The envelope that arrived yesterday still stared at him from the table where he'd left it.

He knew what his father's letter would say without opening it. Still, he couldn't just toss it out. Maybe it wouldn't say what he expected. He could always hope.

Kris slipped his Swiss Army knife from his pocket and slit open his father's latest message.

Why did he torture himself this way?

He smoothed the single sheet out on his worktable and ran his fingers slowly under the words.

It was the same argument. College. Important. Disappoint.

You'd think his old man would've given up. He'd been gone from high school for six years. What college would take him now? Sure, Dad had contacts and could probably get him in somewhere. And if he started at Indiana University's Kokomo campus, he could knock out that associate degree, making other universities more agreeable. In theory.

There were things he promised himself he'd never do again. Most could be avoided by not attending any institution of higher learning.

If only his dad would accept that with no explanation.

The phone rang.

"Hey."

"Son, just wanted to see if you received your dad's letter. We hadn't heard from you." Mom. Dad called in the big guns.

"I got it, just haven't had time to read it all." Was there something he missed?

His mother grew quiet. "We need an answer as soon as possible."

"You know I can't go back to school, Mom. I'm actually making some bread with my art. And the handyman stuff keeps me busy and meets my needs. I'm not starving." Please let that resolve all her questions.

"But what about Ralph?"

His palms began to sweat. "What about him?"

"Right, you said you hadn't read the whole thing. Your cousin Ralph would like to stop by to see you. He's moving to California and is asking for places to stay on his way. We told him we'd check with you."

Cousin Bane-of-My-Childhood-Existence Ralph? Just what he needed. That cretin crashing in his guestroom. "I doubt he wants to visit with me. He didn't enjoy hanging with me when we were kids. Why would he now?"

"I don't think he plans to hang with you, sweetie, he's just lining up places to stop and sleep before traveling on. He plans to leave New York City in the morning. He'll stay with us overnight tomorrow, so he could be to your place by Tuesday evening. Won't you let him, for me? He is your father's only sister's only child." Mom was super at the guilt stuff. No wonder Dad had her call.

"Sure, I guess. I can do one night."

"Good. Now suppose you catch me up on what's going on with my favorite son."

"I'm your only son, Mom."

"Are you limiting my choice from all the sons in the world? Seriously, Kris, you don't have to narrow the competition. You win." She giggled and he remembered why he loved his mother.

If she only understood what their secret was doing to him.

Chapter 2
Tuesday, November 3, 1970

Windy was on her second day of trying to work with Heather elsewhere. She'd broken down in tears three times yesterday, but only once today. So far. She couldn't even explain why she did. It was just that all at once she missed her baby and it overwhelmed everything else.

Fortunately, she'd been able to escape somewhere private each time and pull herself together, so no one saw her except for Frazier who seemed willing to curl up near while she pumped. Pumping ensured she was alone and also encouraged her tears. Cold water on her face, a retouch of makeup, though, and she was ready.

Until the next bout.

Heather handled her first outing yesterday like a champ. Windy knew she would. When she arrived after her walk to her grandmother's house, Gramma had Heather in her little carrier on the floor, rocking it with her foot while she washed dishes. She dropped a kiss on Gramma's cheek.

"How was your day, sweetie?" Gramma set the pan in the drainer.

"About to ask you the same thing. Did she cry much?" Windy stooped to trail her finger down the side of her daughter's face.

Gramma glanced down at her. "Nope. She slept fine. And she took everything you pumped. Do you have more?"

Windy pulled the sealed bottles from her shoulder bag and popped them in the fridge.

When the dishes were done, Windy bundled up Heather and Gramma drove them home.

That was yesterday.

Today she could've waited for her grandmother to show up at the mansion rather than traipse over, but Windy couldn't stand it any longer.

Instead she again sailed the same autumnal breeze of eagerness.

The walk did her good. Worked off some of that baby fat. Maybe it'd help her into her regular clothes a mite sooner.

Dry leaves crunched beneath her feet and the crisp air blew away those things that weighed on her. Not that the concerns wouldn't blow back to her shoulders. Still, it was a nice reprieve.

Gentle autumn currents tinged with fireplace scents and framed with fall colors in the trees and piles on the ground danced design ideas in her head. If she could only capture it all with her lens.

She'd put her camera into overtime with Heather. That child was photogenic. Windy had a collage planned for what she'd already taken. Maybe Kris would construct a frame to go with it for her. That'd be sweet. She'd print them in black and white. Give it a rustic look. She could dry some heather, use it to trail in between the photos. The more she pondered, the more she enjoyed the idea. It added umph to her steps.

Sunny mentioned before she left that they'd gotten a call. Someone wanted to reserve a Valentine's wedding. Said it was hush-hush, but that she'd like to see their package deals. Business was picking up. Some days no one called. More often than not, though, they received at least one. And some days several inquiries came in. Stormy gained skill with each client, zeroing on their tastes and preferences. It made Windy want to stretch her abilities as the artistic consultant.

Of course, every bride requested the old sycamore photo shoot in hopes a cardinal would land. Many lucked out. The rest never realized the bird on the branch was an ornament. Pat donated it to the cause. It kept the disappointment to a minimum. It also upped the delight when couples thought there were two. Not that Windy wanted to deceive. Still, how do you explain that to a bride-to-be? Tell her that the cardinal tradition didn't guarantee they'd experience a long, happy life?

Five more blocks and she'd be at Gramma's door, holding her baby again.

A second wind increased her energy and she picked up her pace. A couple school kids rode by on their bikes and waved. She was used to that. This was a friendly town. She tried to remember what it had been like living in Los Angeles. Busy. Big. Broken. That's all she could conjure. Dad always busy, her mother hid in their big house, and that broken leg. Yep. One thing she'd never forget.

Before she lost her balance, though, Windy'd never felt so free strolling atop the block fence in the back yard. And when she returned from the hospital wearing a cast, only to learn her mother left them, more than her leg was fractured.

Some things can't be forgotten no matter how hard one tries.

This wasn't the time to ruminate. Life and potential lay in front of her. She had the most beautiful daughter on the planet. When she pulled Heather close, everything in the world became golden. Even with her crying at 3:30 in the morning.

So, she needed to get this right. She'd catch up on sleep when Heather was older. For now, her goal was to plow through, prove she was capable.

She turned the corner and Gramma's house came in sight.

Mrs. Jordan, her grandmother's neighbor, waved from her front stoop where she put up fall decorations.

Windy waved back. When she was a teenager, Mrs. Jordan had her babysit for her daughter, Judy. She knew that place inside and out. About as well as Gramma's. It was the same floorplan.

Then she arrived. Skipping up the steps to the porch, she wiped her feet on the mat and let herself in. Fresh cookie aroma wafted past. No cinnamon or chocolate? Hm, maybe spritz? That was her favorite. Windy loved the Swedish pressed cookies, especially when Gramma made the pink and green ones for Christmas—the pink were supposed to be red but they never were that vibrant. But boy howdy, they tasted yummy.

With crossed fingers, she hustled to the kitchen.

Gramma was pulling a tray from the oven. Swedish spritz all right.

Windy glanced about for some already cooled and popped one in her mouth, talking around the crumbles. "Hi Gramma. Where's Heather?"

Gramma kissed her cheek. "She's upstairs."

Alarm shot through her. "Alone?" What if she woke?

"Relax. She's fine. How about some cookies and milk? We can sit at the table." Gramma lifted the last of the cookies onto the cooling rack.

Sit at the table with her favorite cookies? Something was up. This screamed heart-to-heart talk. "What's the problem, Gramma? Did something happen?"

"Just join me in the dining room. We'll enjoy the cookies."

It can't be good if she's dodging questions.

Windy let Gramma push her toward the table and took a seat before popping another cookie in her mouth. If it was bad, she wanted as many spritz as she could eat. Before she lost her appetite.

"How are they?" Her grandmother nodded to the platter of cookies. "Been a few months since I made any and that last batch wasn't worth its salt."

"They're fine, Gramma. But you're not. What's going on?"

Her grandmother cleared her throat. "I have company, sweetie."

"That's no problem, Gramma. I'll just keep Heather with me until your company leaves. Don't worry. I don't want you to feel you can't be a good hostess." She patted Gramma's hand.

But the next instant Gramma encased her palms around Windy's fingers. "That's not it. I'm happy to continue watching Heather. She's no trouble."

Windy slipped her hand away and studied her grandmother's face. "Then what is it?"

A baby's cry came from the living room. Heather hadn't been there when she arrived. Someone brought her downstairs. Her baby cried for food—Windy could feel it. She stood.

Gramma grasped at her arm. "Windy, you need to listen a minute."

"But Heather's crying. I'll be right back." She pulled free, hustled to the front room, and slammed to a stop.

"Hello, Windy."

She knew that face, that voice. A little older, but so was she.

And that face, voice, person held her Heather.

"What are you doing here?" She reached for her baby, careful not to snatch. She didn't want to risk Heather. Neither did she want that person touching her daughter. Ever.

Heather no longer cried.

"I came for a visit. Hazel invited me."

Windy glanced at Gramma. "You knew where she was? All this time?"

Her grandmother wouldn't meet her glance.

Windy's legs gave way. She dropped to the couch. "So, how've you been, Mother? Long time, no see."

She'd been right. There was no desire for her favorite cookie now.

"I've kept in touch with Hazel through the years. She decided we should visit. I finally got up the nerve." She stepped toward Windy.

Instinctively, Windy pulled Heather closer.

Her mother stopped moving. "I'm sorry. Guess this wasn't a good idea."

Gramma rushed in. "No, Cheryl, it's just gonna take a while. Like I told you. Right, Windy?"

No matter how hopefully Gramma pleaded, this was not a good idea.

Against that inner child wanting to lash out, Windy chose not to start anything petty or infantile. She'd fought too hard to be included as a grown up. "Maybe space is what's needed." Panic began to rise. She'd stopped dreaming years ago of the day when her mother would return. Yet here they breathed the same air. She couldn't wrap her mind around that fact. She stood, her adult self running low on maturity. "I think I'd better leave. Are Heather's blankets upstairs? I'll get them."

"Wait, sweetie. You don't have to go. Let's all sit together. There's a lot to be said." Gramma tried to hold her back again.

This time Windy shook free. "I should digest this a bit. Please excuse me, we need to get home." She raced to the stairs but slowed remembering Heather was in her arms. At the top she leaned against the wall, drawing a ragged breath. This was a stomach punch. Her grandmother had blindsided her. The only adult she always trusted let her down. Completely.

Did Daddy know? Did her sisters? No, there was no way they knew. Sunny would freak and Stormy would probably be locked up by now.

Maybe that's why Gramma started with her, thinking she would be the easy one. Sort of break the ice.

She was wrong.

No matter. "Heather, sweetheart, I'll feed you at home. Let's grab your blankets and escape this loony bin."

She found the baby carrier and things in her old bedroom. Once Heather was snuggly fastened in, she covered her and went downstairs. "Nice to see you again. I'll be going." No kisses for Gramma this time. She reached for the knob.

"Windy, wait. I'll drive you. Cheryl, I won't be but a few minutes." Gramma grabbed her purse and held the door.

Windy stared at the mother figure she loved so dearly, who had dropped everything to take her and her sisters in, who knew her inside and out. Why would Gramma do this?

She shrugged and walked out to the porch while her grandmother closed the doors behind her. At the car, Gramma unlocked the passenger side before her own. Windy got the baby strapped into her car seat.

No words were spoken the entire ride. But when Windy climbed out, Gramma reached for her hand. "Sweetie, I tried to soften the shock. But now you know. Focus on getting over it so you can start healing. This is a pain point for you, and Sunny, and Stormy."

"What about Daddy? Did you tell him?"

Gramma pursed her lips and nodded. Guess that was a fun conversation.

"Gramma, I don't get it. I thought you understood. I can't talk now. I gotta get Heather inside." Windy put the baby in the carrier.

"I'll be by in the morning. You'll feel better after you have some time."

Gramma really didn't understand. "No. Thank you, but I think I'll keep Heather with me." She couldn't say it out loud, but trust had been broken. That would take time to heal too.

She closed the car door, not glancing at her grandmother for fear of what she'd see in Gramma's eyes. It might cause her to change her decision.

But she did turn and wave from the porch. If only to pause before having to tell her sisters the news.

⁂

Kris pulled in his driveway just as a VW van parked in front of his house. Decked out with lots of bright colors, the paint job on the vehicle was hard to miss.

There was no mistaking the driver either. Ralph. Though he did look different with his shoulder-length, shaggy hair and sporting a full beard. "Dude! Nice pad. Gramps is letting you stay for free? That's wild man. Gimme some skin."

He charged up the walkway and wrapped Kris in a bear hug.

Kris pulled loose. "I do things for him in exchange."

"Whah? Not gonna say hi or nuthin? It's been a while, dude. You got bigger." He scanned Kris up and down before breaking into a grin. "So, what's shakin' man?"

"Get your bag and I'll let you in. Pizza okay for dinner?" Kris unlocked his front door. A headache followed his cousin's arrival.

Ralph didn't cool his enthusiasm though. Instead, he bounced from the front steps toward his van. "Sure, man. I've got dessert for you too."

Kris entered, leaving the door ajar, and dialed Pizza King by heart. With an order to adjust his usual to the extra-large size, he hung up to catch Ralph checking out Gramps's things—stuff that he'd decided not to take to Hazel's.

"Wow, dig this crazy frame. Can you imagine the bread?" Ralph weighed it in his hand as if it were gold.

"Not mine to sell. It's Gramps's. Pizza'll be ready when we get there. I'll drive." Just to be clear on that.

"Groovy." Ralph followed him to the truck. "So, lay it on me, man, what's your bag?"

"I work handyman jobs during the week. Weekends I do my art. Got a few commissioned pieces ordered that I need to finish." Kris shrugged, unsure why he included that last part. Maybe to make sure Ralph knew he earned his keep and didn't sponge off Gramps.

"Gee, man, don't inundate me with all your words, can't take you rattling on." His cousin crossed his arms in front of his face like he needed to ward off blows, laughing as if George Carlin had written his lines.

But if the guy craved scintillating conversation, he'd come to the wrong place.

"Hey, what's the deal on foxy ladies? Think we could locate a couple sweet chickiepoos and let our freak flags fly?" Ralph hung his head out the window, resembling a giant afghan hound. Hope he kept his tongue in his mouth.

"Not seeing anyone right now."

Ralph pulled his head in. "Bummer, man. Really hoped we could find some righteous action, maybe some submarine races someplace other than my van."

"Nope. Want to see Gramps tonight?" He doubted Ralph or Gramps wanted to see each other. Still, he needed to offer. For Dad's sake.

"Nah, he's got some new old lady who's really an old lady. Not into that scene, man." He snickered at his joke.

"Hazel's cool. Makes great cookies. Always has some in her kitchen." Kris would go over for those oatmeal chocolate chips. And Snickerdoodles. Her Swedish spritz weren't bad either.

"Maybe next time I slide through."

They arrived at Pizza King. Kris went in and paid for the order while Ralph waited in the truck. It gave him a moment for his ears to rest. The guy never stopped talking. Ever.

One night. He'd hang in there one night. Then in the morning wave goodbye.

As he opened his door to climb in, Ralph dangled a plastic bow from his fingers.

"What's this? You goin' girlie on me?"

Took him a minute to remember. Windy left a barrette in his truck. The last time he gave her a ride, back before Heather came. She took it out of her hair because it caused a headache. He'd forgotten and she hadn't been in the truck since.

"Belongs to one of the women I work for. She forgot it."

"Whoo-oo-oo, Kris's been getting his freak on."

"Shut up, Ralph. She's my boss." He didn't need to know they were friends too.

"You got a thing for her?"

"No." Did that come out too fast? With too much volume?

"Sure, man, whatever you say. Maybe I oughta stick around and meet your foxy boss."

That was not a good plan. "Thought you had to be in California."

Ralph slid in his seat hooting with laughter. "You fell for that? Nah. The man's getting too close. My number turned up so I'm switching stations to O Canada."

Dodging the draft. He should've known. Aunt Ruby always allowed that kid to get away with murder.

Ralph would probably argue it was easy to say that since Kris's draft number was so far out it was outasight. However, if his number did get called, he'd go. It's what he believed was right. If his country called him, it was his duty to answer. Since Kris hadn't gotten the call, he felt no draw to enlist. Honor didn't equal zeal.

Plus, sharing that information wasn't on his to-do list.

"You don't approve? Hey, the man is breathing down my throat, dude. It's the only way."

"Your life. I'm not making your choices for you." This was none of Kris's business. Ralph was a big boy now.

He pulled in his driveway, climbed out, and grabbed the pizza. Ralph followed. He'd been quiet the rest of the trip. Which suited Kris. He set the pizza on the dining room table before getting plates and glasses from the kitchen. Plus, he had cans of pop in the fridge. "What do you want to drink?"

"A brewski's fine."

"Don't have beer. Got Dr Pepper, Coke, Sprite, Fanta Orange, and Yoo-hoo." He waited for the verbal jabs. So what if he preferred variety in his soft drink choices. Sue him.

"Seriously? You never grew up, did ya? Well, why not. Bring on the Yoo-hoo."

Kris grabbed that for his nineteen-year-old cousin and a Coke for himself. He'd never acquired a taste for alcohol and if he spent money on something, why waste it on something he didn't like? Besides, who cared if he drank? He wasn't out to impress anyone.

When he made it to the dining room, Ralph had already inhaled two slices. Good thing he ordered the extra-large.

"Got any platters? We need some sounds." Ralph glanced around.

Kris held back the sigh. "Who do you like?"

"The Stones, man. Got'm?" He stared at Kris and cocked his eyebrow. "Or Steppenwolf? Led Zeppelin? Uriah Heep? Deep

Purple? Black Sabbath? Kris, man, you gotta have somethin'. Where've you been?" The guy shook his shaggy head in total disbelief.

"I've got the Beatles, Beach Boys, Temps, Bread. Take your pick." He wouldn't be shamed for his preference in music either.

"Beatles. Abbey Road?"

Kris left to set the album on the stereo.

He returned to only one slice left. Ralph was reaching for it. He should've bought two pizzas.

After dinner, Ralph pulled out a plastic roll and some cigarette papers as "She Came in Through the Bathroom Window" started. "Here's the dessert I mentioned. You'll love this. It's Columbian." He opened the baggie and Kris knew exactly what it was.

"Marijuana?"

"What? You don't like Mary Jane? What's wrong with you, dude? You're more square than your old man."

"Hey, if that's your bag, fine. Just go walk the neighborhood. Don't smoke it in Gramps's house." *And don't call me if the cops pick you up.*

Ralph pushed back from the table and stood. "Sweet. Your loss, dude." He tramped out the front door and headed down the sidewalk.

It was too much to hope he was really leaving. Especially since he didn't take his van and his duffle remained in the middle of the living room.

An hour later Ralph came tripping along, eyes bloodshot and a cheesy grin on his face. "You missed some righteous stuff, man."

Kris waited on the front porch in a chair, his coat zipped to his chin and his hands freezing despite shoving them in his pockets. He couldn't figure out how the guy made it back since walking sure wasn't his best skill at the moment. Ralph wobbled and weaved up the steps and plopped in the chair next to him.

"You're definitely wasted."

"Don't harsh my mellow, man." Ralph turned his cheesy grin his way, his breath stout enough to share his high.

"'Bout ready for bed? Already took your bag up."

"Sure, man."

Kris helped his cousin to his feet. "You gonna be okay to drive in the morning?"

"Yeah, man. No sweat. If I go. I might wanna hang here and live off Gramps too." Ralph wrinkled his nose, giggling.

Kris started to argue but knew it wasn't worth it. "You wouldn't like the terms."

Ralph's eyes closed and he morphed into a dead weight.

Kris tossed him over his shoulder and hauled him upstairs to the guest room, dropping him on the bed. He'd better fumigate the place once Ralph left.

Normally he'd have had time in the workshop tonight, but not with company. He needed to get the guy back on the road as soon as possible.

However, come morning, Ralph didn't feel so good.

Kris wasn't about to leave him alone in the house, checking for what might bring the best price at a pawn shop.

So, he poured coffee down his cousin, fed him some Cheerios, and guided him into the truck. When they pulled up in the back parking lot of Ferguson House, Ralph whistled. "This is where you work, man? What do you do? Haul firewood and polish the Rolls?"

Kris ignored him. "You hang with me. No traipsing the mansion, no investigating the rooms. You get me fired and I'll fire you. Dig?"

"Dig, man. You're not a morning person, are you?" Ralph climbed from the truck and started for the rear door.

Kris whistled, though not how Ralph had. "This way." He led him to the carriage house. The girls let him pull together a workshop in a side room. Made it easier to fix things as needed. Sunny usually left a clipboard of tasks she wanted accomplished on his desk—sawhorses and a sheet of plywood. He checked to see what she wrote and noticed he'd lost Ralph somewhere inside the building. It wasn't difficult to find him.

"Hey pretty mama, what's shakin'?"

Windy didn't appear upset. She stared him down. "Probably those loose bee-bees in your head. *Dude.* Excuse me."

Ralph reached for her arm. "Don't run away. I don't bite. Unless you want me to." He growled, then giggled.

Kris gagged.

But Windy turned, a large pair of scissors in her hand. "I don't bite, either, but I know how to use these. Come any closer to my child and I'll prove it to you."

Child? Heather was there?

"Oh, hey, little mama, I didn't see you had company. My fault. I'll get out of your hair." Ralph spun, hands in the air.

Kris grabbed him by the shirt, pulling him up on his tiptoes. "Don't you ever speak to her again. You will not touch her or her baby. Am I understood?"

Ralph nodded like he was in a contest for world's best nodder. "Yeah, man, sure. Not messing with a fine mama and her baby. I dig."

Kris spoke to Windy though his gaze never left his cousin's face. "I'm going to help this one get on the road." He lifted Ralph a touch higher. "You dig that idea?"

"Yeah, man, whatever you say, man."

Kris shoved him toward the truck before glancing back at Windy. She'd cracked a smile and winked at him. He was sure grateful for that.

Once at home, he monitored to ensure only Ralph's things went in his bag. Then he walked him to his van.

"You got problems, man. You might not know it, but you're hung up on that chick. I don't mess with nobody else's old lady. What about you? Gonna move in on someone else's old lady?" Ralph tossed him the package of weed. "Here. Go find your mellow, dude. You need this more than me." He started his VW.

Kris slipped the baggie back in the rear window and ambled to his truck, breathing a sigh of relief to have his cousin gone.

But now that Ralph was headed for Canada, what did he tell his parents?

Chapter 3
Wednesday, November 4, 1970

Windy chuckled watching Kris guide whoever that someone was out to the truck. At first, he'd startled her, this stranger on their property. However, when she spotted Kris in the room, she realized it'd be okay. Something to take her mind off that person at Gramma's house. She didn't want to think about her anyway.

Plus, the encounter reminded her how to stand up to idiots. She'd met a lot of them at college—guys who figured when a girl was nice, she was giving them a come on. Made her stop being overly friendly at first meetings.

One more reason she kicked herself about Tim. He never seemed to take advantage. She believed he really loved her and that they would be getting married or she never would've let her guard down.

But she did and regretted that.

Yet, she did not regret giving birth to this beautiful tiny human who was sucking on her fist. Yeah, it was about that time.

She set the scissors aside and scooped Heather out of her carrier. "Let's go and I'll get you fed, little love." With a kiss on the baby's forehead, she headed for their bedroom and privacy.

Less than an hour later they were back in the carriage house. It was a bit nippy, and she added to Heather's bundling. Still, the decorations for the Friday night wedding wouldn't get done if she stopped. The bride planned a harvest festival theme so Windy had raffia and burlap for tying up pumpkins and gourds. There were sprigs of winter berries and a couple of cornucopias with colorful squash set about. It kept with the earth tones the bride chose for her bridesmaids and the groomsmen. For a splash of contrast, Windy brought in purple candles and some brass items. It worked perfect in her mind. The hard part was creating that picture her brain painted.

Kris returned, wandering her way. "Looks good. You understand color."

She smiled. "Thank you, kind sir. And thanks for the rescue earlier."

"I don't think you needed me. Ralph was already terrified when I got ahold of him."

That caused a laugh. "Ralph?"

"Yeah, he's my cousin. My parents asked me to let him crash for the night. Couldn't figure out why they wouldn't ask Gramps and then he showed up and I knew." He chuckled, something he rarely did.

"I can hear Gene going on about those darned hippies."

That image made them both laugh.

"Hope you didn't have trouble with him."

Kris shook his head. "He was supposed to leave this morning anyway, but I kinda guess he hoped to stay here and go underground."

"Underground?"

He plopped on a chair and sighed. "Yeah. He told our parents he was going to California for a visit. But he let it slip with me that his draft number is up so he's heading for Canada."

Canada? Like Tim? She bit her lip. "Oh."

Kris covered her hand with his. "Want to talk?" Somehow, he just sensed.

She shook her head no, then reconsidered. "Maybe." Windy took a deep breath and let it out. "Hit a little too close to home, I guess." She glanced down at Heather who slept in her carrier at her feet. "Heather's father is in Canada."

Kris's expression changed and she realized he judged Tim.

"No, he didn't realize I was pregnant. I went to tell him and he'd left me a note. He was flunking, no more scholarship. So, no more school deferment. His number was about to be called. I've no idea how to reach him. I'm guessing he doesn't know how to contact me since I dropped out to come home." She squinched up her mouth as she analyzed what she confessed. It was true. She never considered leaving him word where to find her, in case he ever tried. Should she try to find him?

"I'm sorry. He lost out."

Windy peeked at Kris. No judgment. Just stating a fact. "Thanks."

"Wonder what his folks say." Another statement. Something Windy hadn't considered.

"No idea. He never mentioned his family much. Only that they lived in the Boston area." Would they care to know about their grandchild? How could she reach them? Should she try? What were his parents' names?

"I'll bet my Aunt Ruby's gonna freak when she learns what he's done. Be all over my dad trying to find some legal loophole for her baby boy."

She glanced at him and realized they'd gone in two different directions. Well, she needn't explain that. She was just glad he triggered the notion. Maybe she should see what she could do to get Heather her daddy. "I'm sure Tim's parents are devastated too."

Kris grew quiet, even for him. Finally, he pushed up from the chair. "I'd better get to work." He tossed her a small smile before heading for his office workshop.

Wonder what Kris thought of her now that she'd told him that. Had he assumed she'd been married and something happened? Or that she'd been assaulted? Or she was one of those girls? Whatever he'd imagined, he didn't let it stand in the way of them being friends. He was...kind. She almost repeated that "nice guy" term, but Kris was more. He was genuine and deep. She knew that if she ever needed anything, he'd be there for her. Not that he'd said anything, but instinctive knowledge fed that truth.

As it stood, she'd do the same for him. She liked him, enjoyed his company, and appreciated those not so little things. Such as nearly tearing his cousin's head off for her. She chuckled. A gentle giant. It was so out of character to imagine him violent. Still, he possessed a depth of passion most missed.

Then there was the cradle next to her bed. Kris showed up at her baby shower to bring his handcrafted gift. She couldn't imagine another man doing such a thing. They'd be worried someone might comment on their masculinity. Not Kris though. He didn't care what others thought. He just lived his life and was kind in the process.

He was a good friend to have.

"Windy? You in here?" Stormy thundered in.

"Yeah." The atmosphere changed. Windy would bet money Sunny told Stormy who showed up at Gramma's yesterday.

"You didn't call me?"

"Couldn't think about it. Had to escape." Which was true. In fact, the only reason she told Sunny was she counted on her big sister to fix things, so she wouldn't have to.

"I can't believe it. Sunny made me promise not to go see Mom. But I want to tear her hair out." Stormy paced up and down the aisle.

"You're only getting yourself more upset."

Her sister spun on her. "What about you? Aren't you upset at all?"

"Yes, I'm angry. Just not sure what to say. The main point? I won't go there. Or see her. Or allow her to get her hands on Heather again. One of these days she'll leave. She's good at that. Then we'll go back to normal." That was her hope, at least.

"Open your eyes, kid! It'll never be the same. Gramma always knew where to find her. She allowed us to believe she left and never had contact. But that woman's kept tabs. She knows all about us and we know nothing of her except she walked out. Gramma did that. How can we ever trust her again?" Stormy plopped into the chair Kris had vacated. "That's what hurts the worst. I trusted the old biddy." A tear started down her cheek.

Windy pulled a tissue from her pocket and handed it to her sister. With all her crying jags lately, she kept several on her. Funny, she hadn't cried over this. Maybe she was still in shock, like Gramma said. And avoidance.

Stormy wiped her eyes. "I want to call Rob, but he's got a ton of meetings this week and I can't interrupt. Sunny says she's working on it. What's to work on? I can't imagine what she has planned. But I promised so I'm here. Not there. Maybe you should give me a job. It'll keep my mind off things."

"You don't have any appointments today?" Windy handed her a skein of raffia.

"Not until three this afternoon. What do you need me to do?"

Windy explained her idea and they worked together until Heather got hungry again.

"I'm going to take her in to feed and change her. Finish this row and then make us some lunch. I'll meet you in the kitchen."

Stormy nodded and continued tying raffia bows while Windy took Heather upstairs.

While feeding her daughter, the notion from before bloomed into an idea. She and Tim had enough friends in common. Surely one of them would know how to reach his parents. How many of her friends did she have addresses for?

Well, classes were still going. Some hadn't graduated yet. She'd contact them at school. That got penciled onto this evening's agenda.

But what would she say? No one there understood why she left. She never stopped to tell anyone. Perhaps she needed to consider who she should ask. She couldn't just blurt that she and Tim had a baby. Not even to his parents. She must get word to him first. Somehow.

Forty-five minutes later, Heather was full and Windy had a plan. Heading to the kitchen she decided there was enough family drama. She shouldn't bring Sunny and Stormy into it. Not yet anyway.

Stormy fixed Lipton chicken noodle soup and BLTs. Far better fare than Windy imagined for lunch. They sat at the table, Heather in her carrier at her feet. Made it easy to rock the little seat with her toe.

Sunny came in, dipped herself up some soup, and joined them. "So, I've been on the phone with Dad and Gramma. I'm getting a strange vibe from Dad. It's like he wants us to talk with her."

"Oh no, that can't be right. He's got to be ready to race home and kick her out." Stormy's eyes gleamed.

"Nope. He's cool as a Miles Davis solo. And he says we aren't to get upset with Gramma." She pursed her lips and nodded.

"He can't mean that. She betrayed us. Where's he get off telling us how to feel?" Stormy had a point.

Sunny took a breath. "He says she never does anything without trying to be helpful. If she did this, it wasn't to betray anyone. It was to make things better. We don't have to like it; we just have to respect her motives."

That made sense. The truth was Windy didn't like it. Still, she could see how her grandmother might think she was helping. It didn't help. Still, she'd accept the motivation. "I can do that."

Stormy stared at her. "You can? After she blindsided you?"

"I doubt that was her intention. I chose to walk over there and without knowing pushed the issue. Bet she figured to come here with her cookies and milk talk, explain it all and give us time to choose to do what she wanted. I messed up her scheme." Windy shrugged. "I can't fault her for that part."

"You're nicer than me, kid. Right now? I don't care to lay eyes on that old lady. Or her guest." Stormy shook her head.

"I didn't say I was ready to talk with her. Plus, I still won't see Mother. I can allow it didn't go as planned because of my actions. That's all I'm saying. Maybe in a few days I'll be ready. Gramma and I can talk. We'll pretend none of this happened. However, I won't go there again until her guest is gone." And now that she'd spoken it, she cemented the plan in her brain.

&

KRIS GLANCED AT THE CLIPBOARD again, glad for rough sketches and the clear handwriting. Sunny envisioned a Christmas wonderland out back once Thanksgiving was past. She hoped if it snowed, they'd have structures in place to get covered with the white mounds. They'd give it a magical appearance—her words. If they didn't have snow, maybe they'd drape some fake stuff to make it passable. He wasn't sure about this. Still, not his job to question things. Just come up with what they want.

Sunny was nice enough. Never got pushy and often asked his opinion. He understood why she and Pat were together. Sunny had class.

Stormy, now, she was a powerhouse. He never wanted on her bad side. She was a little scary.

But Windy? There was something about that girl. He wasn't in the market for a relationship, was perfectly content being friends. Still, he had the notion she was underestimated by her family. They all realized she had talent, loads of talent. They just never realized she was savvy. Not only book smart, but able to handle herself, like with Ralph today. Plus, she had integrity.

It was the first time he'd heard her story. He'd kinda guessed. Her defending the dude, well, that showed loyalty. However, if he ran for the border, only leaving a note, he wasn't the type to settle down to fatherhood.

Kris caught his reflection in the window over his workbench. Would the guy staring back step up? He'd like to think so. Not that he was rushing or anything. Still, a family would be nice. In the future. Way, way in the future.

Enough daydreaming. He had work to do. A couple hours later, he had the framework clamped. He needed to get Sunny's approval before he continued though. Getting it all together to learn it wasn't what she wanted would be a royal pain.

He headed for the rear door and spotted them all sitting in the kitchen eating. And talking. Stormy was upset. Enough that he took notice and considered slipping back to his hideaway.

Windy must have seen him. She popped up and pulled the door open. "Come on in, Kris. You need your lunch."

He caught the glare Stormy sent Windy's way and the exchanged glances she and Sunny shared. Something was going on.

"I can come back. Just wondered if you wanted to check if I've got your idea, Sunny."

She hopped up. "Sure, let's go take a peek." She grabbed a jacket and strode out the rear door.

Guess he was supposed to follow.

Windy called after him. "I'll bring your lunch to you. Sandwich is almost put together."

Had he stirred up a hornet's nest or just bad timing?

Well, it was none of his concern. He wasn't paid to stick his nose into their business.

Sunny gave her approval. In fact, she seemed tickled that he caught her vision. Felt good to do something right.

She headed back as Windy showed up with his lunch. He'd told them he'd bring his own, but Sunny explained that they couldn't pay as much as they'd like, so feeding him was included. He doubted they realized what they were getting into at the time, but he was happy, food was great, and they paid steady. He made up the difference with his commissioned pieces.

"Hope you are in the mood for chicken noodle soup and a couple BLTs." Windy figured out early that he enjoyed eating.

"Cool." He grabbed a sandwich wedge and dunked it in the soup mug.

"So, this is what Sunny's got you building. I wondered. A winter wonderland set for photo shoots. Maybe a service. If anyone's brave enough."

He nodded. "Guess she figures it can be adjusted for Christmas, New Year, and Valentine's Day pretty easily."

"I see that. Kris, you do a good job. I'm impressed with your ability." She ran her finger over a joint, not looking at him but at his handiwork.

She'd said ability, not talent. Somehow that meant more to him. Elevated him to craftsman. Beyond just lucky. "Thanks."

"Well, I'd better get back inside. I left Heather with Stormy. She's having a bad day, Stormy is, not Heather. Thought the baby might calm her a bit." She smiled and waved.

He slurped a sip of the soup and remembered. "Thanks for lunch."

Took him the rest of the afternoon to finish the first structures. That was plenty for one day. He put away the tools he kept at Ferguson House and loaded his personal items in his truck before checking with Sunny to see if it was okay to head out.

She thanked him and wished him a good night.

He started his Ford and drove for home. Dinner tonight would be hot dogs and chips. About four dogs ought to do it. Then he'd get more work done on Mr. Hingst frame.

But the phone was ringing as he opened his door. He raced in, hoping he made it in time. He did.

"Kris, dude, what'd you do to me?"

"Ralph?"

"Yeah, man. Me, your cousin that you set up."

What was he talking about? "What do you mean?"

"I mean the baggie you hid in my van. I got Mounties surrounding me. I thought the man was bad. These dudes are tough, I'm telling ya."

Then Kris remembered. "Ralph, I only returned what you handed me. I didn't want to shove it in your face, so I tossed it in your rear window. It's your own stuff."

"Why didn't you get rid of it? You knew I was crossing the border."

"Sorry?" What else could he say? "Want me to phone my dad?" *Say no.*

"Yes. Dude, you owe me. Call Uncle Frank, but not my mother. Here's the numbers here." He read off the name and listing for the Canadian officer in charge of the case.

"I'll do it now. Sorry, Ralph." He hung up before his cousin castigated him further.

However, now he had to phone his father. The one person he avoided talking to. At all costs. His plans were scrubbed for the second night in a row. Thanks to his cousin and his dad.

He dialed the long-distance number, counting the rings while grasping for an opening. Should he explain? No, the less said the better.

"Norman residence." His mother answered the phone.

"Mom, hi. Could I talk to Dad?" Please don't let her badger information before he spoke with his father.

"Kris, honey, what a surprise. How are you?"

"The same as Sunday night. I need to speak with Dad. Please, Mom. It's urgent." *C'mon, Mom, just this once.*

She sighed loud enough to make sure he was aware. "Well, I guess. You'd think a mother could get some time to talk with her son. But if you insist." She held that last sound like the clink of crystal echoing away.

He knew her strategies and he wasn't giving in this time.

Finally, he heard her muffled, "Frank, it's for you. It's Kris. He says it's urgent."

The line grew silent and about when he was sure they'd lost connection his father's voice boomed. "Kris, what's so important?"

He blew out a breath and gave the shortest explanation he could manage. "Ralph decided to visit Canada. He got arrested by the Mounties. He needs help and asked me to give you the information."

Dad cleared his throat and dropped into his business tone. "Fine, give me the name and number."

Funny thing, he didn't ask questions. Just repeated what Kris gave him. Most likely as he wrote it.

"I'll get right on this. Thanks for calling, son."

"Night, Dad." The phone disconnected on his last syllable.

Well, he'd done his good deed and hadn't gotten into a big discussion with his father. He was calling that a win.

Kris set a water-filled a pan to boil before digging out hot dogs from the refrigerator. He grabbed the mustard while he was there.

The cabinet over the counter held the large bag of Lay's potato chips and a package of buns. While the dogs boiled, he grabbed a plate. He'd heard some guy on TV the other day. He was excited about an oven that cooked with microwaves. Said all the big stars in Hollywood had one in their kitchens. According to that guy, a person could cook a hot dog in less than a minute—he called it zapping them. Apparently, they even zapped steaks and baked potatoes in record time. He might have to save for one of those gizmos.

Eventually his hot dogs were ready. He forked them onto the buns and turned off the stove. Should he take the food to his workshop or eat first? He glanced out the window.

Before he could decide, the phone rang. He could go for weeks without it ringing, and with no complaints. Twice in one evening was a lot. He set his plate on the table and hustled to the living room to answer.

"Kristofer, what were you thinking?" His dad.

"What are you talking about?"

"Why would you tell Ralph to run for Canada to avoid the draft? Then toss marijuana in his van so he'd be arrested?"

Kris didn't know which was harder to believe. That Ralph would spin such a tale or that his father would swallow it.

"First, I never said go to Canada. He told me he was going. Second, I don't do marijuana. That was his own stuff he tried to palm off on me. I gave it back to him. I'd think you would know me better than to accept Ralph's craziness as truth. You've met us both. Do you really believe I'd do that?" Why must he defend himself to his own father?

There was a long silence. "You're right. I'm sorry." Did his father just say that? "That boy has himself in one big mess and I'm not so sure I'll be much help. Don't know what I'm going to tell Ruby. Well, I feel better knowing you didn't do what he said. If I'm to be any assistance, he's gotta tell me the truth. I'd better go, see what's to be done. Good night, son."

"Night, Dad." Kris put the handset back in the cradle. That apology went a long way. However, that Dad believed those lies, at least for a second, cut deep.

What had he ever done to make his father jump to those conclusions? Was he such a disappointment to him?

Suddenly, Kris wasn't hungry. He set the plate in the refrigerator and turned on the TV. He didn't feel like working in his workshop either. He didn't know how he felt. But he knew what he wanted.

To be someone else.

Chapter 4
Thursday, November 5, 1970

Windy grabbed the ringing phone. "Weather Girls Wedding Shoppe and Venue. This is Windy. How may I help you?"

"You're the one I was calling, lovey. How are you doing?" Gramma.

"Good. You?" Windy stiffened at the voice. She didn't want this conversation.

"It's a little lonely without my great granddaughter around. Just wondering if I might fetch her for the day?" And there it was.

"That depends, Gramma. Do you still have company?" It was the nicest way she knew to phrase it.

"I do. And she'd love to see her granddaughter too."

Windy paused. If she repeated what popped into her brain, it'd be true but impolite—that Gramma's visitor had a decade to visit her daughters and didn't. Why should she be allowed time with her granddaughter?

But she held her tongue. "Today isn't a good day. Sorry." Sorry that this would hurt her grandmother's feelings, but not enough to let her mother near Heather.

"How long do you plan to behave this way, Windy?"

"Gramma, I don't want to talk about this. It will only make us both unhappy. Just tell me when she's gone. I still love you. Bye." She hung up before her grandmother could argue.

As another wave of guilt threatened to pull her under.

Hurting Gramma was not her intention. She hated knowing that was the result. But the mere notion of staying in the same town as her mother, realizing she might bump into her at the grocery, or during a stroll through the neighborhood, kept her hibernating at the mansion. That woman had to leave sometime. All she could do was pray it'd be soon. Today would be the perfect day.

She gathered Heather and wandered to Sunny's office to update her. "That was Gramma."

"Great. I'm almost afraid to answer the phone anymore for fear of who is calling. But we've a business to run and I can't miss a client. Why'd she decide to show up now?" Sunny ran her hand over her forehead, swiping her bangs to the side.

"She was too late a decade ago. She shouldn't have attempted coming back." Windy leaned against the desk and sighed, patting Heather against her shoulder.

Sunny held her gaze. "Recall how we've always said Stormy was like Mom? Can you think of anyone more headstrong than our sister?"

"You mean our mother?" She couldn't call her mom. That was a term of endearment. Windy housed no kindred emotions for the woman.

"Yup. You ain't seen mulish until you've met Cheryl Ann Day. I remember. We need to accept we'll meet face to face eventually. The sooner you and I come to grips, the sooner Stormy'll be talked down."

Not what she wanted to hear. Plus, Stormy wasn't the only pig-headed one. Just because Windy never exploded all over everyone didn't mean she couldn't dig in her heels. When the circumstances called for it, of course. And if any instance demanded dug-in heels, this one did.

"No, I'll wait her out. Besides, how is she going to make us bow to her whims? She's not the Queen of England. She hasn't authority over us. She gave that up when she walked out." Windy couldn't contemplate any reason to give that woman the power to command an audience.

"She's still our mother, like it or not. For Gramma's sake, and Dad's, we might have to swallow our pride long enough to hear her side." Sunny always was the reasonable one.

Windy didn't want to be reasonable. "I've got work to do. We'll be in the carriage house."

Her sister said nothing more but returned to the paperwork on her desk. Sunny didn't like arguing any more than she did.

Bundled for the cooler air outside, Windy, with Heather all comfy in her little carrier, left to finish for tomorrow's wedding. She could possibly salvage time come morning, but with her luck, some crisis would blow that. Best to complete early, make adjustments later.

Everything she could handle from ground level was complete. Now to haul out that extension ladder, get leaves strung from the rafters. Where was it? Kris would know.

She carried Heather with her in search of the one person who'd be able to put his finger on the device in a heartbeat.

He was in his workshop finishing another structure for Sunny.

"Hey, Kris, do you know where that extension ladder got stored?"

He glanced up from his work with the start of a smile. "I'm not allowed to tell you that."

"What do you mean?"

He shook his head. "Sunny made me promise not to say. She said when you need stuff done that requires climbing, I was to help you, but not to allow you to. Said you have a reputation. I got called on the carpet because I let you climb when we worked on the ballroom."

That wiped the words clean out of her mouth, but not the indignation. After a minute of hemming and hawing, she was able to form meaningful sounds. "I can't believe she'd do that. What right has she? I am perfectly capable of climbing a ladder."

"Sunny said you'd say that. She told me to answer, no more broken bones on her watch." That grin still teased at the corners of his lips. Made him better looking. Downright handsome, even. It sort of startled Windy.

Focus. Her sister overstepped. Windy's peeve began to steam.

Kris must have noticed. "For the record, I find enough trouble without help. Please don't add to it." Now he kidded her. She didn't see this side of him very often and it cooled the tantrum wanting to erupt.

"Fine then, I'll protect you, you big baby. Bring your ladder and meet me in the main room." She spun on her heel and headed out, letting him think she wouldn't watch. But she would. After sneaking outside, she tried peeking through his window. Once she figured out where the ladder was stored, she'd no longer need him to grab it. So there.

He sure took his sweet time getting it though. Then he waved at her over his shoulder. Didn't even glance her way. He knew. Curses. Foiled again.

She returned to the main room and plopped in a chair, rocking Heather's carrier with her toe, until he showed up. At one point she forced herself to slow down. She had that little chair moving. Fortunately, Heather slept through it all.

Five minutes later, Kris wrangled the contraption into the room. Still smirking. Yeah, he got her. This time. Still, she'd figure out where he kept it. Then no one would boss her. Too many tried that lately.

Okay, so maybe this vexation was more about Gramma's visitor than her sisters protecting her from her natural klutziness. It still made her hot under the collar.

Kris set up where she indicated and started to climb. About three rungs above the floor, he held out his hand. "What do you want up here?"

She passed him a silk autumn leaf with nylon fishing line attached to the stem and a thumb tack. The plan called for about a hundred dangling below the miniature white lights, so they'd dance in the breeze. If they had a small breeze. But even motionless, they would be pretty.

He went higher, then pushed the tack into the beam. "How's the length?"

"Good." She gave him a thumbs up. "Only ninety-nine to go."

Kris groaned.

"Hey, you're the guy who wouldn't divulge the ladder's secret hideout."

"If I'd known this was what I was getting into, I'd have begged Sunny to let me tell you." He reached for the next.

Funny, he didn't say he'd have told her, just that he'd have asked permission. The guy had integrity. Not that she hadn't already figured that out, but here was proof positive. She appreciated that about him. And that he looked cute standing so tall. Kind of hot, actually. As he stretched to poke the next tack in, she spotted a scar on his forearm. Guess he'd had an accident or two. Like her. Maybe they'd compare war wounds later.

Sunny peeked inside the carriage house. "Kris, you've got a phone call. I think it's Gene."

"Thanks. Tell him I'm on my way." He descended, heading toward the door, but then turned back. "No climbing."

He didn't wait for an answer.

And she never promised.

Once he was out of sight, Windy prepared three leaves for hanging, adjusted the ladder's placement, and scurried up the rungs. Things went fine. Exactly like she knew they would. Then she hustled down, grabbing three more. Heather stirred so she gave her the pacifier and rocked her chair a moment before moving the ladder where she needed it. Then she began the trek up again.

"What do you think you're doing?"

Windy startled, missing a step. She snatched at the rung with one hand, grasping leaves with the other. All at once she dangled in midair by her arm, like a decoration.

Her grip slipped.

She gasped.

Kris caught her, drawing her close. His arms closed about her, making her more secure than she'd ever been, even though she felt his heart pounding while hers raced. His taut muscles encased her, holding her steadfast. As her breathing slowed, she grew aware of his aftershave—a woodsy scent that fit him. It was nearly intoxicating, pulling her mind in a million different directions, all leading to one goal. Kris.

Then he set her on her feet. She was more alone than she'd ever been.

"I told you not to do that." His voice shook. Was he that angry?

"You scared me, or I'd have been just fine." She's the one who oughta be miffed. Besides, he wasn't the boss of her.

"You could've been hurt. Really hurt. And what about Heather? You've got to think of her."

He was right about that. She did need to consider her daughter. But it didn't mean she must be a basket case, solely relying on everyone else to get done what she was more than capable of accomplishing. "Fine. But this stupid trying to protect me from myself is for the birds. I can climb a ladder. As long as no one attempts scaring the daylights out of me."

Kris took her by the shoulders and captured her gaze. "Hey. I've no idea why they do that. But from what I just viewed, maybe it's not a bad rule. I don't want anything to happen to you."

Dang, his eyes were blue.

She shook her head. "Honest. I'm not the klutz they think I am. Yes, I've had a few spills. And have broken a few bones. But I'm healthy and capable. I don't want a nursemaid."

"How about a friend? We're friends, right?"

How could she not agree? "Yes. So as a friend, will you believe me?'"

"As a friend, will you not get me fired? I need my job."

This involved something more. Could it have been the phone call? She sat and motioned him to the other chair. "What happened?"

He blew out a breath. "Ralph got arrested. It's stupid really. You know how I said he was heading to Canada? Well, they found weed in his VW. He handed it to me as he was leaving so, I stuck it back in his window. Never occurred to me they'd search his van. I should have thought about it. Anyway, he spun this tale about me talking him into crossing the border and then planting marijuana on him just to get him in trouble. My dad bought it, at first. Actually, I'm still not sure I convinced him otherwise."

Kris would never do anything like that. She'd only known him since March, but even she knew that was far-fetched.

"That was my grandfather on the phone. The family wagons have circled. But, somehow, the story got to him that I'd set Ralph up. At least he didn't believe it and wanted to hear my side. Guess my dad is trying to get Ralph home. I gotta see Gramps after work, learn what they've come up with."

He was going to Gramma's? Then he'd meet *her*. "You know they have company, right?"

How did she feel about that? What would he think of her? Maybe he'd share his impressions of the woman who gave her birth. Kris would be unbiased. She hoped.

Perhaps the horns and tail really were all in her imagination.

⚿

"NO, I HADN'T HEARD ANYONE was staying with them." He only planned to talk with Gramps for a few minutes. See if he had any advice.

"Yeah, well, apparently my mother dropped in." Windy sounded none too happy about that. In fact, he didn't remember her ever mentioning her mother.

He'd figured she was out of the picture because Hazel raised the girls, and their father flew in sometimes. But none of them mentioned one word about their mom. It must not be good.

"Want to talk? Friend to friend?"

She shook her head. "I'm trying not to think about it and outlast her. She has to leave sometime."

"You won't go see her?"

"It's been over a decade without a peep from her. I'm fine." She didn't appear fine.

"I won't pry. Not my business. But I'll listen anytime."

Her gaze locked with his and her slow smile split his heart. It was sad and sweet all in one.

He tucked her hair behind her ear, just because it called to him. Then he realized what he did. Felt like his face would melt off. "Yeah, well, we'd better get those leaves hung."

"Thanks, Kris."

"No problem." He returned up the ladder and she handed him a couple of the dangly things. It started a rhythm. Soon they had the front of the room covered. He stepped down to stand at the rear for a view. Yeah, she had an eye for color and design. A fall wedding in here would make a pretty photo album. "Nice."

"It's turning out almost like I envisioned. Ready to do the rest?"

"Sure." He moved the ladder and started up again.

An hour later they were finished. This might be his favorite design they'd done so far. He packed up the dangerous device and leaned it against the wall in his workshop until Windy took Heather back to the house to feed her. Then he tucked it away in his hiding place. He knew she'd go through his room, probably the rest of the building searching, though he was equally sure she'd have a difficult time finding where he put it.

Ready to head for Gramps's.

He pulled up out front and took the steps to the porch. Hazel had set out fall decorations, making him think of Windy's style. Her grandmother influenced her.

Speaking of Hazel, she answered his knock and let him in, glancing past him. "All alone, Kris?'

"Yeah, just me. Sorry, Hazel." He caught the sadness in her eyes.

"Your grandpa is in here." She led him to the den. "You guys care for a snack?"

Kris wanted to drool. He'd looked forward to this solely because of the chance at Hazel's cookies. Didn't matter what kind. She could bake.

"That looks like a yes." She matched his grin.

"Please."

She stepped out and Kris sat on the couch. "I'm glad Dad called you."

"Me too. I worry about that boy. I don't understand what goes through that brain of his." Gramps released a sigh. "I talked with Frank, and they've made a suggestion that they're hoping the Canadian government will accept. They'll send Ralph back and he's to enlist. Any branch of the service, so he might go with the Coast Guard, but at least that gets him home and keeps our draft board happy. The chances are slim, but your dad has some clout in high places."

Kris had a sudden vision of all that hairy mess on the barber's floor. Would Ralph still be as baby-faced as he used to be? That he'd like to see. But a photo would be good enough. "Any idea when we'll know?"

Hazel walked in with a plate of oatmeal chocolate chip cookies. His stomach rumbled.

"Give him one, Honey. The boy's starving." Gramps winked and stole a kiss from his wife.

Hazel handed him three and put the plate on the couch next to him. "I'll let you two talk. But Kris, I'd like a word before you leave."

Thankfully, he'd crammed a cookie in his mouth before she made her request so he couldn't respond. He was afraid she was going to ask about the girls, maybe Windy in particular, and if they'd mentioned her visitor. This wasn't any of his business. Besides that, what Windy said to him was spoken in confidence. Hope Hazel understood.

She stepped out and Gramps swiped a cookie before continuing. "I think I've put on ten pounds since we married. I'm eating too well and too regular." He chuckled a moment, patting his belly, before he sobered. "So, back to Ralph. Don't worry about anything. Your dad can handle this and as much as I love that boy, he needs a dose of reality. Hope it ends up being in the service rather than prison across the border."

"I'm sorry, Gramps. I never thought about it. I didn't want an argument and wasn't gonna keep his stash. Should've figured on him having his van searched. Instead, I thought he'd find it eventually."

Gramps sat forward. "You listen to me, Kris. It's not your fault. He knows better than to smoke that stuff. He also knows better than to run to Canada. He made the choices that brought him there. His problem is he thought he was too smart, and it bit him on the backside. You got that? You didn't cause this."

"Well, not on purpose." Kris grabbed another cookie.

"We're all disappointed, son, because we're family. Hope Ralph gets that. If your dad pulls this off, that boy's not gonna feel the love. At least not at first. There may be some fallout. But remember, we can love him without agreeing with his choices. And they're his choices. However, when we must clean up after him, we earn the right to address them. Understand?"

Kris nodded. "Okay, Gramps. Guess I'd better go see what Hazel needs." He stood.

"About that. Don't let her put you in the middle. She's hurting. This trying to help her family blew up in her face. But it's fine to say you can't do anything. Got it?"

That lifted a weight. "Got it. See you later, Gramps." He patted his grandfather's shoulder on his way out.

Hazel waited in the living room. Another woman sat with her. He spotted the resemblance to the girls. They each had a bit of her, though Stormy appeared to be a younger carbon copy of her mother. "Kris, this is my daughter-in-law, Cheryl. Cheryl, Kris is Gene's grandson. He's been helping the girls, but you oughta see his artwork. One exceptionally talented young man."

Heat crept up Kris's neck. He hoped she didn't say that to get him on her side. Hazel wasn't like that. Was she?

"Nice to meet you, ma'am."

"And he has manners too. Kris, please sit a moment. We need to talk with you."

As much as he wanted to tell her not to waste her time, he complied, wishing he were somewhere else.

"Kris, I'm grasping at straws now. I'm not trying to rope you in, but hoped if you met Cheryl, you might have a less biased opinion when the girls say things." She eyed him, waiting for him to deny that they spoke to him about this.

"I just work with them, ma'am. They're my bosses."

"But you're also friends, right? At least with Windy. I've seen you two together. Kris, I'm not requesting you take my message or maneuver them to come over. But if one of them starts to share, maybe you'd ask questions? Get them to think?" Hazel blinked hard, the edge of tears warbled her voice.

Cheryl patted her hand. "Hazel, I'm glad you introduced us, but please don't put him in the middle. This isn't fair to Kris."

"But I'm out of ideas. I've prayed about you coming home for so many years and now that you're here, nothing is working the way I imagined." Hazel broke down and Cheryl embraced her.

Kris cleared his throat. "Cheryl is right. I can't be your middleman." He turned to Windy's mother. "I'm glad to meet you though. You have great daughters and I hope you work it out soon." He rose.

So did Cheryl, who stretched out her palm. "Thank you for saying that, Kris. It means a lot."

He shook her hand, wondering if he'd somehow betrayed Windy in doing so. Yet, what was he supposed to do?

Hazel stood and gave him a hug and kiss on the cheek. "You're a good man, Kris. I'm sorry I put you on the spot."

He leaned, whispering at her ear. "I'd do almost anything for your cookies, Hazel. Wish I could've helped you tonight."

She stepped back with a shaky smile. "Night, Kris."

"Night. Nice meeting you, Cheryl." He made for the door. The sooner he was home, the sooner he could sort his thoughts, because he'd never been so mixed up.

Cheryl seemed a perfectly nice, normal person. Nothing like what he envisioned from Windy's brief description. He couldn't imagine what would've made her leave her daughters and husband and not contact them for over ten years.

But something did. Something that scarred her daughters—he'd glimpsed their wounds in his eight months of working for them. He'd also seen them rise above it all into strong, tough women. Those girls were definitely resilient. Especially Windy.

The memory from earlier when she landed in his arms rushed back. Talk about confusing. That moment hadn't felt friendly. Protective, maybe. She'd terrified him. All Sunny and Stormy's wisecracks about Windy's clumsiness sprang to life before his eyes. She could've broken her arm. Or worse.

Then when he held her, there was something else. Stirrings from down deep. A craving, almost. He wanted to wrap her in his arms while his pulse pounded in his ears. She uncovered a different person inside him, someone he hadn't known was in there.

He would make it his mission to keep her safe, whether she liked it or not.

Hopefully, she wouldn't hate it too much.

Chapter 5
Thursday, November 19, 1970

"Is that the mail?" Windy tried to appear nonchalant as she peered over her sister's shoulder.

"Yep." Sunny shuffled the envelopes into proper categories.

"Anything for me?" Windy crossed her fingers behind her back.

"You've asked every day this week. What's up? You send away for something?" Her sister gave her a side glance and continued her sorting process.

She shook her head, not wanting to explain. Time for phase two. Her patience ebbed. So, she brainstormed an idea last night, remembering that the public library housed all sorts of books. Including directories for all the major cities in the country. That was her next plan, so she changed the subject. "I think we'll walk down to the library. Be back in a bit."

"Wait, it's getting pretty chilly out there. Give me fifteen minutes to get finished and I'll drive. I want to run by Raab's Shoes anyway." Sunny slipped the mail into the proper inboxes.

"Okay, why do you need to go to Raab's?" She moved Heather to her other shoulder and patted her back.

"Pat's mother wants me down there for Thanksgiving, and I gotta get new shoes for my dress."

"You won't be here either? I figured it would be you and me and Pat since Stormy and Rob will be off on their delayed honeymoon. Now we'll be alone." She turned to her baby. "Guess it's just you and me, sweetie."

"You can always go to Gramma's." Her sister didn't bother to glance up.

"You're kidding, right? You and Stormy unearthed ways to get out of going and you're throwing me to the wolves?"

"It's not like that. Besides, when I called Gramma to let her know, she cried. I'm so torn, but I'd already promised Pat's mom. I think I'm starting to rub off on her. As for Stormy, it's their first chance to get away with Rob off from school. This isn't intentional."

Windy stared. "Gramma cried?"

"Yeah. It broke my heart. Please go, for her sake. With Dad not coming home until Christmas, she feels deserted."

"She never should have blindsided us." However, knowing her grandmother cried twisted way inside.

"I guess she realizes that now. Still, there's no undoing. Windy, you don't have to make up with Mom. Just be civil to her and kind to Gramma. If I were staying, I'd go. Honest."

Windy sighed. "I'll consider it. That's all I can promise. Not happy being cornered with no alternatives. Come get me when it's time. I'm going to change Heather." She left the office before Sunny could guilt her anymore.

Besides, she needed to get herself ready to leave.

Fifteen minutes later, Sunny found her in the front room. Stormy had gone for groceries, but it was near closing time anyway. Sunny flipped the sign. They trekked through the back door to the rear parking lot. Windy got Heather in her car seat before climbing into the passenger side. Then they were on their way.

"What're you getting at the library?"

Though Sunny's question might be innocent enough, if Windy shared her plan, she'd get an earful of advice. She was tired of people telling her what to do. What she shouldn't do. Or couldn't do. "I thought I'd go through some of the fashion magazines, especially the bride ones. Plus, I'm gonna check out some books on infant and child rearing. See if there're things I oughta be doing." All logical and truthful. Nothing to raise an argument.

Sunny dropped her and Heather off by the Kokomo Public Library sign. Windy transferred the baby into the carrier. Once inside, she asked at the information desk about the White Pages directories. The library aide guided her to the area and then returned to the front.

Windy realized they were grouped first by state, then by city. Kept duplicate-named communities from being confusing, she imagined. Made it easy to find Boston, Massachusetts. And the three listings for Burketts: Charles T.; George M.; and Harold R. She had an inkling that the Charles T. might be her best guess (T for Timothy maybe?) but to be sure, she wrote each of the names and addresses in her notebook, sticking it in her purse before returning the directory to its place.

Then she moved onto the magazine section. Windy made more notes, plus found great ideas to build on before moving to the non-fiction area and selecting a couple of books. Most were published post World War II. There had to be something more current. She settled on two and headed for the checkout.

Sunny slipped in about then, making her jump. Good thing she wasn't caught with the Boston white pages and having to explain. Sunny took her stack and led the way to her parked Camaro. "I found the cutest pair of burgundy platforms on clearance. They're faux snakeskin and fit like a dream."

"What are you wearing to go with?" Windy buckled Heather into her car seat and climbed in the front.

Sunny closed her door and started the ignition. "You know that maxi dress with the big geometric print?"

Windy knew it. Empire waist with a Nehru collar and sheer puffy sleeves. "Are you sure the color will work? That's mainly subdued blended hues."

"I'm positive. The burgundy will offset the pinks in there just fine. You aren't the only one who knows colors, Windy." What had her so snippy?

"Sorry. Trying to picture it in my mind."

Sunny paused with a sigh. "I'm sorry too. Just feeling the stress of going to Indianapolis and guilt about Gramma. But I do think it'll look great together. We can check it out when we get home."

They did, the shoes worked fine. Plus, they were cute with a tiny scale design and big gold buckles to pick up her jewelry choices. Her sister was right.

After dinner Sunny had her nightly phone conversation with Pat, who could afford to call long distance each night and talk an hour.

It gave Windy the chance to get Heather and herself ready for bed and pull out her stationary. With one of the library books as a makeshift desk, she propped up against her pillows and pulled out the address notes. Since she didn't know which were Tim's parents, she'd write the same carefully crafted message to each.

Dear Mr. and Mrs. Burkett,

My name is Windy, and I am hoping to locate my friend Tim, who attended DePauw University with me. He left me a note saying where he was headed,

but not how to contact him. I'm no longer at school
so he wouldn't know how to reach me.

If he is your son, would you please ask Tim to
contact me at the address below?

She gave the information on Ferguson House and decided to
sign with her middle initial. Windy J. Day read less goofy than
Windy Day.

Windy addressed and sealed the last one as Sunny started up
the stairs. She shoved the envelopes in her purse with the notes
and grabbed her makeshift desk, using it as originally intended.

The Children's Doctor by Dr. Lendon H. Smith focused more
on diet and biological chemistry. It had some interesting data, but
nothing she could add to what she was already doing. At least, it
seemed like it from a minute of perusing.

"Hey, you're still up." Sunny came in and pulled her pajamas
from beneath her pillow before she undressed.

"Yeah, thought I'd read a bit."

"Learning anything?"

Windy shook her head. "Not really. Maybe if Heather were six
months or older. At only a month, though, not much."

Sunny left to brush her teeth and Windy set the book aside.

Heather stirred so she brought her into bed with her, getting
her fed before she got upset. It was so comfortable doing this. At
first it had been painful—no one tells you that part. Now she and
Heather had a routine and it was working.

At some point Sunny returned and flipped off the lights,
because the next thing Windy knew Heather stirred against her
and her watch glowed 4:36. She switched sides and fell back
asleep, cuddled with Heather while she nursed. When she woke

again, it was with her 7:30 alarm. The best night's sleep she'd had in a long time. She felt the smile spreading on her face.

Windy got herself and Heather up and ready before heading downstairs. The song "Good Morning, Star Shine" ran through her mind and she hummed the tune while pouring her first cup of coffee.

"Who is this happy person and what have you done with my sister?" Stormy popped into the kitchen and kissed Heather's forehead.

"I just had a lovely night's snooze. Realized I don't have to keep putting her back into the cradle. We can sleep together."

Stormy coughed, spewing her drink. "What? That is so dangerous. You might roll over and smother her."

"I wouldn't do that." But panic went off in her brain, making her doubt her abilities again. She checked Heather who lay peacefully in her carrier. "She's fine. Stop scaring me like that."

"Just be careful, kiddo. I'm off to get ready. We've two appointments. One is for that Valentine's Day package. It falls on a Sunday, but it's what the bride wants. I've got the feeling she's been visualizing this wedding her whole life. Hope we can live up to it."

"Is it still hush-hush?"

Stormy nodded and called over her shoulder. "For now, it is. Let's just hope her groom knows. Ha!"

Windy rinsed her cup and picked up Heather and the carrier, heading for the third floor. Today they had to transform the ballroom into an Autumn festival like the carriage house.

Kris showed up a few minutes later. He carried a load of the decorations which she set around the room. Once everything they could do from the floor was completed, Kris brought in the extension ladder.

The maple beams on the third floor were too beautiful to stick tacks into, so they needed another idea for the dangling leaves. Kris came through with that. They added tiny eye hooks in the wall next to the beams. Then, using fishing line, they melted the tops of the clear line attached to the leaves onto a horizontal string of fishing line. The heat secured the connection. Then they strung that horizontal line between the eye hooks and voila! It appeared they dangled from the beam, but with no damage.

After the first rows, Kris descended the ladder. They gazed from the back wall at their handiwork.

"Looks nice." Kris was the king of understatement.

She socked him on the bicep. "Nice? It looks great. We make a good team."

He rubbed his upper arm. "You hit me."

"Big baby."

"I'm a big baby? Really?" He stared her down.

"I announce we make a good team and all you do is whine about that tiny little touch to your giant bicep?"

That made him crack a smile. "We do make a good team. You seem happier today."

She dropped into a chair. "Guess I am. Not all my problems are solved, but I got sleep. That helped."

"Cool. So, what's the problem?"

"How do you zero in on that one tiny thing?"

He shrugged. "Gifted. What's up?"

"Looks like I have to go to Gramma's for Thanksgiving. I don't see a way out that won't hurt her or be plain petty. The thought of going twists my stomach. Great, you just shattered my good mood." She socked his arm again.

"Ow!" Kris rubbed his shoulder and grinned. She was so easy to get going. "If you'd quit picking on me when I try to help you, maybe we'd find a solution."

"A solution? You're sweet. Now back to reality. I have to sit in the same room as my mother and pretend she's a normal stranger I met at a friend's house. Everyone there'll be on her side."

"It's really bumming you out, huh?" He nudged her, shoulder to shoulder.

"Yeah, it is. Sunny said Gramma cried on the phone. That's too much. I can't say no to her now, and I dread going. So, what's your idea, big baby?" She nudged him back.

"I'm supposed to go too. What if I pick you up and we stick together? You can use me for a shield." His turn to nudge.

"Not as good as you kidnapping her and leaving her on the moon, but hey, I'll take it."

"Wow. On the moon? Can she at least wear an oxygen mask and bring a sweater? I hear it gets brutal up there." He winked.

She giggled. "Sure, why not. I don't want to be mean."

"Gramps said dinner was at two. I'll pick you up at one thirty."

"Make it one forty-five. Less time to deal with her away from the table. I know, I'm sounding childish, but any avoidable encounters, I'm all for." She stretched her arms in front of her with her fingers laced. "And I should go feed Heather. I'll be back in a bit."

Since they'd figured out the method and the hard part was done, Kris continued attaching the long string to the eye hooks. Wasn't difficult, though it had been more fun when they worked together.

By the time she returned, he'd finished and was folding up the ladder.

"You don't need me?"

He shrugged. "Not unless you notice something I missed." Which could happen.

"Guess we'll go downstairs and check in with Stormy and her appointment." She wiggled her fingers and hefted the carrier with Heather in it, heading for the staircase.

He propped the ladder against the wall. "I'll carry her for you." No need of her falling with Heather.

She let him take the carrier and they descended to the first floor.

The bride brought her whole group of women with her—moms, bridesmaids, flower girls—more than one? Oh well, he'd learned this didn't have to make sense to him. It wasn't his scene.

The little girls noticed he had a baby and rushed over.

"She's so cute." The older of the two stuck her finger out for Heather to grasp. "She's a girl, right?"

Kris nodded while Windy stepped alongside. "Yes, her name is Heather."

The littler one piped up. "That's my name. Can she hold my finger?"

"Sure. Your sister will need to pull hers away so you can have a turn." Windy smiled and stared at the older girl until she complied. "Now hold your finger out by her hand."

"Oh, she's got my pinkie. She's moving it!" The child was enthralled.

"Christie, Heather, it's time to try on your dresses." Stormy motioned them in the direction of the stairs along with the rest of her group.

The girls both waved. "Bye, Baby Heather." "Yeah, bye-bye Heather."

Windy waved to the girls and took a step toward the hall.

Kris threw a last glance up at the kids in time to catch the little one, the other Heather, running her sweater sleeve under her nose, leaving a glossy sheen on the weave as she pulled away. *Ugh*.

He followed down the hall. Since he must hide the ladder in its special place, he'd better hand Heather off to Windy. They were headed into Sunny's office.

"So, tell Gramma I'll attend dinner but I'm coming with Kris. We don't need a ride. He's promised to be my shield." She grinned.

Had he volunteered for more trouble?

"Got the feeling others could use shielding more than you, however, just as long as you are going. Oh, hi, Kris."

"Hey." He set Heather's seat on the desk. "Better get back to work. Later." He waved as he exited and hoped the giggle behind him wasn't about him. The safer plan was to keep moving. Which he did.

The day continued without incident and quitting time finally rolled around. With the ladder well hidden, he closed up shop and headed home. But something had nagged at his brain all afternoon. He hadn't been able to pull it out and look it over. Now that work was finished, the nagging jumped an octave.

He'd offered to pick Windy up to go somewhere.

That sounded dangerously like a date.

Is that how she took it? Did he want her to think that?

Biggest question, had he meant it that way?

He dropped his keys in the bowl by the front door and wandered where habit led. After opening and closing each food-bearing cabinet in the kitchen, he moved to the refrigerator and stood staring at the shelves. Nothing appealed.

What was wrong with him? He was always hungry.

Apparently not for anything in his house.

Pizza King time.

He called in his order and headed for the truck. That's when he spotted it again. Windy's barrette. It was an imitation tortoise shell carved like a bow on top of a metal closing device. It belonged to her. That made him want to pick it up and touch it. There was something about it that reminded him of her. Smooth lines, soft designs, muted colors that were surprisingly distinct when studied closely.

Why was she so in his brain? Especially now? They'd worked together for over eight months. Of course, he'd seen her when she was most vulnerable—you don't let a woman rest her head on your lap while she's in labor and not feel a little close to her.

That brought heat to his cheeks, and he was sure they glowed like Rudolph's nose. Good thing it was cold out so he could blame it on the weather.

He set the barrette where she'd left it and pulled out of the drive. Twenty minutes later he was back with his Supreme. He took it on out to his workshop. Maybe a little art therapy would help. He'd already given Mr. Hingst his piece. That success brought in two more orders. Might as well get started on them.

An hour later he had the frame glued and clamped and his pizza was gone. He dropped the empty box in the trash, then headed for the house, Windy still on his mind. It was like she peeked out from between other thoughts and memories, smiling and waving.

He'd better face it. This was greater than friendship. He was becoming interested. In her. Doing that meant opening up to her about stuff. Things he'd never talked about with anyone else.

Would she still respect him if she had all the facts? That was important. He was fairly sure she liked him, at least as a friend. But there'd be nothing more without her respect.

He needed to know this. And he didn't want to know.

A clear answer required them being on the same page.

He summoned his courage and pulled the phone to him, dialing Ferguson House.

Windy answered on the second ring.

"Hey, it's Kris. Hm. How's it going?"

"Hi, Kris. Long time no hear." Her laugh had a musical quality that he enjoyed.

"Yeah. I wanted to talk to you. Do you have a moment?"

She sobered. "Sure. Everything okay?"

"Um, fine. I got thinking..." He should have planned this out better. After a breath, he continued. "You know about going to Gramps and Hazel's for Thanksgiving?"

"You aren't backing out on me, are you? I'm counting on you for this. I can't do it without you, Kris."

Great, he'd blown it already. "No, I'm not backing out. Just getting this all wrong. I should've explained better." He cleared his throat. "I'm asking you out, Windy. If things work, maybe we could try a real date. I'd like to know you better." There, he'd said it. The rest was up to her.

She got awfully quiet, and he grew concerned they'd lost the connection. In more ways than one. "Windy, still there?"

"Yes, I'm here. I'd like that, Kris. I need to confess something. I'm nervous about dating now that I'm a mom. Are you sure you want to ask me out?"

That's what held her back? "Positive. I get that dating is different when kids are involved. But we've got lots to learn about each other. Let's take it slow, see where it goes. Sound okay?" His heart pounded loud enough to make him worry about hearing her.

Still her words came through nice and clear. "Good idea. We've got things in common, and I enjoy talking with you. Yes, I wanna get to know you."

A weight lifted off his chest. "Whew. We've got a few days of working together before Thursday. We could go out before then. But I figured if we made Thanksgiving our first date, it'd relieve some pressure."

"I think I'd like to try it without a lot of family staring at us. Even if dating isn't our thing, we're still friends. That won't change."

He wished he could be as sure as she was. "Okay. May I take you to dinner and a movie tomorrow?"

Her smile came through the phone with her voice. "Yes. When shall I be ready?"

They set the time and he learned what foods she liked and what she didn't like before hanging up.

Already an idea started. He'd discovered a little Greek restaurant with excellent food uptown. Then they could head to the Isis to catch *The Boatniks* with Robert Morse and Stephanie Powers.

Simple, easy, fun. They'd have an opportunity to talk.

Not that he was a great conversationalist. Somehow with her, though, he didn't feel so awkward sharing his thoughts. She accepted him where most wrote him off.

However, would she accept him if she knew his secret?

Chapter 6
Saturday, November 21, 1970

Windy stole one last glance in the mirror. It'd been a while since she'd entertained these butterflies—anticipation, excitement, trepidation. They all fluttered about her stomach, and she feared they might try a ghastly exit if she didn't calm down.

And it wasn't all centered around Kris. This was the first time since Gramma's visitor debacle that she'd left Heather. Tonight, Sunny would play favorite aunt.

Stormy had promised Rob she'd attend a school function with him, or she'd be hanging out at the mansion vying for her niece's attention.

Windy had no qualms about her daughter's safety. It was just that being away from her was plain hard. If this, whatever it was with Kris, bloomed, they'd have to include dates with Heather along.

Like a family test run.

Where did that phrase come from?

She was getting way ahead of herself. Kris was a nice guy. That'd been established.

And he was good-looking. That was an understatement, especially when he gave a rare grin.

More than that, he drew her attention because of his gentle kindness and view of life. He saw stuff others often missed. He wasn't concerned with people's opinions of him. It was more important to be true to himself. She respected that.

However, Windy was smart enough to know that a relationship required more. There must be agreement on their values. They needed to explore those issues to determine if they were compatible. Her gut told her they were, but maybe that was her heart running ahead, like it tended to do.

"What do you think?" She turned to catch Sunny staring at Heather, not even glancing her way. "Will this work?"

"You're fine. It's not as if Kris is a blind date. He's seen you at your best and worst." Sunny still had her gaze fixed on the baby.

"I know. That's what makes me the most nervous."

A door closed downstairs.

"Didn't you lock up?" Windy turned questioning eyes on her sister.

"I flipped the sign. No need to lock Kris out. He might park in the rear, enter through the back porch out of habit. I'll go see." Sunny set Heather on her hip and went to the first floor.

It gave Windy a moment to wipe her sweaty palms on the rust-colored corduroys she'd paired with her brown patterned silky shirt and crocheted vest. She wore her hair straight, Peggy Lipton style, with her bangs clipped straight back. Once upon a time she'd gazed in this mirror feeling satisfaction at her reflection. Those days were gone. She spotted only the imperfections, lingering baby weight, circles beneath her eyes that had faded but remained no matter what she did. This was who she was now. Hope it was good enough for Kris.

Sunny peeked in without Heather. "He's here."

"Where's my daughter?"

"Kris has her. He's rocking her in the chair." Her sister winked giving her an idea.

She grabbed her Nikon and tiptoed down the steps. If she leaned over the banister just right, she should get a clean shot.

He never glanced up. Instead, Kris's eyes were glued to Heather's.

Windy hoped she caught his gentle expression, praying the photo would turn out. She slipped her camera back up to her room and grabbed her shoulder bag before returning to the first floor. "You appear comfortable."

He didn't raise his head. "I am. She hates for anyone to break their gaze, doesn't she?"

Windy chuckled. "Yeah, she's kinda the Queen of the Stare."

Sunny took the baby from him. "Oh, how can I reach you? Not that I'm anticipating anything, but to be safe."

Kris handed her a piece of paper and put his finger to his lips.

Sunny giggled. "Alrighty, then. You kids enjoy yourselves. My niece and I are going to have some fun. Wave bye-bye to Mommy." She helped Heather bat her hand.

Windy blew kisses and forced herself to follow Kris out. Leaving her baby was harder than she'd anticipated.

Kris slipped her hand in his and led her to his truck. After opening her door, he scooted around to his side and climbed in. "Ready?"

"Ready." She hoped she sounded more convincing than she felt. "Where are we off to?"

"I found this place uptown. It has unique stuff on the menu and isn't far from the Isis. Ever been to Coney Island?" He glanced her way as he finished.

Just in time to catch her grin. "I babysat for the Volikas kids when I was in high school. Until they'd grown enough to help at the restaurant. Yeah, I've been there a few times. The bakes are wonderful, but I love the sauce they put on their coney dogs."

"Oh." He became quiet.

"Hey, it's a great choice. I love their food. Are you upset because I'm familiar with the restaurant?"

He shook his head. "Not really. I forget you grew up here. I'm still discovering places."

"Well, you found a great one. Getting hungry just thinking about it." She hoped that was all it was, and he wasn't holding something back.

"Good."

A few minutes later he parallel parked on Union Street near the restaurant's entrance. But when they arrived, the inside was dark.

She pointed to a sign taped on the door.

Closed—due to busted water pipe.

"Oh no. I was counting on a bake." Just thinking of the hamburger/meatloaf creation served on a hot dog bun had her mouth happy. And now...

"Any ideas?" He shoved his hands in his pockets and gazed her way.

"Do you have your heart set on the Isis? We could eat at the Casa Grande. Then check the theater at the mall." She crossed her fingers, not knowing how he'd react at this frustration.

"Sure." He held her door and then climbed back in. "The Casa Grande it is. I could go for a T-Bone tonight." He grinned, making Windy's heart skip a beat. Yeah, that grin should be patented. Made her thoughts of food fly out the window despite the rolled-up glass.

The conversation lagged until they arrived at the restaurant and were seated. Getting the menu into her hands stimulated something. She could finally form words. "Not sure what I want. They've got turkey, but we'll be having that next week. Maybe I'll go with the roast beef. Are you still sold on the steak?"

He nodded. "Yeah. I'm a little pizza'd out."

"You eat a lot of pizza?" Funny, she'd never imagined what it might be like for him after work.

"More than I should. I've got Pizza King's number down by heart." He grimaced. "Sometimes it's the easy way. Other times I warm up hot dogs or open a couple cans of Chef Boyardee."

"Do you know how to cook?" She hoped that wouldn't be too personal. Still, wasn't that the point? To learn about each other?

"When it's only one eating, there's no need for fancy. I grill as weather permits. But it's just me." He didn't seem upset or embarrassed or defensive, just matter of fact.

"Back in the dorm, I used to sneak cook using my iron. I could wrap a hot dog or a cheese sandwich in aluminum foil and press it on the cotton setting until the food was heated through. I guess that's sort of the same. Only we had so many house restrictions it was crazy." Something about clandestine cooking made it taste a little better.

"What did you study in school?" He'd set his menu aside and turned his full attention on her.

"I was an art major. Tried several mediums, but found I was most comfortable with my camera. I minored in music mainly for Dad. With Sunny chasing her finance degree and Stormy becoming a teacher, I was concerned he'd think he had no influence. Where did you go to school?"

Now he got uncomfortable. "I didn't. My folks pressed but it wasn't for me. I took some trade classes, but it got to be too much. So, I moved here with Gramps. They figured my grandfather would side with them, but he gets me. Let me set up my studio in his old workshop out behind his house. Even helped me find my first commission. Dad mentions school every time we talk. Guess he still hopes."

"Have they seen your work? That should change their minds." Kris was so talented, his ability to create things from a simple sketch was amazing. Maybe he'd let her photograph him, a sort of collage of the steps to the completion of a project.

He scrutinized her face. "You've just thought of something."

"You could tell?" Really?

He nodded. "Your eyes narrow when the idea is churning and widen when you get it. You should never play poker." That brought a laugh.

"True. I can't hide my emotions very well." She wasn't telling him anything he didn't already know.

"You don't like negative feelings. I've seen you avoid them. You change the subject, or when you're stuck you search for something positive out of it or crack a joke. Sometimes you gotta deal with the bad stuff."

She smoothed her napkin across her lap. "Do you do that? Allow yourself to really feel the bad stuff?"

"Sometimes. I either deal with it or dismiss it. That's how I move on."

"So, what's some bad stuff you've had to deal with or dismiss?"

The waitress arrived to take their order and she could've sworn he looked like a death row inmate getting a last-minute reprieve.

No, she wouldn't press that one tonight. She could revisit it later if things went well. Then another thought hit her. "Sunny doesn't know we aren't at Coney Island. I better call her. Excuse me." She swiped her bag and headed for the phones.

After digging a dime from her wallet, she dialed the mansion. Busy signal. Great. Sunny must be talking with Pat. Hope she was paying attention to Heather too. She returned to the table. After dinner she could try again.

Kris peered up as she approached. "Everything okay?"

"I guess. The line was busy. Pat calls Sunny every night and they talk quite a while. I hope she's watching Heather. There's no one more responsible than Sunny, though. I'm sure all is fine." She sat and the waitress appeared with their salads.

Dinner soon followed and Windy decided she was too full for dessert. Besides, she had some weight to lose.

Kris paid the bill and they left for the mall. Once inside, they perused the movie choices.

"What's caught your interest?" He was letting her choose?

Maybe she should pick something he'd enjoy so he wouldn't regret this date. "How about *Dirty Dingus Magee*. I like to laugh. What do you think?"

"When does it start?" He stared at the signs. Couldn't he see?

"In fifteen minutes."

"Okay, that sounds good." He clasped her hand and led her to the ticket counter where he paid for two seats and then to the concession stand where he bought a large popcorn. After checking her preferences, he added a couple Cokes to the order. He was forced to release her to carry the snacks. However, once in the theater his hand found hers again.

The tingles didn't make her crazy, just increased the sweetness of his touch. She discovered a contentment she'd never known and wanted to draw inside the sensation, letting it wrap all around her. Like one of his hugs might. She closed her eyes a second and let herself get lost in the moment. It felt so right.

Frank Sinatra and George Kennedy were funny enough, but Windy's thoughts were drawn to the guy sitting on her left. Now that she had a daughter to consider, she wouldn't date for fun. So, could she see a future growing between them? Kris seemed natural holding Heather before they headed out. From what she'd seen, he'd make a good father.

But what if Tim contacted her? Didn't she owe him the chance? The guy didn't even know he had a child.

There were too many questions tonight. Her brain wanted her heart to take over. And her heart? It just longed to sit there and hold Kris's hand. Forever.

⚘

KRIS SMILED TO HIMSELF. This was better than he'd imagined. Sitting here, holding her hand. She liked westerns. The choices hadn't been that great. A part of him was worried she'd catch on while they chose. The Isis only had one show playing so that made it easier. But everything was good. They'd had an easy conversation and he realized he knew her more than he first thought.

He'd been concerned they'd feel awkward with each other, but that didn't happen. Much. But her zeroing in on the school topic wasn't fun. She could've kept asking about the hard stuff in his life, but she let it go. Maybe she read him a little too.

Her hand fit so perfectly with his. The contentment of just sitting together would overwhelm him if he allowed it. When he reached for popcorn a minute ago, she did too. Their other hands met. So silly, but the gentle electric pulses from her touch woke his heart.

Yeah, he was in trouble.

Maybe he should focus on the movie. He'd be hard pressed to tell anyone the plot. The audience seemed to like it, roaring on occasion. Hope she was getting something out of this film. He was more into enjoying her company.

The show ended and the others cleared the theater, but he and Windy continued to sit. He peeked at her and realized she slept sitting up straight. Wow. He knew she'd been tired. It was hard to miss the weariness in her eyes. She must have really needed the rest.

He hated to wake her, but the cleaning crew was starting. "Windy." He tried to be as gentle as possible, wiggling his fingers against her hand. "Windy, we need to go now."

Her lids fluttered open, and she scanned the room. Then she gasped. "Oh no, Kris. I'm sorry."

"It's okay. You've been tired for a while. One good night in six weeks isn't enough." He brushed her hair from her cheek.

"But you paid for us to see the movie. This is a date. You deserve my attention."

"I'm not upset. However, I do think I'd better get you home." He helped her to her feet and pulled her close a moment, rubbing her spine.

She melted into him, and he worried she'd gone back to sleep until she glanced up. "Thank you. I've enjoyed our evening. Haven't been this relaxed in forever." Her warm laughter floated around them.

He turned her so they could walk, though his arm held her to his side. The chilly night air gave him a boost of energy and he imagined it woke her more. The rustling leaves in the night's breeze added to the music of the atmosphere as cloudy skies blocked the stars and hid the moon.

He unlocked the truck and helped her in before getting himself inside and turning the ignition. It fired to life. He flicked on the heater and pulled out onto the highway.

At the stoplight, he glanced down and spotted her barrette. Should he give it back to her? Yes, if she asked for it. Until then, the barrette represented a piece of her. For when she was gone.

Would she be gone? He didn't want to consider that. If anything, this evening convinced him he wanted to pursue her even more.

He parked in front of Ferguson House and came around to get her door. Walking her to the steps, he hesitated. Should he? Shouldn't he?

Before he made up his mind, the door yanked open. "Windy, I'm so glad you're home, get in here." Sunny didn't wait, but hustled deeper inside, expecting Windy to follow.

She grabbed hold of his hand first and pulled him along with her. "What's the matter? Where's Heather?"

"Up in the bathroom. Doctor Schwartz was here. Told us to give her lots of steam tonight and bring her to his office in the morning." She opened the bathroom door.

Hazel, holding the baby, and Cheryl, sat on the edge of the clawfoot tub. Heather was down to her diaper. The room was filled with eucalyptus scented vapor.

Windy's grip tightened on his fingers.

"The doctor said to rub Vicks on her feet and to steam until ten o'clock. Then feed her like normal and see how she sleeps." Sunny relayed the orders, though she had to know Windy's glare fixated on her mother and grandmother.

"What are they doing here?" Windy's voice lost all warmth.

"I couldn't reach you, so I called Gramma. She's the one who told me to call Doctor Schwartz. Mom got the steaming started while we waited. The doctor said it was the best idea."

Windy released his hand and moved to her baby, taking her from Hazel. "What happened?"

Neither Hazel nor Cheryl spoke. Instead, they kept their attention on Heather.

Kris closed the bathroom door, replacing the towel that'd been shoved at the base.

"You going to tell me what happened to my baby?"

Hazel glanced up then. "Windy, settle down. Heather is congested. She's caught a cold somewhere. Sunny thought she felt a little warm, so she took her temperature. It was over one hundred, so she called me when she couldn't reach you. She tried to find you first. Your sister was concerned for your baby and did the right thing. You should thank her."

He could see it in her eyes. She didn't feel like saying thank you.

"What do I need to do?" At least she was thinking proactively.

"Just keep her head up to help her breath better. This came on suddenly. First the fever and then the congestion. The doctor isn't positive it's only a cold. He wants to check her for strep in the morning, even though it's Sunday. If it's merely a stuffy nose, this should help clear her. But if there's strep involved, he'll know tomorrow when you take her in." Hazel pushed Windy to focus on Heather's immediate needs.

Windy set Heather against her shoulder and patted her back while she paced the bathroom.

Sunny pulled at his elbow. "What happened? No one answered at Coney Island and the Isis manager said he even stopped the film to make the announcement."

"Coney's had a pipe burst so they closed early. We went to The Casa Grande instead. She called you but the line was busy. Said you must be talking with Pat." He shrugged.

"I told him not to call tonight because I was babysitting. Oh, what a mess. Thank you, Kris, for bringing her home when you did."

"She fell asleep in the movie. Windy's more tired than she lets on." His gaze returned to the woman trying to pace. Her eyes looked enormous in her face, but they couldn't hide the purplish hollows beneath them.

Sunny patted his arm and moved to whisper to her grandmother, who nodded and whispered to Cheryl. They rose and left the room.

He ensured the towel was in place. Then he slipped out of his jacket since the room's temperature got to him. Afterwards he padded over to keep step with Windy. "Would you like me to hold her awhile? I can spell you."

She shook her head and buried her face closer to Heather.

He shrugged again to Sunny who shrugged back. They sat on the edge of the tub and watched her continue her walk.

Half an hour later, Sunny checked her watch. "It's ten. We can bundle her up and get her ready for bed."

Windy slowed and wrapped a blanket about Heather. She hadn't said a word since Hazel made her listen.

Sunny turned off the faucets and wiped the mirror before opening the bathroom door.

"Would you like me to take you in the morning?" He needed to do something.

Windy raised her eyes, glanced from him to Sunny and back, then nodded. "Thank you."

Sunny smiled, patted Kris's shoulder, and left the room.

Kris sidled to the same side as Heather, peeking at her sweet face beneath the blanket. He kissed her on top of her head. It was time he left. So, he trailed his finger down Windy's cheek and headed out the door.

"Kris?"

He turned back.

"Thank you. It was a nice evening until we came home."

"No problem. I had a good time too." He waved and left.

Sunny waited downstairs. "Is she okay?"

"Exhausted, worried, and angry. Okay isn't the word. She'll focus on Heather now. Maybe that'll cool her down. She gets it about you needing help. But not about your mother."

"I know. Gramma decided to bring her, but she's the one who remembered about the steaming and got it started before the doctor arrived. I'm just glad he still makes house calls." Sunny brushed her bangs from her face and rubbed her earlobe.

"Better go. I'll be here in the morning." He waved and let himself out.

As he climbed into the truck, he noticed his pulse was pounding. If anything happened to that little girl...No, nothing would happen on his watch. She had him wrapped around that tiny pinkie of hers. He now realized he loved her as if she were his own. Good grief, he'd been the first to hold her, after the doctor and nurses and her mother, of course. And Aunt Stormy. So, he might as well be her father.

He threw the truck into gear and pulled away from the curb. His protective nature kicked into high. Not simply for Windy or Heather, but for both of them. Agreed, it was too soon to push, they'd promised to move slow. Yet he knew, as well as he knew his name, the three of them belonged together. They were growing into a family.

The thought thrilled him as much as it terrified him. Could he handle it? Was he capable of becoming a good father and husband? The provider they deserved?

That was yet to be seen. One more reason to take it slow. Going to the doctor with them tomorrow was a step. The sort of stuff a father and husband would do. Right?

So, why did this scare him?

Chapter 7
Sunday, November 22, 1970

W indy held Heather in Doctor Schwartz's outer office while he got the exam room ready. Kris had driven them, parking in the side lot. They spotted the doctor arriving at the same time. No nurses worked since it was Sunday, so he asked them to give him a second to get things started.

Her nerves were going to make her jump out of her skin. She hadn't gotten a wink of sleep for watching Heather all night. Fear of hurting her kept her from pulling the baby into bed for more than just feeding time. So instead, Heather slept in the cradle. Windy leaned over the edge checking her until the alarm rang at six.

She ought to get rid of the alarm clock. Heather handled that chore much better.

Kris put his hand on her knee.

She glanced at him, realizing she'd been bouncing it up and down, over and over. Her nerves needed an outlet.

"You can come back now, Windy. Wanted to make sure I was set up." Doctor Schwartz motioned to her.

She gripped Kris's hand before following the doctor to an exam room. It was one designed for kids with cute cartoons on the walls and a smaller examination table. She sat in the chair and pulled Heather closer.

"How about you undress Little Doll and put her on the scale. How did she do last night?" He warmed his stethoscope in his hands.

"She ate less than normal and woke twice. Both times she nursed but not great. I took her with me into the bathroom when I got my shower today hoping the steam helped." Windy studied his every move and expression.

"Fine. It's that time of year. She's still itty bitty to have to deal with a bug, though. Sounds clearer this morning. That's good. But her throat has me concerned. The congestion is in her head, but I'm thinking she might have strep. Has she been around other children?"

Windy started to answer when she realized Doctor Schwartz looked past her. "Oh, doctor, this is my friend, Kris. Heather's father is...out of town."

"Oh, I see. Has she been with kids who could've exposed her?"

Her cheeks must be glowing because her face felt like it was on fire. "I don't think so..." Then she remembered. "Yes, two children at the shop. They wanted Heather to hold their fingers." She never thought about them making her baby sick. What kind of mother was she? "If she's got strep, doctor, what do I do?" It was time to focus on Heather's needs and not her own embarrassment.

"With these little ones, continue feeding her. You can offer her water in a bottle too. I'll give her a shot today, which should help. Watch for a fever. If it spikes, head straight for the emergency room. If it's merely coughing in her sleep, keep an eye on it, make her comfortable. If she's not eating like normal by tomorrow, call and we'll fit you in. Oh, be sure to wash your hands and be careful. You don't need to come down with strep yourself."

He gave the injection and Windy winced.

Heather froze, then hollered.

Windy picked her up. "Okay to dress her now?" She met Kris's gaze. He had paled watching Heather have a needle inserted into her tiny little hip.

"Sure, get her dressed. I'll meet you out front." The doctor left the room.

Windy put the baby gown back on Heather while whispering soothing sounds and then wrapped her securely. The baby calmed.

Kris toted the empty carrier.

Windy needed to feel Heather in her arms at the moment.

They walked to the reception desk where she wrote a check for the visit. An afterhours appointment was expensive. Then Kris guided her to the truck where she strapped Heather into her car seat, and they headed for home.

Once underway, that instance in the office rushed back. "Kris, I'm sorry about that."

He glanced over. "About what?"

"About Doctor Schwartz's assumption."

"Oh, that." He shrugged. "It was a natural mistake. Don't worry. I'm a big boy." He even flashed her a grin.

She really liked that grin.

"Guess we missed church again. I've been finding excuses to stay home to miss the drama. Almost wish for that now instead of knowing Heather's got strep." Why had she let those little urchins near her baby?

"Hey, no blaming yourself. You're the best mom I've ever met." He grabbed her hand.

Windy absorbed strength from his touch. He believed in her. "Thanks." She wiped a tear away with her other hand.

When they pulled in the drive, Sunny's car was gone. She probably left for church. Hopefully, she'd go to dinner, too, though both she and Stormy had declined to attend since Gramma's visitor arrived.

Kris walked her to the door.

"Do you want to come in?" As much as she longed to be with him, right now Heather was her focus. But he'd been so supportive, she had to ask.

"I'm here if you need me. How about I make lunch while you take care of Heather?"

That was a wonderful idea. "I don't know if we have hot dogs..." She tossed him a wink.

"I can handle it. Go on. You don't want her getting too fussy with her throat sore." He was right about that.

"Thanks." Windy picked Heather up out of her carrier and headed to their bedroom. "Mama's got you, little love. Let's get you fed." She curled up on the bed and set her to nursing.

Heather was such a good baby, never a big crier, so content. When she was awake, she tried to focus on things, her immense blue eyes so round taking in her environment. How was it to be tiny, dependent? Windy craved to cuddle with her, let the world spin away. She stroked the downy white fuzz that covered the little head. Most of the dark hair she'd been born with had turned auburn and fallen out like her dad predicted, replaced with microscopic hairs so fine they were almost transparent. Her baby would be blond. Like her.

Tim had sandy colored hair, so it wasn't a stretch to figure Heather's would be light. He had blue eyes too. What color were Kris's eyes? Right, they were blue as well and he had those beach blond waves. No wonder the doctor took him for Heather's other parent.

He'd make a good father, of that she was sure. Did he want to be? He didn't seem opposed.

But what if she and Kris built a relationship and Tim showed up? She never put his name on the birth certificate. It was easier that way. If she'd been after child support, maybe she would've. But back then she never imagined seeing Tim again, even if she'd secretly wanted to.

Did she still want to? That was the million-dollar question.

She couldn't answer that. At this point, if he returned, it would complicate things. A lot. But she never would have given herself to him if she hadn't loved him. And she really thought she loved him enough to get married.

That is, until Kris.

Not that she was declaring herself marriage-commitment-in-love with the big guy, but what she did feel made her question her emotions for Tim.

Windy heaved a sigh. This was too much to think about. She was too tired, and her baby needed her. If she could just sleep, she'd be able to sort it out and move on.

She switched sides and Heather kept eating. That gave her hope. This beautiful girl without any birth marks. Not even the white baby acne other babies got. She traced her finger over her daughter's perfect miniature ear. Heather's complexion was flawless.

The baby stirred and Windy blinked. The room was darker. She glanced at her watch. Five-thirty? Oh no, she'd just slept the day away.

And Kris. He fixed lunch for them.

She buttoned her top, picked up Heather, and headed for the stairs.

Kris sat in the hallway, his head resting on his knees.

"You'll be stiff sitting there like that. How long have you been up here?"

He jolted. "Oh, Windy. You're awake. How was your nap?"

How did he sit there and sleep? Wasn't he the least bit put out?

"I'm so sorry, Kris. I didn't mean to doze off. I keep doing that to you."

He rose to his feet, unfolding all six foot plus of him—how tall was he anyway? "You needed to sleep. You've needed to for a while. I saved our lunch. We can have it for dinner. Oh, call Stormy."

She headed down the steps. "Did she say what she wanted?"

"No." He followed.

"How long ago did she call?" Windy took the landing into the kitchen.

"She stopped by while I was cooking. I told her you were feeding the baby, so she slipped upstairs. Guess she realized you'd crashed because when she came down, she said to have you phone her."

"Better do that, then. We'll be right back." Windy slipped off to Sunny's office and dialed.

"You're just waking up?" Stormy sounded concerned.

"Yes. I didn't realize I'd fallen asleep, but I'd been awake most of the night. What do you need?"

"Was just checking on Heather then. But now I want to make sure you're okay. Is Kris still there?"

Windy's lips pressed to a thin line. "You know he is. You can see his truck out your window. He's been a proper gentleman, Stormy. Nothing went on. He's only here to help. Did you go to Sunday dinner at Gramma's?" How would she handle that change of subject?

"I did. I hate that she's been crying. Sunny said she planned to stay awhile and maybe talk things out. That was more than I could do. I played nice and Rob kept a close eye on me. He noticed when I was about to say something I'd regret and squeezed my hand. We left soon after dessert."

"Sunny isn't back yet. Wonder what all is being said?" And if her sister had made peace with their mother.

"Oh, I doubt she's still there. Pat showed up for dinner. Apologized that he couldn't make church but wouldn't miss a meal. Gramma loves him for that. I'm betting Sunny and Pat took a drive. She'll be along eventually." Which translated meant she might arrive any moment, so don't get into trouble. Good grief.

"Kris is reheating lunch so I'm going to go now. Bye." She hung up before Stormy tried to give her a lecture.

Why did they assume she and Kris would do something? They'd never even kissed. And she'd already made that mistake once. Did they really think she hadn't learned anything?

Sometimes her sisters were overbearing.

She wandered back to the kitchen that smelled wonderfully Italian as Kris set two bowls of pasta on the table. After getting Heather into her carrier, she sat.

"Spaghetti leftovers are better than fresh cooked." He winked.

"I'm starving and this smells amazing." The guy was full of surprises.

He took the other chair and offered her the Kraft Parmesan cheese container. "Didn't know how much you wanted."

She grinned. "No such thing as too much cheese."

"We have an understanding, then."

And they did. An easy understanding that only grew better.

Oh no.

Her mind conjured the letters she'd sent. For the first time, she hoped none of the people were Tim's parents. That they'd no clue where he was or who he was. And, most of all, that he wouldn't try to contact her.

If she didn't hear from him or them, she could rest knowing she'd tried. But if Tim contacted her...

That was one thought she'd not ponder. At least, not until she absolutely must.

෫

KRIS RUBBED THE BACK OF HIS NECK.

"Oh, man, you're stiff from sleeping in the hallway." Windy's gaze filled with concern as little lines formed between her brows.

"It's no big deal. I wanted to be close in case you had a problem. I didn't mean to sleep either. Guess we both needed it." He grinned, hoping that would end her uneasiness.

But it didn't. She hopped up and began to massage his neck. He was sure she meant it to help him relax, but the touch of her fingers going up into his hairline and down onto his shoulders stirred him, like electrical charges running down his spine. Pleasant, invigorating, exciting. Was it becoming harder to breathe in here?

He patted her hand. "I think I'm good."

"Sorry, I'm not the best at giving neck rubs." She sat again.

"It's not that." How did he explain? It sounded goofy to say her touch drove him crazy. But that's what it was. "We'll have to try it another time. I'm hungry. Aren't you?" Get this focus off him.

She chuckled. "Yeah, I am. I'd better keep up my strength. My little girl needs me." With her fork poked into the nest of noodles, she twirled strings of spaghetti into the perfect sized bite and popped it in her mouth.

He'd never tried the twist around the tines method. His mother rarely served the dish but when she did, she insisted on cutting the pasta and scooping. She claimed twirling was gauche. But somehow Mom's manners lacked the gusto he saw in how Windy enjoyed her food. He caught her eyeing him as he succumbed to his old habit. Her way required private practice before he'd attempt it for an audience, even if it was just her.

After dinner, she boiled some water and left it to cool. Then she set out a bottle. "Maybe she could use something to drink." She glanced down at Heather who watched every move her mother made.

"I'll feed her for you." He volunteered before he thought. But sure, he could do that.

"You just want out of washing dishes. Okay, you cooked." She flashed him a smile that set his pulse to throbbing.

"There's probably time for both. The water won't cool that fast." He put his dish in the sink.

"You're right. Wash or dry?"

"You know where everything goes. I'll wash." He turned on the faucet and grabbed the bottle of Palmolive.

"Deal, buster." She nudged him and snagged a dishtowel. "You're pretty handy in the kitchen."

"I learned from the best. Mom's a great cook. I worked as her sou chef whenever I saw the chance. Junior high is when I discovered power tools and woodworking, but the school insisted on two weeks per semester where the boys and girls switched home ec and shop teachers. That way none of the kids could plead ignorance. I think it was hardest on the male instructors, trying to watch their language and all." He handed her a plate.

"Sounds like a great idea. Girls should know about power tools and boys about the stove and oven. What kind of grade did you get with the switch?"

Why did he bring that up? The only saving grace from that experience was his partner was a born leader. He took over. Having Larry tell him what to do kept him from making a lot of mistakes. "I did all right, got a B+." Thanks to Larry.

"I'd have loved to have a chance to take shop. Hey, would you show me how to use some of your tools? Maybe I might make something."

Have her in his shop? That set bubbling in his gut. Was it fear or excitement? He'd love for her to see what he did, share that part of himself, but the way her sisters talked, Windy was an accident waiting to happen. Could he risk that?

"You're awful slow answering there, Mr. Norman. You don't want me in your domain?" She took the big pot from his hands.

"No, it's not that. I'm happy to show you my shop. Even teach you some things." How should he say this? "I use stuff there that requires close attention. If you're not careful, you can get hurt pretty bad. Will you watch out?"

"You've been listening to more of Sunny and Stormy's propaganda. They have no idea what I'm capable of. And neither do you. Do you think all my art projects in school were with crayons and watercolors? I did some really creative stuff that could've gone wrong if I didn't pay attention. There were sharp tools and caustic chemicals. And I never got a scratch. They can't let go of my falling off the block wall, because it happened when our mother left. They've tied the two things together." She tossed the dishtowel on top of the drainer. "So, are you going to listen to them or treat me like an adult?"

He raised his hands in surrender. "Fine. But if you get hurt, you better protect me from your sisters. I think I can take Sunny, but Stormy still scares me."

She punched his arm. "Big baby. If anything, I'm the one you need to fear." She laughed at that.

But she was right. The way he'd fallen for her, she could rip his heart to shreds with little effort.

She started drying again and he tested the water. It was warmer than room temperature, but not hot to the touch. "I think it's ready. Want me to fix the bottle?"

"You know how?"

"Yes." He wasn't stupid. Maybe he did need to show her his workshop, so she'd realize he had a brain. Especially before she learned his secret.

"Only about two ounces. I don't want her to fill up on it, just keep her throat comfortable."

He nodded and got the bottle ready, even doing a final test on his wrist. The water was fine.

Heather watched the whole exchange and when he picked her up, her eyes locked with his. "She's got another staring contest going."

"That's my girl. Take her on into the other room. I'll finish here and meet you there."

He did, settling in the rocker and testing Heather with the bottle. She went for it. Then stopped. She peered as if to say, "Not what I'm used to, Bub." However, she was willing to take it and began to drink. Every so often she'd stop and swallow, then start again. He wondered if her throat felt better.

Windy wandered in and curled up on the sofa, tucking her feet under her. He caught her eyes growing heavy. All those carbs from dinner at work. Heather would need to eat in a couple hours. He might as well let her grab another nap. Besides, rocking this little one was pleasant.

As he rocked, Heather's lids lowered, then blinked, then lowered again. Soon they stayed closed. Her tiny lips parted letting water from the nipple drip down her chin. He set the bottle on the floor next to him and wiped her mouth with the edge of the blanket before settling back in the chair with her. It was tempting to close his own eyes, but fear of dropping the baby kept them open. The house was so quiet and the baby's body heat so comfortable, it would be easy to drift off.

Who knew he'd enjoy rocking an infant like this? He couldn't remember seeing his father rock his little sisters, but then his dad was always busy. He hadn't thought about his sisters in some time. They were both in high school now. Did they miss him? Neither wrote often since he left, but then, he hadn't written them either. He could call, but long distance added up fast. And on his budget, that wasn't good. He didn't want to wreck things by spending before he'd saved.

However, it was getting better. Doing that project for Mr. Hingst helped a lot. He'd gotten two referrals out of it. More connections might result from getting those completed, which he needed to do. He had done little more since he clamped the second frame. Now he was prepared to do the designing and staining before adding the wrought iron touches. Maybe by next weekend they'd be finished if there were no more emergencies.

He heard the back door creak. Seconds later Sunny entered from the hall. She spotted the two sleepers. Moving on tiptoe into the room, she spoke in a whisper. "How are they doing?"

He nodded. "Windy fell asleep earlier with Heather. We just finished dinner and I gave the baby some water. It got so quiet, I think she dozed again."

"Nope, I'm not sleeping, just resting my eyes." Which Windy never opened. "I'm appreciating the peace."

"Ah. Well, if you want to sleep, that's fine too. Kris and I can watch over Heather." Sunny perched at the foot of the couch.

Windy cracked her lids then. "How did dinner go?"

"It was...different. Gramma, Mom, and I sat in the living room and talked awhile."

"What? No cookies at the dining room table?" Windy cocked an eyebrow.

"No, no cookies. Gramma asked me to hear what Mom had to say. So, I did. She never tried to convince me she did the best for us nor begged me to forgive her. She just gave me a glimpse of her side, right or wrong. It helped a little. I've missed her more than I realized." Sunny ran a knuckle under her eye.

"I never missed her."

Kris glanced over, catching Windy's firm jaw.

"That's not true. You cried yourself to sleep every night for a month."

"Because I broke my leg." Windy grabbed a pillow with braids of fringe around the edges and pulled it close beneath her crossed arms.

"Whatever you want to tell yourself. I was there." Sunny glanced at him, and he got the impression she wanted him to leave.

Perhaps he was in the way for a needed conversation with Windy.

Heather's carrier wasn't in the room, so he stood and put her in her mother's arms. "I need to go. Now that you're here, Sunny, you can take care of them. See you tomorrow."

He grabbed his jacket from the cloak tree.

"Kris, you don't have to leave." Windy begged with her eyes.

He shook his head. "I'd better. There's work to be done on a project in my shop and morning comes early. We'll talk then." *Besides, you need to face that chat with your sister.*

Sunny met him at the door. "Thank you. For everything."

He nodded and stepped into the November chill, which cooled his body and his emotions. More than warm fuzzies were involved with building this relationship. Frankly, they'd have better odds if they were both in healthier places with their own lives.

Maybe he needed to give his sisters a call. Just to remind them they had a big brother.

Chapter 8
Thursday, November 26, 1970

Windy woke with a scratchy throat. It took a moment to connect the dots in her head but when she realized it might not be post-nasal drip, panic rose.

She'd made a bargain and she was determined to keep it. But if she claimed strep now, everyone would think she was just trying to duck out of Thanksgiving at Gramma's. Especially after that chat with Sunny who guilted her into making sure she attended the dinner. Why couldn't she have caught the stupid infection when Heather did? Now her baby was doing better, but she might end up exposing her family and making them all ill.

Or maybe she had already.

She'd read up on strep after Heather got sick. The Encyclopedia Britannica was a wealth of information. It said the incubation period for adults was two to six days. They were contagious even during that time. Great. Who had she exposed?

She thought of everyone she'd been in contact with. It would take sharing utensils, cups, or straws.

Or kissing.

And she hadn't kissed Kris.

Yet.

Maybe not for a while now. If she coughed or sneezed, she could spread the germs, but she'd not been doing either. Much. Some. Mainly at night, a little tickle in her throat.

So, the customers were all probably uninfected. What about her sisters? They hadn't shared contact items. Plus, she'd been vigilant about washing her hands because of what Doctor Schwartz said. Okay, that meant everyone else was most likely clear.

She and Kris had hugged a few times. Briefly. *Please don't let him be exposed.*

This day would be hard enough. How did she handle it and keep her family safe?

Windy glanced at the clock. Dinner wouldn't be until two o'clock. Maybe it wasn't strep. If she gargled with warm salt water, that might be all she needed. She climbed out of bed, giving a sleeping Heather a check before running off to the bathroom. After that she raced downstairs for a cup and the saltshaker, returning to allow the faucet to run until the water had heat. Then she mixed up a small pile of white crystals in the water, swirling it before taking a mouthful and juggling it over her tonsils. The sting made her eyes tear. Ouch. Something told her it wasn't just drainage.

Now what should she do?

A cry from her bedroom grabbed her attention and she hustled to her baby girl, who'd awakened and wanted food. Would nursing make her daughter sick again? Or had she built up enough antibodies? She couldn't let the baby starve. But would this end up a vicious cycle, re-exposing each other?

She brought Heather into bed with her and set her to feeding while trying to keep her face turned away. It had been a long time since she'd uttered a prayer outside of listening to her grandmother say grace, but she thought one now. *Please, God, don't let Heather get sick from me.*

Since Gramma wasn't caring for her baby, there hadn't been a reason to pump. But now there was. Could she pump enough plus feed her angel until she built a supply? She'd have to. *Body don't fail me.*

Sunny left for Indianapolis last evening to spend the weekend with Pat's family. Hopefully, she didn't get this and expose all the Whitcombs.

Stormy hadn't spent as much time with Heather. However, if she got this, imagine the fun her delayed second honeymoon would be.

Windy groaned.

Heather stopped and stared up at her.

"Sorry, lovey. We're in a bit of a pickle."

Her baby latched on again.

So, what did she do about today? Should she let Kris know?

Heather fell back to sleep.

Windy put her in the cradle, then she slipped to the kitchen for the pumping equipment she'd stuck on a top shelf. Might as well get started.

She didn't have as much milk as she hoped. But she put it into the refrigerator and prayed that pumping between nursing would replenish her supply. Then she set about getting ready, taking the cradle into the bathroom while she took her shower. Heather slept through it, which helped.

Once she was dressed, she gargled again and winced. She'd just have to suffer through. Then she carried Heather in her carrier downstairs. She had five hours and forty-five minutes to figure out a plan.

She tried pumping again an hour later. Basically, she was making herself sore and not producing much. Plus, her head had started to pound, and she was fairly sure she had a fever. She found the thermometer where Sunny stored it in the downstairs medicine cabinet, only to discover the proof. One hundred point four. Great. Just great.

Who should she call? Gramma would be up to her elbows in turkey and potatoes. No way to call her sisters. Besides, she hated to ruin their holiday. If she hadn't already.

Kris. Poor guy, he was her only hope. She dialed his number.

"I think I have strep." She hadn't even given him a chance to say hello.

"You need me to come over?"

"Tell me what to do. If I back out now, no one'll believe it's because I'm sick and don't want them to get it. If I go, they might all become ill. What do I do?" Her head felt worse with each word she spoke, not to mention how it hurt her throat.

"Give me five minutes." He hung up.

She knew he was driving over. He shouldn't come. She didn't want him sick too. Yet knowing he was coming helped. Brain activity worked at a premium. If he'd think for her, that'd be better.

Kris parked out front.

She unlocked the door before crashing back on the couch.

Heather slept in her carrier next to the sofa.

He didn't bother to knock, just peeked around the jamb. "Hey."

"Hey, yourself. What do I do?" Tears filled her eyes, and her throat grew tight.

"Don't worry." He went to the phone and dialed. A moment later she heard his side of the conversation.

"Yeah, Windy's sick. She got strep from Heather...Yeah...She's worried no one will believe her...No, she needs to stick around home. Her eyes are glassy and her cheeks flushed...I'll take her temperature and call you back...Yeah. Okay. Thanks."

He returned to her. "Gramps said to stay away, not to worry about it. Where's your thermometer?"

She pointed to where she'd left it on the table as a weight slid from her shoulders. They'd believe Kris.

He washed it off and shook it down before putting it in her mouth. "Gramps said he'd make sure to send food over to us. He told me my job was to care for you and not to come over."

That brought more tears. She reached for the tissue box.

He moved it closer for her. "Have you taken any aspirin?"

She shook her head. Ouch, she needed to not move her cranium so much. Why hadn't she taken anything?

He pulled out the thermometer and handed it to her. "I always have trouble finding the line."

She looked. "It's 102.8 degrees. No wonder I feel lousy." She gave it back.

"I'll get you some water. Where's the aspirin?"

She told him about the medicine cabinet and closed her eyes.

He shook her shoulder. "You were out already. Sorry. Take this and go to sleep. I've got Heather."

Windy obeyed though the pills scraped going down. Soon she was drowsy. She woke to find herself under a blanket and Kris in the rocker holding Heather. They seemed great so she closed her eyes.

Later her throat woke her, throbbing enough to make her ears ache. The light in the room had changed, shadows in different places. Voices, soft but insistent, drifted from the hall. She'd never be able to call out to them, talking hurt too much. She threw off the covers and tried to sit up. Whew, that was an adventure. As the world stopped spinning, she rose and wobbled toward the direction of the sounds.

Her grandmother and mother were there talking with Kris, who held Heather.

"Wha?" She couldn't finish the sound, it was too painful. However, it was enough to get their attention.

"Go back to the couch. We're here to help."

Gramma tried to guide her, but she shook her head, pointing at her mother.

"Stop it, Windy. You're too ill. Kris is doing fine, but the baby needs to eat so we brought formula. I know you didn't want to introduce that, but you can't risk Heather. Plus, Kris can't stay here all night. Think."

Windy squeezed her eyes closed to block the tears. More mouthing the words than speaking, she made her bottom line clear. "You okay, not her. Send away."

"You might not understand this, little girl, but I'm getting older. I need help too. If I'm going to be here all-night taking care of you and your baby, I need your mother to assist me. Get over yourself. Stop being so selfish. You don't have to forgive her. Just let her stay."

Little girl? She was a grown woman with a child. How dare she call her a little girl.

The room started spinning. She grasped at the wall.

Gramma caught her and led her to the couch. "Lie down. I'll take your temperature and then get you some aspirin and a cold rag. I need to know how high it is before I phone the doctor."

Doctor? This simply got worse and worse. However, she had no more fight. She laid on the pillow and surrendered her mouth to the little glass tube.

It was still over one hundred. Just not as bad as before. Though she couldn't tell that from the way her throat was killing her. Gramma brought her two more aspirins, a cup of water, and a cold rag for her head that felt like ice when it touched her. Soon it soothed and she closed her eyes again.

The next thing she knew, Doctor Schwartz was at her side. "Hey, there, Windy. Heard you've caught strep from Heather. Got a notion you've run yourself down to where it's hitting you harder. I hear you're not getting enough sleep."

She tried to respond but could only mouth her words. "Until today. Lots of sleep today." She added a smile. Poor guy working on a holiday.

"Well, you need it. Let them take care of Heather and you. If you wake up and can pump, fine. Just don't feed her. Let's not get her sick again. Plus, formula is fine for babies. Rest. You'll be a better mother for it." He patted her hand. "I'll give you a shot of penicillin, too, and hope it helps you improve faster."

He pulled out a syringe.

She turned away, not wanting to watch the needle coming, and winced when it happened.

Then he left.

Kris returned to the rocker with Heather, this time giving her a bottle of formula.

At least she wasn't in her mother's care. Windy closed her eyes. All she saw was a shattered family photo sporting a hole where Mom oughta be.

It was too late to fill that hole. Too late to heal the break. Too late.

⸎

HEATHER DRAINED THE FOUR-OUNCE BOTTLE of formula, so Kris set it on the floor next to the rocker. The little stinker was still wide awake, happy for the attention he gave. Man, she looked like Windy. Would she be as stubborn?

Kris turned her to face him straight on.

Heather's steady gaze scrutinized his features. Did she remember him from before? Was his voice familiar to her now?

Had she any idea of how she'd wrapped herself around his heart?

He broke eye contact to glance at her mother. Windy was out cold. The congestion in her head caused little snoring sounds. She'd be embarrassed to learn that and call him weird that he considered it cute.

Kris realized the word cute was nowhere in her brain at the moment. She'd hate discovering he saw her this way. He knew she was too weak to fight it now. Yet, if they built this relationship, wasn't part of it to be vulnerable enough to allow their rough, unvarnished sides to show? Get to the rustic. For better or worse, right?

Only Windy had no choice about being seen at her worse. He still kept his worse from her. Not exactly equal, but he wasn't ready yet. Okay, maybe it wasn't fair. However, as long as he had say-so, he'd keep that secret. That he'd almost revealed. Good thing BAYER was written in block letters.

Hazel wandered in and planted herself on one of the fireside chairs. "You've got a magic touch, Kris."

"It's not difficult." This was the easy part.

She smiled. "How long do you plan to stay?"

Somehow, he expected her to ask that. Her granddaughter's reputation had been splattered enough. Still, he'd told Windy he'd take care of her, and he'd keep his word. "As long as she needs me."

"Well, Cheryl and I are here. You don't need to stick around. You might run to my house for a late meal if you want." She smiled again, but he realized she was attempting to push him out the door. Mentioning food was dirty pool.

He shook his head. "No, I said I'd stay. Not going to lie to her."

"Can I be honest with you, Kris?" That made him wonder if she'd been truthful before. Yeah, he knew she had been. He just didn't go for that opening.

Hazel continued. "If Cheryl and I have time alone with Windy, she might listen. She doesn't understand. You see, even though my granddaughter tries to avoid negative things, she also digs in her heels if someone challenges her beliefs—once she thinks she understands something, she sets it in cement in her brain. In her memory, her mother's the source of every evil thing that has ever transpired. Her daddy's a saint. So, she's just gotta hang on until everything works out in the end."

She paused, as if giving him time to respond. What was he to say? She might've clarified things, but none of it changed what he told her or his determination to keep his promise.

"Aaron is my son and I love him dearly. I'm certainly not saying he drove Cheryl away. Still, there's a lot Windy doesn't know. Cheryl deserves the chance to tell her. Can you understand that?"

He nodded. "Yes, ma'am, I can. Can you understand I gave my word? I won't go back on it until she releases me."

He'd never seen Hazel appear so defeated. "I understand." She breathed a sigh. "How about you put Heather in her carrier and help me get Windy upstairs to her room? She'll do better in her own bed."

That he could do. After securing the baby, he scooped Windy up and headed for the stairs. She never woke. Her almost white hair hung long over his arm and her head lolled toward him. He pulled her closer, his heart thundering to have her in his arms. She'd have complained that she weighed a ton, but he knew better. She felt light as a feather.

This was his first view of the girls' bedroom. He didn't know what he'd imagined—truth was he hadn't thought of it—but it wasn't like he expected. Two twin beds stood perpendicular to the left wall. A third one was shoved lengthwise against the right, in the corner. A familiar little cradle sat next to it. He recognized which one was Windy's.

Hazel pulled the covers back and he laid her down.

"I'll return to Heather." This room was not where he belonged.

"Thanks, Kris. Would you ask Cheryl to come up?"

He captured her gaze.

"To help me get her changed into her nightgown. Even I realize she's in no condition for a talk right now."

Kris nodded. Scooping up the cradle to take with him, he left to do as she asked.

Cheryl was rocking Heather. She glanced up, guilt at getting caught beaming off her like neon.

It wasn't his place to judge. "Hazel needs you upstairs."

She waited until he set the cradle down, then handed him the baby and headed for the stairs without a word.

He sat in the rocker, turning Heather to face him straight on. "Glad you can't understand what's happening, sweetness. Your mama needs more than her throat to heal. If I understood prayer, I might do that. But I don't. So, we'll cross our fingers and hope the praying people around her will."

She stared back and waved her little arm in the air.

"You get it. I bet you get a lot more than I do about some stuff. Your mama is pretty special. Think there's a chance for us to become a family?" To utter the words out loud made them more real.

Heather blinked. She never blinked first. Was it a sign? Good grief. Why was something as natural as a baby's blink getting him excited? Yet somehow inside he knew she understood the question. The problem was interpreting her answer.

He settled her at his shoulder and continued to rock, searching for meaning in her blink. With eyes closed, he tried to figure all the reasons for working toward that goal and recognize each sign warning he should walk away.

No signs shouted to stray from this destiny. He couldn't imagine what would require him to change course. In his mind, he saw the three of them living in his grandfather's house. He'd make enough from his art that the handyman work became a sideline. Windy could take her photographs and do as she desired without a struggle. They'd build together. And little Heather? She'd grow up knowing she was loved and valued for who she was. That was the vision that repeatedly played. That was his goal, his destiny.

Now to get Windy on board.

Hazel came downstairs carrying sheets and pillows. "If you plan to stay, you can sleep here on the couch. Cheryl and I will take Sunny and Stormy's beds."

"What about Heather?"

She pulled her lips tight, and he knew she didn't like the decision she'd made but chose it for expediency. "If you'll care for her tonight, Windy will sleep better."

He nodded. It was her concession. He wouldn't argue.

Hazel went to work fixing up his bed on the couch. "Heather'll need to be changed as well as fed. There's boiled water on the stove top in the pan. It'll be room temperature. You can warm it a little before making the bottle. It's one scoop for two ounces of liquid. Four ounces should do her at a feeding."

"Thanks, Hazel. I've got this." He'd read the bottle's markings before and remembered the ratio. Plus, it couldn't be that hard to change a diaper, right?

"You've changed a baby before?" She didn't seem sold.

He hadn't, but he'd seen it done. "I can do it."

"How about you show me now, so I feel better about it. Besides, it's been a bit." She found Windy's diaper bag over by the cloak tree. "Oughta be enough disposables here for tonight. You can use the Pampers and we'll return to cloth tomorrow. I'll get you a wet rag." She left the room, so he laid the baby on his newly made-up couch-bed.

Hazel returned with a warm washcloth, and he undid the pins as a sudden thought flashed through his mind. What if she's dirty?

Heather wasn't. Only wet. He slipped the old diaper out, holding it between his fingers.

Hazel smirked. Thankfully, she didn't say anything as she took it and left.

He put the clean disposable one beneath her little bum and brought it between her legs before pulling the back edges over the front, a side at a time. Those diaper pins appeared lethal up close. He slipped his fingers between the baby and the diaper at the waist, holding the thing together and protecting her from getting poked while he pushed the point through the many layers and out to close. One side down.

Hazel returned to watch the repeat performance and he stabbed himself. Ouch! Vicious pin. At least she had to the good grace not to laugh out loud. It'd be easier without an audience.

With the other side pinned, he adjusted the baby's gown, and pulled the drawstring.

"Good job. I'll trust you with my great granddaughter tonight." Hazel's smile built his confidence. "Good night, Kris. Please call if you need anything."

He nodded. "You too. Night."

Hazel retreated up the stairs.

Kris laid Heather in her cradle. He'd worried when he made it that it wouldn't be big enough, but seeing her in it, he realized he'd somehow done something right. After slipping off his shoes, he stretched out on the couch. Then leaned over to rock the cradle.

The next thing he knew he was awakened by noise. Heather. Not actually crying but fussing. He threw off the covers and padded to the kitchen to make the bottle, encouraging the water to warm with words he rarely used.

Heather's grumbling had grown louder. If he wasn't quick enough, she'd wake the whole house.

Then he realized he needed to change her before he fed her. Oh, she'd not like that much.

However, he finished, got her back to sleep, and just laid his head on the pillow when he couldn't remember. Did he turn off the fire from under the water? He could picture it all boiling away before the next feeding. Or worse, be so scalding it took forever to cool.

He tiptoed to the kitchen to find he had remembered. The burner was off. So, he returned to bed, where he fell asleep in time for a repeat performance at 4:47.

When he had her down and collapsed onto his bedding, it hit him. This is why Windy was so exhausted. He'd understood mentally, but until tonight, he couldn't really imagine. Like someone reading books about all the wars of history. Until one was physically in the battle, there's no real empathy.

So how could he help her?

Sleeping overnight at the mansion, indefinitely, wouldn't work. Of course.

Could he search for opportunities to support her throughout the day? Maybe give her a breather? Hopefully, this forced rest would bring her the stamina she needed to be the mother she worked so hard to be.

But would she accept help from him?

Chapter 9
Saturday, November 28, 1970

W indy rubbed her face and stretched. She was rested, for the first time in a while. Plus, her throat wasn't killing her.

She sat and caught her reflection. Her hair was tangled and matted but the purple beneath her eyes was all but gone. She stretched again and threw back her covers.

A glance showed the other two beds were occupied. For an instant, she thought it was her sisters. Then she remembered. She glanced at her watch. 6:04. She wouldn't wake them. Even her mother had helped take care of her. She hadn't wanted it. Still, if she was assisting her, then she wasn't holding Heather. Which made her feel somewhat better. And a little petty. But she'd protect her daughter, petty or not.

After slipping into her robe, brushing her hair, and using the facilities, she tiptoed downstairs through the living room. Kris slept on the couch, on his stomach with his arm over the side holding the cradle.

Heather snoozed, too, or Windy would have succumbed and picked her up. Her arms ached to hold her baby.

Her belly rumbled, making Frazier raise his head. He'd slept on her bed and then followed her downstairs wanting his own hunger handled. She'd see to her empty tummy first. Probably ought to be gentle with it. Oatmeal would be nice on this crisp morning.

As she reached for the box, her arm brushed her breast, causing her to notice the fullness. She ought to pump while the cereal cooked. Rather than returning upstairs, she found a tablecloth large enough to cover her in case anyone walked in and sat in a kitchen chair to multitask. As she partway filled another bottle, she realized she had no clue if her pumpings would be safe for Heather. Maybe even the shot would taint them. If her milk wasn't usable, when might she go back to nursing? Better call Doctor Schwartz's office.

Her pumping and the oatmeal finished about the same time, so she closed her robe and dipped up a bowl. She'd made a full pot of coffee but settled for half a cup after she fed Frazier.

"Hey, what are you doing up?" Kris peeked around the corner.

"I'm better and couldn't take lolling a moment longer. I promise I'm not overdoing, but I had to move." She smiled, hoping he wouldn't worry. Poor guy appeared tired. "I think I'll try a shower next, but don't be surprised if I go back to bed after."

He nodded, satisfied with her answer.

"Want some oatmeal? I'll get you some if you grab your coffee."

"Sure." He pulled a mug from the drainboard and poured a full cup before pulling out another chair and dropping on it. "I get why you've been so tired."

"Has Heather kept you awake? I'm sorry. I apologize for making you stay." He never complained and was such an incredible help.

"I told you I would. I won't lie. She did fine. Normal baby stuff. But I'm getting good at making bottles and changing diapers."

"How many times have you stuck yourself with the pins?" Gramma shared about watching how he poked himself.

"I stopped counting. My thumb's a pin cushion now." He held up the digit and gave her a lopsided grin. She was positive if she looked up nice guy in *The Encyclopedia Britannica*, Kris's picture would stare back.

"I appreciate all you did. My only concern is that you'll get strep. I'd hate it if you did." That'd be the worst payback.

"Don't worry. If you're better, do you mind if I run home? I could go for a shower and change of clothes. I'll hurry back." And he would. She'd bet on it.

"Get some rest too. I confess, though, I love knowing you are here."

His eyes lit from within, and she thought his posture straightened a bit. "I'm here for you, so I think I'll wait until Hazel is up before I leave."

As if on cue, Gramma padded into the kitchen from the stairs. "Good morning, all. Windy, should you be up yet?"

"I'm fine. Needed a change of scenery. Kris is going home to grab a shower. I better get one, as well. Can't stand myself. Then I gotta call Doctor Schwartz with a question."

"He won't be there today. This is Saturday, honey. His answering service will get the question to him."

Saturday? She hardly remembered Friday. Wow. "Guess I missed some things. Well, then, I'll phone his exchange. First, though, I'm gonna get clean." She smiled at Kris, telegraphing how she felt before racing up the stairs.

Her mother was in the bathroom, so she waited her turn in the hall until she came out. She still didn't care to speak to the woman. Yet, she was aware her grandmother didn't look after her alone. Being in debt to Cheryl Day was loathsome. When the door opened, she acknowledged her with a nod, then she scampered inside, slamming the door.

Windy brushed her teeth, then climbed in the shower to let the water loosen all the tightness. As it streamed over her head a thought popped in.

You hate your mother.

The shampoo bottle slipped from her hands.

No, she didn't hate anyone. She simply preferred to never see some folks again. One in particular. She could live her life and they'd never have to have contact.

You hate your mother.

No, that wasn't a part of her makeup. She searched for the good, found the positive in situations. It was her nature.

You hate your mother.

Stop it! That can't be true. Could it?

Hot streaming water blended with the scalding tears pouring down her face. How could she hate anyone? That made her a horrible person, to hate. Was she a horrible person?

She grabbed the shampoo and washed her hair twice, like the directions said. Then again, just to feel cleaner. She scrubbed her body as if washing away all the bad stuff. But she couldn't. No matter how many times she rinsed and repeated, she still noticed the stain of hate.

Finally, she turned off the faucet and dried. It was sorta hypocritical sending up a prayer, but it was her only idea. "God, I don't want to hate anyone. Gramma says You are love. Can You help me with this, please?"

Nothing really changed but she found the strength to dress in clean pajamas and head downstairs.

Her mother sat in the rocking chair holding Heather. Everything in her wanted to rush over and snatch her baby away, but a small voice inside whispered, "No hate." She took a deep breath and retreated to the kitchen.

Gramma was making a bottle.

"That reminds me about calling Doctor Schwartz. I need to learn when I can start nursing again, and if the milk I've pumped is safe."

"The doctor said to wait three days without fever. Your milk might be okay, but it'd be better to toss it." Gramma never glanced up but kept working.

"Oh, well, that answers my question. Thanks."

"Windy, come with me." She didn't request, just directed.

That talk was coming whether she wanted it or not.

When they got to the living room, Gramma handed the bottle to her mother, making Windy's blood pressure rise.

"If we're about to have that discussion you've been so hot to force on me, then I better hold my daughter while we do it." That was all the concession she could give.

Her mother stood, allowing Windy to sit in the rocker, before giving her Heather and the bottle. Then she sat on the sofa's edge.

Gramma pulled a fireside chair closer. "I realize you don't want to talk about this. Still, there're things you must hear. Your dad agrees. No one's forcing you to do anything. Just gather all the facts."

"My mother walked out on me when I had a broken leg. She never waited to see how I survived. Just sneaked away while I screamed in the emergency room. What else do I need to know?" She glanced at the woman who gave her birth and spotted the pain that filled her eyes.

Part of her wanted to speak comforting words so she wouldn't be the cause. However, another part whispered, "Good, now you understand."

Windy didn't like that second part, but she understood it.

Her mother took a deep breath. "Aaron and I married quickly after we met at a party in Los Angeles not long after the war. Everything was so hopeful. I had appeared in a few pictures, small parts, but was starting to build a resume. Your dad was doing well with his music. We got introduced to the movers and shakers, we were on our way.

"A few months after our wedding I discovered I was pregnant with Sunny. It was considered desirable to have experiences to help win roles. So, I figured having a baby would be good for my career. Besides, I loved my little girl. Then I became pregnant again. Immediately. Two beautiful little girls. It was a lot, and there weren't many ingenue parts for child-bearing women. Before I could start auditioning again, you came along."

Her mother wadded a tissue in her hands. "Please understand, I loved you girls the best I knew how. But I was seventeen when I met your dad, barely eighteen when we married. Not even twenty-one when I had three daughters. If I'd had a mother, maybe I'd have been equipped. I didn't. I had no clue what to do."

Fine. It was tough, not what she signed on for. Windy stroked Heather's face.

"You are already a better mother than I ever hoped to be, Windy. I was beaten down. Between what my doctor thinks was postpartum depression, my career tanking, and not knowing what I was doing, I lost who I was, like descending into an abyss. I bet you remember me being in my room a lot. I couldn't face anything. I knew I'd fail as I had in the past. I was a lousy wife and parent. I failed at my acting career. Everything I touched became worse. I was terrified I would hurt you even more when you came home. I know this isn't rational. Nothing about this is. It's what went on in my head until I got help."

"Help?" Was this woman safe around her baby?

Her mother nodded. "I checked myself into a mental clinic. It was run by some nuns, and they spoke to me about God's love. I learned I had to forgive myself. Knowing I needed to do that and doing it were two different things. The second took much longer.

"That's why I got in touch with Hazel. She'd always been kind. I discovered Aaron sent you girls to live with her. So, she kept me up to date with your lives. I've been so proud of your accomplishments. You all three are capable, strong women. Hazel finally convinced me it was time to let you know my story." She swallowed and blinked several times. "I knew it would be difficult. I'm not asking for forgiveness or a relationship. Just sharing my part and saying I'm sorry. I am here if you want more."

Windy blinked hard too. She didn't know what to say. However, she didn't hate her mother anymore.

She wasn't sure what she felt, but hate was gone. For now.

⁂

THE SHOWER HELPED MORE than he thought it would. Kris pulled on fresh jeans and a clean sweatshirt and felt more human.

He was aware that leaving opened the opportunity for Hazel and Cheryl to have their chat with her. Bet Windy knew that too. Maybe he shouldn't keep trying to protect her from her family. Perhaps she should listen to their story. Besides, it always backfired when he stuck his nose in other folks' business.

How long should he take getting there? Interrupting that conversation would be awkward.

Though that thought slowed his steps, he still went straight away after cleaning up. And grabbing a second breakfast. Okay, so he was hungry.

This time he parked in the back lot, entering through the rear. The kitchen was empty, so he ambled for the living room.

Windy lay stretched out on the couch, Heather slept beside her in the cradle. "Hey, you're back already."

"Yeah, the shower woke me enough. Still hanging in there?"

She nodded though she closed her eyes and rested her forearm on her head. "They got their way."

"Figured they would."

She blew out a sigh. "I hate to admit it, but I think Gramma was right. I needed her side. Doubt it fixes anything, but I might have a smidge of sympathy for her. Now. There was more to the story. Doesn't make it all hunky-dory though. I still don't feel like I ever had a mother. Aside from Gramma and Sunny."

"Could you sorta get to know her? Who she is now? As a person."

She peeked up at him. "You are wise, Kris Norman. Can I ask you to do something for me?"

In that moment she could request anything and he'd do it— run to China backwards for real take out, climb the Eiffel Tower with his teeth while she rode his back just for a photograph. He was long gone down that magic trail. "Sure. What would you like?"

"I need to hear your voice. Would you read to me?" She reached over and handed him a book laying open on the table, page side down. "Between overdoing a little, and with the emotional dump I want something soothing. This is Sunny's. I found it upstairs and thought I'd read awhile but I gotta close my eyes. Will you please read for me?"

He'd never expected anything like this. A part of him wanted to ask if she wouldn't prefer original Chinese takeout. But he cleared his throat and turned to look at the words that danced all over the page. He tracked with his finger taking it slow, attempting to memorize what he saw in order to spout it back and sound like an intelligent being capable of doing what she asked.

Why didn't someone just shoot him now?

He licked his lips and forced out the first word. Then he grasped at an idea. Use the pictures to tell the story. Yeah, that's what he'd do. He'd invent the plot to go with the illustrations. At least this book had some of a bird named Jon...a...than, Jonathan. Oh yeah, people talked about this story. *Jonathan Livingston Seagull.* Okay. "Jonathan Livingston Seagull was a bird like the other birds in his area. He liked flying and going places..." What had he heard? "Uh, he got fantastic at flying. He'd soar really high, and then he learned how to do tricks. But the other birds called him a show-off. They yelled, no, they squawked at him to mind his manners. They said he wasn't so special."

He turned the page. No more pictures yet. He took a breath and kept going. "But he knew he was. Not just himself, but each bird was special with unique gifts to offer. Jonathan tried to talk to his family about it, but they told him he needed to be like the other birds. They didn't get it. No matter how he explained. No one understood what he said. They only wanted to do what they'd always done." He turned another page.

Still no more pictures. "Jonathan decided to move on. Do what he longed to do. What he was called to do. He would never be happy being a seagull crammed into a pigeonhole. So, one day Jonathan took off flying where he wanted. He did tricks and flips." He turned the page and found illustrations. Apparently, they came with the start of new chapters.

Now it was just one bird. Okay, what could he say about a single bird?

"Kris, would you help me in the kitchen for a minute?" Hazel's call was the relief he needed.

"Be right back." He set the book down and headed down the hall.

Hazel sat at the table and pointed to an empty chair. "What's that drivel you're spouting in there?"

"What do you mean?"

"I mean, it's a great story, but I've read *Jonathan Livingston Seagull*. That wasn't it. Why didn't you just read it to her?"

He was suddenly standing in the middle of the field. A bull charged him. He couldn't move. Kris knew how this ended. He'd been waiting for the day it did. Still, he wasn't ready. Not yet.

"Kris, can you read?"

Air. He needed air. Nothing would go into his lungs.

Hazel dumped a small paper bag filled with rubber bands on the table and handed the empty sack to him. "Hold it to your mouth and breathe into it." She rubbed his back and he tried to suck in air.

And then it worked. Oxygen burned its way down his windpipe, into his lungs. He let it out and tried another breath. And another. His body was working again. He set the bag down and wiped the sweat from his forehead. "How did you figure it out?"

"You're not the first person I've seen who's managed to fool people into thinking you can read. That's why you wouldn't go to college."

He nodded. "I can read a little. When I take it slow, and it is written large and clear. I run my finger under it and make myself focus on one sound at a time."

"But Windy doesn't know?"

He shook his head. "No, no one does, except my mom. I've never told a soul."

"I can't believe it wasn't caught when you were in school. But then, I've seen it happen before. My first husband had the same problem. Said the letters wouldn't sit still. I helped him with all his homework. In fact, that's one reason we rushed to get married after graduation, so that I could read all his mail to him. Like his draft notice." She grimaced and began putting all the collected rubber bands back into the paper bag. "You have to tell her."

"Yeah, I'm just not ready. It will happen."

Hazel didn't look convinced.

"This strep thing has messed with plans. I won't keep the secret from her much longer." Especially now. "Better get back to her." Not that he wanted to continue pretending. Still, he'd told Windy he'd return.

"Fine. Remember, she's gonna pick up that book soon. Then she'll wonder what in the world you were doing."

He nodded. That was what scared him.

Back in the living room, Windy had fallen asleep. He got his reprieve. After putting *Jonathan Livingston Seagull* back on the table, he checked on Heather who'd started to stir. "C'mere little one."

With Windy on the couch, that left the floor for changing her. He spread out a small blanket, gathered the supplies, and got the baby into dry drawers. Then he took her to the kitchen and handed her off to her great grandmother while he fixed her bottle. Soon he and Heather were back in the rocker, having another staring contest while he fed her.

He was quite sure not all infants were this docile. He'd heard stories of babies crying all day. Some even screamed. But Heather was so even-tempered. Sure, she fussed when she woke hungry at 3:00 a.m. and it took too long to get her bottle. Yet that was not the usual.

What if he and Windy had kids? Would they be this mellow? Every kid was different. Maybe one would have his problem. Could he handle it? Could she? Normally he wouldn't worry about it, but the whole thing with Cheryl had him wondering. Windy's mother seemed so normal now. Yet she'd left her children for over a decade. He couldn't understand it. Leaving your children when you don't have to...Did she have to?

Kris hadn't asked Windy or Hazel or even Cheryl for any details. Windy shared she had some sympathy for the woman who gave her birth. It was enough to make him wonder.

"Whatcha doing?"

He glanced over.

Windy leaned on her elbow watching him rock the baby.

"You made me lose. I was going to beat her at her staring game."

Her laughter filled the room, making the world all right. "You never stood a chance."

"All I gotta do is outlast her. She'll drift off and I win." He winked and resumed the contest.

"So that's your strategy. I'll have to keep it in mind."

"Patience wins." He learned that ages ago. Wait it out. Hang in there long enough. The others will give up, go home.

"I see. Looks like this round goes to you. She's out. Want to put her in the cradle?" Windy sat as she asked, curling her legs to her side.

She looked more tempting than he could imagine. Hadn't she a clue how beautiful she was?

"Sure." He leaned over to lay the baby in her little bed. As he rose, Windy was so close. Too close. He drew closer.

She pressed her hand on his chest, slowing his momentum. "Kris, I want you to, I really do. But I'd hate making you ill."

"If I haven't gotten sick already, I probably won't."

"It'd be awful if our first kiss gave you strep." She was weakening.

"Fine, I can wait. Patience wins." He straightened, towering over her.

She rose to meet him. "I promise, when I am well."

"You've got a deal." The tickle came on sudden. He turned his head in time for a giant sneeze.

Her eyes grew. "I knew it. I've given you strep!"

"It was just a sneeze. Don't overdramatize."

She punched his arm.

"Ow!"

"Overdramatize? Did I hear you correctly?"

"I didn't stutter. Nor did I get violent." He narrowed his lids and waggled his brows.

"Who's the big baby who has to cry out when the little girl touches his arm, poor wimpypoo?"

"First big baby, now wimpypoo? Are you impugning my masculine reputation?" Fancy words he learned from his father the lawyer. He could come up with a few. When he wanted.

"What reputation?"

He pulled her to him, but as he lowered his lips to hers, Heather gave a cry. "Hush, little one, I need to teach your mother a lesson."

Windy ducked, slipping away from his arms. "You'll have to do that another day, big baby. I don't want your sneezes."

Just as he opened his mouth to retort, the tickle returned. "Achchoo!"

Heather startled. Windy scooped her up.

He grabbed for a tissue. The tickle hit the back of his throat. Great. As sure as he knew she teased, he'd caught her case of strep.

Chapter 10
Monday, December 21, 1970

"**O**ur hush-hush client is coming in today." Sunny joined Windy at the breakfast table.

"Think she's really on the level? Not just a big dreamer?" Windy forked the last bit of egg from her plate. She was attempting to get more protein in her diet to help with stamina, so her beloved Cocoa Puffs were getting stale in the cabinet.

Sunny took a sip of her coffee before continuing. "I'm thinking the secret might be out, the way she's talking. Her maid of honor and the best man are coming with her so they can choose their outfits. She plans to pick up the invitations today. Said she's putting them out tomorrow with Christmas cards."

"She thinks she'll package and address fifty invitations tonight?" Windy couldn't envision that. Talk about focus.

"She's got assistants. The gal who's her maid of honor might be helping her. You'll get to meet them because they want to plan the photo shoot. The newspaper engagement shot will only be of her. No couple photos until he arrives a few days before the wedding in February. So that means the sycamore pics will have to wait."

Windy nodded and drained her mug. "What time should we expect them?"

Stormy wandered in just then. "Yeah, when is my first appointment again?"

Sunny sent Stormy a look. Windy had no trouble interpreting it—*why can't you keep track of this on your calendar?* But she didn't verbalize her thought. Instead, she let them know the client would arrive in an hour.

That lit a fire under Windy. She scooped up Heather, who'd been cooing in her carrier and raced to their room to get changed. Then she hustled out to Kris's workroom in the carriage house. "Good morning."

"Hey." He was gluing a large wreath together that had fallen in the wind, snapping in two. The crash had wakened her and Heather and Sunny last night. It was nice that it was fixable. Even better if it were secured so it wouldn't to blow down again.

"I was wondering...I've got to take some photos in a bit. The client should arrive in forty minutes. Would you be able to watch Heather for me?"

"Sure. We'll do fine, won't we, princess?" He grinned at the baby who cooed back at him.

Windy had watched the bond form between Heather and Kris. Sometimes it made her want to cry, it was so sweet.

The poor guy caught strep and stayed home for most of the week following Thanksgiving to ensure he was no longer contagious. She'd missed him so much, but he wouldn't let her come help. Neither would her sisters or grandmother.

However, Gramma did promise to take care of him personally. Somehow, she'd not gotten sick—an answer to prayer according to Gene and the family.

Now he was back. Yet they never had time alone. Both were so busy with clients and work and events. These few minutes to ask his help were a godsend. Just not long enough for what was on her mind.

She loved hearing his voice. Baritone and smooth, like milk chocolate. It sent tingles up her spine when she thought about it.

He set his tools on the workbench and turned her way, pulling her to him.

She snuggled in, drawing peace in the middle of the busyness. Mightn't be an opportunity for romance, but a hug never hurt.

"I needed that. We'll meet you in the front room when you're ready. I've gotta get inside before she catches another cold." With reluctance, she drew away.

His lips pulled tight, and she knew he'd hoped for more. So had she. Their day would come. "I'll be in as soon as this is clamped."

She nodded and took Heather to the house, determined to find a private chance to talk.

Stormy set up in the front room.

"I'll be right back. I need to grab my camera. Can you watch Heather a moment?"

Stormy agreed, at once taking Heather out of her carrier to play with her.

Windy chewed her lip, knowing how much her sister wanted her own baby, before racing up the stairs. She returned in two minutes, fresh film installed.

She'd refurbished a small room off the parlor into a private studio. Small being the operative word. It was large for a closet, enough for one person to sit. So, she'd maneuvered light diffusers around the ceiling area—with Kris's help to appease her family— allowing special photos to be taken for the newspaper. Now she readied it for this bride-to-be since that's all the shots they'd get today.

Just as she'd finished, Kris came for Heather. He raised her up and blew raspberries on her belly, making Windy laugh as well, before taking the baby elsewhere.

Then the client arrived. A perky blonde followed by a tiny Asian woman and a really big guy. A Kris-sized big guy carrying a baby a few months older than Heather.

Stormy started introductions. "Sally Ann, this is my sister, Windy. She'll be taking your photos today."

Windy shook the girl's hand. "Nice to meet you."

"And you too. These are my friends Hien and Beau Salem, the matron of honor and best man. The little one is their Owen. I really appreciate all you've done here. When I saw your ad in the Trib, I just knew this was where I wanted our wedding. Steve agrees but won't be able to leave Viet Nam until closer to our day. So, what is our next step? I've too many ideas and need help." She giggled and her friends smiled.

Stormy led them into the seating area and presented her with a photo album. "You're doing fine. We've got the invitations for you to take when you go. Your photos will be ready by Friday." She glanced up at Windy for confirmation.

That would work. Windy nodded back.

"The next thing is to choose the maid of honor gown. Yours has arrived. You can try it on to see what alterations are needed. We also have some tux styles. We might need to special order, though. It'd be good to get that picked today, too, just to be safe. This album contains photos of all the bridesmaids and groomsmen attire we carry. Why don't you begin looking here?"

Sally Ann opened the cover and oohed. Hien sat beside her on the sofa, perusing with her. Beau bounce-stepped with the baby, occasionally raising him above his head. The little guy grasped at his father's hair and pulled while Beau laughed.

It should have brought a smile to Windy, but somehow seeing this father with his son only made her wonder what Tim would do with Heather. Would he be playful like Beau and Kris? Would he be loving and tender? Little girls needed their daddies. She couldn't imagine her life without hers. The times they were separated were so hard. Still, she'd held on to him every way she could. Daddy was her lifeline, even at a distance. Where was Heather's lifeline?

Would Kris be willing to be hers? He gave that impression, but their time to talk had all but been filled with daily urgent chaos. She craved opportunity for the two of them. Okay, maybe the three of them. Heather must be considered in their decisions. Still, couples required getting to know one another on a deeper level.

Stormy brought out Sally Ann's dress while the girls continued through the album. They both glanced up and Sally Ann dropped the photos to race to her gown. It was long-sleeved, reminiscent of the recent *Romeo and Juliet* movie—long sleeves with solid capped tops, sheer and billowy from above the elbow to the wrist, and a sweetheart neckline, with an empire-waisted fitted bodice, and a full skirt covered with lace and seed pearls. Windy agreed it was perfect for the girl.

"Oh! Stormy, it's gorgeous, just like you promised. Can we go try it on?" Sally Ann fingered the folds cascading from the waist.

"Have you chosen something for Hien yet? I need to get that pulled from our closet."

Hien stood and brought the book to Stormy. "I believe this is the one she prefers."

Windy slipped by Stormy to glance over her arm. The dress was in red. It had a design similar to the wedding gown, only ballet length with a wide satin sash at the waist.

"That's a great choice. We'll have to take your measurements and order it for you, but I have one for you to try on. Be prepared, it'll be too big."

Hien winced. "That is the story of my life. By the way, do you have a regular seamstress for your alterations? My sister-in-law is local and is incredibly talented. I just thought of that."

Stormy glanced at Windy before speaking. "We've been having our grandmother do the quick things, but major alterations get sent to Indianapolis. That's what takes so long. Maybe if you leave your sister-in-law's contact information, our sister Sunny can get in touch with her."

Beau wandered up, feeding Owen a bottle while he spoke. "Shouldn't you ask Thea first?"

"I will call her so she will not be surprised. This might be for Thea." Hien patted his arm, wiped a drip from her son's chin, and turned back to Stormy. "Her name is Thea Carpenter. She has much experience. They live in Indian Heights so that is closer."

Stormy gave Hien a piece of paper to write down the information while she retrieved the dress Sally Ann picked. She returned with two. "Try on the pink one, it's smaller than the red. This way we'll check the fit plus you'll see the true color."

The girls nodded and Stormy led the way upstairs while carrying the three gowns. When she came back, she offered Beau the photo album to look at tux styles.

"I don't know about that stuff. I think Hien and Sally Ann should pick for me. I just obey and show up." He shrugged. "Besides, this little guy's trying to get active. He turns seven months the day after tomorrow." Beau tickled his son's belly.

"Your first?" Windy had to ask.

"Yeah. We got married last year. That's how Sally Ann and Steve met, at our wedding. He gave Hien away. I'd never met him before that, but he's been a good friend to my wife. I'm grateful for all he did to help her get to this country. We ended up becoming friends, so now we're standing up for him and Sally Ann."

Windy had a feeling there was more to their story. However, this wasn't the time for personal questions.

Somehow it was never the time to ask personal questions, at least for her and Kris. Would they ever get that chance?

⸎

KRIS CARRIED HEATHER AGAINST his shoulder, hoping the front room had cleared. He'd sit and rock her while she drank the bottle he fixed.

Nope, Windy and Stormy were talking with some guy. Some big guy holding a baby.

As he wandered in, the dude looked his way, question lines forming between his eyes.

"Kris, this is Beau Salem. Beau, Kris. He's watching my Heather for me." Windy hurried over and kissed her daughter.

The big guy, Beau, came closer, glanced at Heather, grinning before offering a handshake.

Kris tucked the baby bottle under his arm and shook the man's hand.

Stormy peered from him to Beau and back. "Seriously. How tall are you guys?"

Kris shrugged. "I'm about six four."

"Me too." Beau nodded. "Play b-ball? Bet Bobby Knight had his eye on you."

Kris winced, remembering the scholarship he turned down. "A little, played center. You?"

"Had too much to do on the farm, no time. Besides, I'm not that coordinated. Ever have trouble finding shirts with long enough tails?"

"Yeah. How 'bout pants? Inseams are never long enough."

Beau grimaced.

Windy and Stormy shared a glance before they busted into laughter. "The hazards of being a tall male, I guess."

"It's a fact. If you don't want to embarrass yourself at some place your wife wants you to take her." Beau winked.

"Bet she'd understand my dilemma. Everything is always too long." Windy waggled her wrists and her sleeves dropped below her fingertips.

Kris held in the chuckle at Windy's floppy arms. Guess Beau's wife was short.

"I need to measure and pin Hien so they can make a final decision." Stormy scurried upstairs.

Kris glanced at the tall guy. He was fully focused on his little one. That gave him the opportunity. He pulled Windy aside. "I meant to tell you this morning. I stayed up last night until I finished the final project. They should be dry when I get home. I only need to deliver them, and I'll have some free time. How about you? Think we might get away tomorrow night?"

She nodded. "I am so ready to spend an evening with you."

He grinned, her answer warming his heart better than a down vest. "Then we have a date. Should we plan on Heather or will one of your sisters babysit?"

"Just you and me. This time. Oh, I have a break in the middle today, an extra-long lunch. Could we talk then?"

He nodded. Of course, the job he was supposed to do that he put aside to watch Heather still waited. He pulled Windy close with his free arm. Let it wait.

Heather yelled and grabbed her mother's hair.

"Ow! You little stinker."

Kris held back his laugh while releasing the tiny fingers. "Big baby." He winked, kissing the top of her head before moving to the kitchen. He'd make a chair there work.

He got settled and Heather inhaled her four ounces. Something told him she might want more, but he'd wait for her to inform him.

That guy in the front room, Beau, he didn't have a problem playing with his baby son. There was a bottle on the table, not one of Heather's. Had he fed the baby while the women were doing their thing?

Kris never felt unmasculine helping with Heather. In fact, he was happy to do it. But he hadn't seen many men interact that way. His father certainly wouldn't have helped with his sisters. However, he'd been a busy attorney, not usually home when they were little.

Where'd he acquired this appreciation of the small and helpless? One more trait that made him different.

Maybe not. Not if Beau enjoyed helping with his child. But then, his child was a male. Funny, the baby boy had jet black hair though. Plus, a hint of Asian, sort of, about the eyes. Maybe he was adopted.

"Excuse me, please?"

Kris glanced up and a petite Asian woman stood smiling at him. "I think I took a wrong turn. I am looking for the front room and my husband."

Nope, not adopted. "This way." He motioned for her to follow and led her down the hallway to where Beau sat in the rocker with his son. Their son. Yeah, Windy's comment earlier made better sense now.

He returned to the kitchen with Heather and placed her in her carrier, rocking it back and forth. Hopefully, that would help her drift off. It was time for her morning nap.

Later Windy took charge of Heather so he left for his workshop. The wreath was dry, but he added a couple screws for good measure before reattaching it to the display. This time he anchored it so the wind couldn't send it flying. Then he performed some smaller repairs to their Christmas themed decorations on the front porch and lawn. After lunch, he'd tackle the back yard. The garden looked decent with a soft powder of snow. If he kept his tracks to a minimum, created some trails for people to walk through so the dusting remained undisturbed, then he'd call it a day and get his deliveries completed.

He'd also add the finishing touches to Windy's present. He'd put a lot of time and thought into it and hoped she liked it. She'd spoken of wanting to create a collage of Heather's photos, but she had yet to do it. Maybe with his gift that would help. He released a sigh, the smallest nip of fear that she wouldn't want it trying to surface. She would like it. Of course, she'd like it.

Lunch rolled around and he went inside. Windy had fixed tomato soup and grilled cheese sandwiches. Perfect for a chilly December day. He washed before pouring them each a glass of milk. Then he sat.

Windy brought the food and put Heather's carrier on the floor by her chair.

Just as he took a bite, she touched his arm. "Kris, why did you make up the story about *Jonathan Livingston Seagull*? I was reading last night. Couldn't figure out where you left off. Then I couldn't find anything you'd read to me. What gives?"

He choked.

She jumped up and pounded his back.

The bit of crust lodged. He couldn't breathe. Panic rose. Spots appeared in the air.

She hit him square between his shoulder blades and the piece flew out.

He quickly grabbed it up and tossed it in the trash before sinking into the chair again and gulping his milk. Mortification settled over him.

"Are you okay?" Her eyes were full of compassion. She actually worried for him.

He nodded. "You just surprised me."

Windy returned to her seat. "So, what happened?"

He gave her a questioning stare. "I choked?"

"No, goof, before that. Remember my question? About *Jonathan Livingston Seagull*?"

Of course, he remembered. He just wished she'd forget. "Oh, that." Keeping his eyes on his soup, he swallowed hard and dropped his voice to a whisper. "I can't read."

"What?"

He stared her in the eyes. It was time. He had to face it. "I can't read. Well. I can't read well. Or much. Just some. If I take it slow. And it's clearly written."

"Oh." She returned to her lunch.

"You're not going to say anything?"

"What should I say? You could've told me. Maybe you didn't trust me. Never wanted me to know. Which makes me wonder, if that's the case, where do you see us headed? It's not the type of secret you keep from someone you want to build a relationship with. I mean, you're pretty much aware of all my secrets, some a lot messier with bigger stigmas than an inability to read. But hey, I've been wrong before."

She stood and dumped her sandwich in the trash before pouring her soup down the drain and setting her dishes in the sink.

"Windy, wait."

She froze with her back to him.

He pulled her around to speak face to face. "I haven't even told my dad. He doesn't know. I didn't tell you because I don't want you to think I'm stupid."

"I don't think you are stupid. A stupid man hasn't your imagination." She paused. "Your dad doesn't know?"

He shook his head. "Even Gramps hasn't been told. Hazel figured it out when she heard me read to you. I promised her I would tell you. That was my plan for tomorrow night."

"I kinda jumped the gun again, huh?"

That brought a little smile. She wasn't totally angry at him. "It's a hard thing to admit. I'm a grown man. It shouldn't be like this."

"You are a grown man. I don't see you differently. But it does make me concerned about what you haven't told me." Her fingers brushed his cheek.

He enclosed her hand in his. "I will answer any question you have. I won't lie to you. Bring a list with you. Tomorrow night you'll get every one of them answered. Okay?"

"Okay."

He leaned in when someone cleared their throat.

Stormy stood in the doorway. "Don't let me interrupt." She winked.

Windy stepped back from him. "Glad you are here. Stormy, will you babysit tomorrow night?"

"Yes, I'd love to. Shall I come here or want to bring her to my house?"

"You come here. Bring Rob if you want and enjoy the fireplace. That way her stuff will be convenient for you." Windy tossed him a grin.

Yes, they'd have a nice evening. Tomorrow.

He dropped a kiss on her forehead, cleaned up from his lunch that he didn't finish, and returned to his workshop for the supplies needed to create the sand trails through the garden.

By five o'clock he'd finished for the day and packed up. Today's confession had terrified him even after he got the words out. Yet Windy didn't think less of him. They'd make this work.

He still had to answer all her questions. She'd come up with some doozeys, he was sure. He had no fear about answering them.

She might not like his answers, but his secret was out. He was done hiding it from her. That weight was off him. Sorry, Mom.

He hurried home to double check his art and then phone to see about delivering the pieces. Some were meant as Christmas gifts, so he was careful how he phrased things and to whom he gave the message. He needed to wait for two customers to return his call, but then he'd start the deliveries. Only one wanted to pick it up on his own. Kris gave him times on Wednesday, making sure to keep tomorrow free. That was his and Windy's day. He'd waited too long. He'd bet she felt the same. At least, he hoped she did.

Back in his shop, his Christmas gift to her was dry and ready for the wrought iron touches. Should he give it to her during their date? Patience may win, but he was excited.

What he ought to do was plan for tomorrow evening. They definitely needed to go to Coney Island for dinner. Then they'd take a drive, look at the Christmas lights. That would be sweet. Maybe they could find a pretty spot to park. Take a walk where he could kiss her in the moonlight while snow fell.

Yeah, he was a dreamer.

The phone rang. He heard it through the rear door as he stepped to the porch. After hustling in, he got it after about six rings.

"Kris, glad I caught you." Dad. "It looks like Ralph will get to come home as long as he enlists. He needs to have an official escort back. I'd like you to go as my representative. I have a connection with a lawyer up there and I'm sending my assistant. But I'd feel better if you were there. I don't think Ralph could pull anything over on you. He might with strangers. The Mounties will escort you all to the border."

Icy fingers crept up Kris's spine. "When?"

"My assistant will drive. Pick you up Wednesday morning and bring you home for Christmas. If the two of you trade off driving, you should make it." His father had done it. Found a way to ruin things. Again.

"Dad, I have plans here."

"You weren't coming for Christmas? Your mother is expecting you. You don't want to disappoint her."

"I..." What was the use? If he didn't help, Ralph might get stuck up there. Dad couldn't make the trip. He'd not been away from the house since the accident. At least they had the income to pay the doctor to come to the house. That wheelchair was a pain— no matter how Ironsides made it look. "I'll go up with your assistant, but I'm coming back here. I can't be gone that long. Besides, as I said, I have plans."

"Plans that are more important than your family?"

"I didn't say that. But they're important to me. I can't miss them. Who's the assistant you're sending?" *Let's try a different subject because I'm not changing my mind.*

"Someone new to the firm. I've given your grandfather's old address so there shouldn't be a problem finding you. I'm guessing they'll arrive tomorrow evening and you can leave first thing Wednesday morning."

"Tell them I'll be out. The key will be under the mat." He wasn't going to change those plans.

His father's sigh rang loud enough for Kris to catch the meaning. Dad was exasperated. "Good night, Kris. Thanks for your help."

Though somehow, instead of being thanked, Kris felt as if he'd just been smacked.

Chapter 11
Tuesday, December 22, 1970

W indy twirled in front of the mirror wishing she had a full skirt like she used to wear to school that fanned out around her. The anticipation of getting to be alone with Kris, no interruptions, brought a physical excitement that tingled over her skin, making the fine hairs stand on end.

Was she dreaming too much into this? She kinda figured he wanted to be with her as much as she longed to be with him. That was good, right?

His confession yesterday roamed through her brain for the millionth time. Did it bother her? How did he handle those notes from Sunny? Then she pictured her sister's precise penmanship. Each letter clearly formed with a slightly larger than normal size. And she didn't write volumes. Her messages were concise. Windy imagined how if he slowly ran his finger under each symbol, pulling those that blended together into words he'd memorized, he could do it. Given enough chance to concentrate. That explained why he had her read stuff when they went to the movies.

No, it didn't bother her in a way that considered him less in her estimation. He'd more than proved his intelligence so often over the past year. But it did bother her in one way. She wanted to shake his teachers and parents, demand why they didn't see this and help him when he was younger. She wanted to champion him. But would her standing up for him make him feel inferior?

This was a place where they needed to discover their balance.

She had other questions too. Since he'd said she could ask what she chose, she'd taken a lesson from Sunny and created a list of about five queries, knowing that they were only starters. His answers could easily lead to more she hadn't considered.

Those yet-to-be answered points increased the anticipation. There'd be a lot to discuss.

To be fair she needed to grant him the same permission, though there was little she hadn't shared with him. Well, maybe a few things. Like those letters she'd sent. Letters she dearly wanted to make disappear if it were possible. So far there'd been no responses. Hopefully, there wouldn't be. But who knew?

That notion changed her anticipation to anxiousness. Would that door ever close?

"Hey, Kris is downstairs." Sunny stood in the doorway. "When will you be back?"

"I doubt we'll be late. We all have work tomorrow, plus it's been so busy I'll want to fall into bed by ten. I just don't know what he has planned."

Her sister nodded. "Stormy and Rob are already playing with Heather. She's going to be spoiled when you return."

"Not my little girl. She's too sweet."

Sunny's laugh floated back as she descended the stairs.

Windy checked her hair one more time. She'd chosen to fasten the sides with barrettes and let the rest hang long. Her navy turtleneck sweater with the tiny daisy prints all over it paired well with her navy cords, giving her a longer look. Add in Sunny's new platform shoes and she actually appeared much taller than her five-foot two status. Funny how standing next to Hien made her feel gigantic. Windy bet she had four inches on the woman. And her husband was about the same height as Kris. They had to get looks, but obviously didn't care. What showed brighter was their love for each other.

She entered the first floor where Kris held Heather above him and slowly turned her in a circle. Her baby wasn't afraid or upset. Instead, Heather stared at Kris, not breaking eye contact. Windy smiled. She should take a photo of that.

Which reminded her of Kris's Christmas gift up in her room. Should she run back and get it? Would he want to exchange gifts away from their family?

She took the chance to be prepared, in case he did, and slipped upstairs to add it to her shoulder bag. Then she returned. "All ready."

"About time. Thought this guy would hog Heather forever." Stormy took her niece from Kris.

Kris didn't seem to mind. His gaze rested on Windy.

Warmth raced up her neck and cheeks as a slow smile spread over his face. She had the definite notion he approved.

He followed her to the cloak tree, helping her with her jacket.

"We won't be too late, will we?" As soon as the words were out of her mouth, she worried he'd take it that she didn't want to be with him very long. "Rob's gotta get up early for his drive tomorrow and we all have work." *Please understand my meaning.*

He gave her a lopsided grin. "Nope, not late. Dinner and maybe go look at Christmas lights."

Her anticipation bubble returned. "I like that. A lot." She flashed him a smile before turning to blow kisses to Heather.

Stormy turned the baby so Windy could see her face. "Say bye-bye, Mommy. Have fun." She helped Heather wave.

Windy blew one more kiss and headed out the door while Kris held it open for her.

He got her passenger door on his truck before climbing in his side and starting the engine. "I thought we'd try Coney Island again. Hope this time it'll work for us." He cranked up the heater.

"Good plan."

He switched on the radio as the Carpenters sang "We've Only Just Begun."

"That's our song, in a way. We're just beginning this relationship." Somehow the words filled her with hope. For a moment she pictured a future with Kris. They could make it, she was convinced.

"Yeah, I was thinking the same thing." He paused. "Windy, I gotta ask. Are you sure you're okay with my not being able to read like everyone else?" His eyes stared straight ahead, no glances her direction. Was he afraid of her answer?

"Yup. Only part that irritates me are those who might've helped but didn't. No idea if you masqueraded so well that they missed it, or they simply never checked. But you deserved better."

"Don't feel sorry for me. That'll get us nowhere. We can't grow this thing on pity." Now he looked her way.

"No pity, Kris. I'm amazed by you, how you've fought past, how you've used your talents to do so much. I promise, there's no pity."

"Good." He relaxed again. "Do you have more questions?"

"Yup. Made a list." She grinned.

He glanced over. "Oh-oh. Guess I asked for it. Wanna start now or wait for the restaurant?"

"We're almost there and I don't want to get distracted. I'll wait." She tossed him a wink.

He chuckled, though he sounded a wee bit nervous. Sort of.

After he found a parking spot, Kris hopped out and got her door. Windy realized that it was the little things he did that endeared him to her.

Louie Volikas greeted them, bringing glasses of water and taking their orders.

Windy requested her favorite, a bake, while Kris ordered that plus a coney. After Louie left, he leaned in close. "I never can make up my mind, so I get both."

She smiled and reached into her bag for the list. "Are you ready?"

Kris inhaled, his eyes growing, and then exhaled. "Ready. Let's do this."

"First question: You've mentioned your parents. Do you have any siblings?"

He blinked. "Yeah, I have two younger sisters. Jan is sixteen and Suzy is fourteen."

"Don't you ever talk?" Even when in different cities, she and her sisters regularly communicated. Always. She couldn't imagine life without some connection to Sunny and Stormy.

Kris found a few grains of salt on the table and began pushing them around with his index finger. "They can't just make long-distance calls whenever, and they're usually gone doing something when I call them. Jan sent me a letter the other day. Only I haven't read it. She doesn't know either. Maybe later, would you mind reading it to me?" His voice dropped lower as he asked.

His request put her heart in a vice, giving it a tight squeeze. Must be hard to even verbalize. "Sure, happy to." She'd keep it light and simple. It was too important that she didn't let him see she hurt for him.

Windy cleared her throat. "Question two: how many steady girlfriends have you had?"

A nervous chuckle slipped from him. "Okay, I get where this is headed. I dated Marsha Myers for a while my senior year. We went to prom together and then kept seeing each other. She was nice, but when she left for college, we agreed we were only friends. She wrote me a few times, but I never answered."

The reason was left unspoken.

She flattened her paper on the table. "Question three: What is the one thing you've done that makes you the proudest?"

He leaned back in his chair, a funny smile spreading over his face—man, he was cute! "I made a puzzle box. You know, it's a cube thing. You push the right spot, and it opens to a secret compartment?"

She'd read about that in a mystery book, she couldn't remember where now. But he'd made one? "That's impressive. Where is it?"

His eyes grew pensive. "At my dad's house. I gave it to him as a gift. I don't think he realized what it was. It sits on the shelf in his office. Kind of like my relationship with him. He has no idea what's inside, but he's got it where he can keep an eye on it."

She wasn't going to leave him feeling like that. "Question four: You're stranded on a desert island. What three things do you need besides basic food, water, fire, and shelter?"

He scrunched up his mouth and chewed his lip. "Okay, I'd want my tools, a source for electricity, like a generator or something. And you."

Heat flooded her cheeks. "Me?"

He nodded. "You can bring Heather. I just figured she'd be one of your choices." He winked, letting her know he knew exactly what he did there.

She cleared her throat again. "Last question: Do you see us making this work?"

Louie showed up with the food.

A glance at Kris told her he had an answer but waited for privacy.

When Louie stepped away, Kris reached for her hand, tracing little circles underneath on her palm with his thumb. "Yeah, I do. We'll talk more after we leave. For now, let's eat."

She nodded, not sure she could speak. And she wasn't about to be the one to pull away, so she waited until he released her to pick up his bake before grabbing her own.

The food, which was always wonderful, had no taste tonight. Instead, all she wanted to do was leave and be alone with Kris. But, because Louie watched her plate, she did her best not to insult him. She couldn't explain, so she chewed and swallowed the best she could.

Forever later Kris paid the bill and they left. There'd been little conversation while they ate. But once they were in the truck, pulling from the curb, Kris glanced her way, gaining her attention. "Yes, we will make it, Windy. I think you were made for me. We belong together."

He said no more but drove through the streets while they viewed houses adorned with Christmas lights and figurines until he pulled into Highland Park, turning into a parking spot. "Do you have gloves and a hat?"

She drew them from her pockets and put them on.

He helped her from the truck and clasped her hand. "Let's walk."

Snow started to fall, softly dancing in the gleam from the pole lights around the parking area. Like glitter sprinkled from the sky. She'd never been so secure. Windy leaned her head against his shoulder.

"I need to tell you something." He stopped under a lamp's glow, standing in the middle of a halo. He tipped her chin, making sure she saw his eyes. "I'm falling in love with you, Windy

Day. I can't imagine life without you." His face lowered toward hers.

She stood on her tiptoes and pulled his head closer, faster. This was too long in the making. Their lips met and the electricity snapping through her exhilarated, excited her like nothing ever before. She fed his hunger, matching it with her own.

He lifted her off her feet, pulling her closer still. Her cheek slid against his clean-shaven one, his voice soft in her ear. "Windy."

"I love you, too, Kris."

And he found her lips again. Making her heart pound, her pulse race, her throat throb. Making her alive.

⁂

KRIS PULLED BACK, breathing hard, little puffs of white steamed from his mouth that floated away in the dark. It would be so easy to not stop.

No. Windy deserved better. He couldn't do that to her, particularly knowing she felt the same way.

Still, this was tough. "I need to get you home." Then he remembered what else he had to do. "Something more I need to tell you." Something he didn't want to. Especially now.

Snow fell harder. He scooped her in his arms and carried her to the truck, savoring the feel of her so close.

Once he'd climbed inside and started the ignition and heater, he found her hand and took a breath. "I got a call from my father last night. They've worked a deal for Ralph. But Dad isn't able to leave the house. At least, not easily since his car accident last January. He definitely can't travel far from home yet." He stroked the back of her glove, hoping she'd understand. "His wheelchair gets him around the house, but he needs to have oxygen available at all times. He still conducts business from his den, but has assistants and interns to help. He asked me to represent the family.

Thinks Ralph won't put one over on me. Dad's sending an intern from his firm to meet me at the house tonight and we leave for Canada in the morning."

Her grip on his fingers tightened and her eyes grew rounder. Was she afraid? "For how long?"

"I'll be back Christmas Eve night. Dad expected me to come home with the intern. I declined." No way he'd be gone from Windy and Heather this Christmas.

"Are you sure? It's your family."

"You're the one I want to build a family with. I know we're still learning, we don't have to rush, but you are where I want to be." He pulled her hand to his lips.

She didn't argue. Instead, she scooted as close to him as she could.

He put his arm around her and drove one handed out of the parking lot.

She rested her head below his shoulder and started to hum, "We've Only Just Begun."

It made him smile. They had no need for words. If she was that content, this would be heaven.

When he pulled in the drive, a VW Beetle sat parked at the curb. Her muscles grew taut the second she spotted it. Even though he had every intention of getting her door, she didn't wait. Instead, she popped out and raced to the porch, pulling the storm door open. Then froze.

He caught up to her, her hand resting on the knob but not turning it. "Are you okay? What's the matter?"

"I don't know." She spun around and pulled his head to hers, firmly kissing him. "Please remember I love you."

Something was way wrong.

She breathed hard a couple times, then pushed open the door.

Stormy and Rob sat on the couch with Heather.

Then, as Kris stepped into the room, someone else stood from one of the fireside chairs. A blond guy with wireframe glasses ambled toward Windy.

"Tim."

Tim? This was Heather's father? A vice tightened around Kris's heart.

"Surprise. How are you, Windy?" He took her hand and kissed her cheek.

"Flummoxed? Stymied? Flabbergasted?"

His chuckle sounded uptight. "I started to write so many times. Then my folks got your letter and forwarded it on to me. I couldn't get the words right. So, I decided to see you. You sure look good."

Kris cleared his throat. A better choice than clearing the invader from the room.

She glanced back at him. "This is Kris. Kris, this is Tim."

Tim stuck out his hand. A normal thing to do in a totally abnormal setting. "Nice to meet you."

Kris accepted his grasp, choosing not to cause a scene. Then Heather cried, so he excused himself and took her from Stormy. "When was her last bottle?" The baby calmed the moment Kris held her. So did he, a little.

"It's been a while. She's probably ready." Stormy motioned for Rob. "We'll get out of your hair. Windy, hon, call me if you need anything. Sunny's in the office on the phone with Pat." They grabbed their coats and beat it out the door.

Tim watched the exchange, and then as if just understanding, he smiled and nodded. "Now I get it. I thought the baby was theirs, but she's yours. Oh, okay."

Kris caught Windy's glance, emotion welling up in her. He was about to claim Heather, give her the out, when she spoke.

"No, Tim. She's *my* daughter."

The guy stared at her, then at Kris, then back at her again. "Oh, sorry. I didn't know. Don't want to get in the middle of things."

Then she hit the guy. Made a fist, punched him. Hard. On the shoulder. Probably left a bruise. "Don't be so stupid. You're Heather's father, Tim. That's why I was getting in touch with you. Thought you ought to know."

Tim cocked his head like a puppy trying to figure something out. His eyes narrowed and he took a step back. "Mine? You think she's *my* baby?" He backed up, hands in front to ward off more blows. "It was only once."

Windy's cheeks pinked, but her mouth rose on one side, a lopsided grimace. "That's all it takes sometimes." Her eyes narrowed. "I came to tell you but found you'd left me a note. A note, Tim. Didn't bother to call. Guess I was lucky to get what I did."

"Hey, I didn't know who might be listening. Big brother is everywhere. I couldn't tell you and I shouldn't even be here. But I wanted to see you again."

"Well, now you have." She shrugged. "Kris, I'll take my daughter. It was a lovely evening. Goodnight. Please see yourselves out." She plucked Heather from his arms and headed for the stairs.

Kris stared after her until she left his sight, never once looking back. Then he glanced at Tim who'd also followed her ascent. Only he kept staring. Was he hoping for an encore?

"She won't be back."

Kris's voice must have jarred him enough so he could react. "She's got a baby. My baby? What am I going to do?" Tim ran his hand through his hair.

"Dude, I'm not the one to ask. We'd better go." Kris indicated the door and pulled up the collar of his peacoat. Yeah, he definitely wasn't the person to ask.

"Oh, right." Tim grabbed his jacket from the cloak tree. "Know where I can crash tonight? I'd figured to land on her couch or something. No idea she lived in a mansion with her sister. She's got two?"

Kris nodded, and guided him out the door, pulling it closed behind him. "How long are you staying?" Let's focus on the important details. No side trails.

Tim shrugged. "No clue. I'd only planned to see her. Maybe talk her into coming back with me. Now that she has a kid, my kid..." He shook his head, still in shock. "I don't know."

Stay on point. "That your bug?" Kris pointed to the little green VW at the curb.

Tim nodded.

"Follow me. You can crash at my place tonight." The words were out of his mouth before Kris thought. He headed for his truck.

"Thanks, man." Tim climbed into his Beetle.

Kris turned the ignition and backed out around the Herbie wannabe. Then he motioned for Tim to follow before taking the lead to his house.

The guy was nothing like what he'd imagined. Not that he'd spent a lot of time wondering what Heather's father looked like, or what type of male would catch Windy's attention. Still, on occasion, a scenario crossed his mind. And nowhere in it had he pictured the bespeckled Ryan O'Neill lookalike who now followed him home.

So why was he following Kris home? Right, he'd opened his big mouth. Again. Well, he couldn't let Heather's father freeze to death sleeping in his car. Could he?

He shook that thought away. Technically all he could offer was one night anyway. What happened after that?

It was none of his business. Whatever happens happened. It wasn't his job to house all the draft dodgers venturing through Kokomo. He squeezed his eyes shut at the stoplight. What a patsy he was.

That reminded him he'd have another visitor tonight too. Dad's intern. They could toss for the guest room. The other'd sleep on the couch. Or share. Who cared? He'd had enough for one day.

At least the evening hadn't all been bad. In fact, most of it had been beyond wonderful. That kiss with Windy blew his mind. His heart still skipped when he thought about it. She was so in his head.

Was she in Tim's head? Like that? He didn't want to think about what they'd had together. It would only mess with what little mental capacity he possessed.

He pulled into his driveway and watched to see if Tim made it. He did, so Kris shut off his truck and headed for the house.

Tim followed with a backpack slung over his shoulder.

The house was still dark and the key beneath the mat. His other visitor hadn't arrived yet. Tim might be in luck for the guest room.

"Come on in." Kris led the way inside, turning on lights as he went.

"Do you live with someone or are you older than you look?"

Kris squinted at the guy until he understood. "It's my grandfather's house. When he got married and moved out, I stayed on. All his stuff." He headed for the kitchen. "Want something to drink?"

"What do you have?"

Kris cringed. It was bad enough to get the ribbing from Ralph. He didn't need to appear juvenile in the eyes of Heather's father. But when he glanced up from the open refrigerator to yell out choices, Tim stood in the doorway. "Take your pick." He grabbed a Dr Pepper and moved out of the way.

Tim didn't judge him. Just grabbed a Coke and popped the top.

"Have you eaten?"

Tim shook his head. "Don't think I can. This is hitting pretty hard."

Kris didn't want to feel bad for the guy. He was blockage on this relationship path. But he understood. There hadn't been much preparation for the big announcement. Tim probably did feel disoriented.

Someone knocked. Kris left to answer it.

He pulled the front door open and blinked. About a million times. "Marsha? What are you doing here?"

"Your father didn't mention I was coming?" She smiled and tipped her head to the side, waiting. "So, you going to let me in? It's crazy cold out here."

"Oh yeah, sure." He held the door and she trundled through with her suitcase. Suitcase. His father expected her to stay with him? Kris shook his head and glanced at his watch. It was after ten. Too late to call Gramps and Hazel.

Tim wandered out from the kitchen, taking a swig of his pop.

Marsha glanced at him, and then Tim, and back again. "Who's your friend?"

"Tim, this is Marsha. Marsha, Tim. I've only got the one spare bed. Tim, you'll be okay on the couch?"

"Sure. Don't think I'm going to sleep much tonight anyway." He punctuated that with a yawn.

"You get the guest room, Marsha. It's up here." He grabbed her bag, leading the way up the stairs to where his last visitor, Ralph, had crashed. Maybe she shouldn't know that. "When do you want to leave?"

"Right away. Out the door by eight?"

Kris nodded.

"You look good, Kris. It's been a long time." She smiled, running a finger down his arm.

That was uncomfortable. He never thought he'd see her again. What was his father trying to do? "Well, if that's the plan, I'd better lock up. Get to bed. Catch you in the morning."

She wiggled her fingers at him and slowly closed the bedroom door.

Kris secured the house, dropping off a pillow and blankets for Tim while he was at it.

This was not how he saw this evening ending. Even with the foreknowledge that his dad was sending someone, this scenario never crossed his mind.

The sooner he got the errand for his dad over with, the faster he'd be with Windy. He hoped.

But what if Tim talked her into leaving before he got back?

"Hey, Tim. I gotta take off in the morning until Christmas Eve. For my dad. Anyway, you're welcome to stay here until I get back. Will that help?"

"Sure. I appreciate it."

"And you might not want to mention around here where you're from." Kris glanced up toward the second floor and raised his brows.

Tim squinted his eyes and then opened them wide as understanding flooded his face. "Yeah, got it. Thanks, man."

"No problem. 'Night."

He'd done it again. Volunteering to help the guy who could destroy everything he hoped for. Yet it was the only idea he had to keep Tim from taking off with Windy before he returned.

Chapter 12
Wednesday, December 23, 1970

Wasn't it what she'd hoped for? Even prayed for, a little. It sure wasn't what she wanted now. Scratch that. It most definitely wasn't what she wanted. Instead, the big desire of her heart was making his way to Canada this morning. She pulled the brush through her hair and clamped it with a barrette at her nape.

What attracted the men in her life to that frozen country?

She'd cried while she nursed Heather last night, cried long after her daughter fell asleep, and woke with tears still in her eyes, having cried in her dreams. Did her eyes look puffy? She stared in the mirror as she hoped Max Factor and his friend Maybelline, could cover it.

A part of her felt the fair thing was to give Tim a chance. This was a long term situation. Maybe she'd been too tough on him last night. Face it, his timing might stink, but she'd not been too gracious delivering the news.

And poor Kris. She should've been nicer to him too. But he understood. At least she thought he did. Plus, she'd told him before they went in to remember that she loved him. No matter what, that wouldn't change. Windy put Heather into her carrier and took her downstairs to the kitchen.

She stared in the open fridge, her mind elsewhere. What if Tim requested a chance to be a father? What if he asked her to marry him and move to Canada? Was she obligated to consider that? Could she be stuck in a marriage to someone with whom she'd made a mistake? Especially when the one she loved was right there and willing to be Heather's daddy? Kris had already proved he was great father material. Great husband material, too, if that kiss was any indication. No, she couldn't go there. Being a husband was more than just kissing someone's socks off.

The refrigerator shelves came into focus. Great, they were out of milk. Windy sighed. Guess it was scrambled eggs for breakfast. Her mind too much on the guy who kissed like no other while memories floated past.

Kris stayed with her when it wasn't good. Waiting at the hospital when she was in labor. Caring for her when she had strep. He listened when she needed someone. Stood by her when Tim showed up. The guy was wonderful husband material. He even trusted her with his secret that he kept from his family. That said more to her than anything else. Besides, he chose her over his family for Christmas. She couldn't wait for him to get back.

In the meantime, though, there was Tim. Or at least she figured he still hung around. However, it wouldn't be the first time he vamoosed.

Heather cooed, pulling her attention that direction. What would be best for her daughter? Was there something about blood that made Tim the better choice? Did she owe him that even if it wasn't what she wanted?

Sunny came and sat at the table. "How are you doing this morning?"

"Fine, I guess. Wish Kris were here."

"Where is he?" She scrunched her face. Didn't she know?

"He never told you? His father called. He's off to Canada today to rescue Ralph and bring him back. He's supposed to be home tomorrow night." Windy put the rattle Heather dropped back in her hand. "I miss him already."

"So, you're getting serious."

"Yeah, I guess we are. I love him, Sunny. He said he's falling in love with me. He thinks we can make a family and I want him to be right. But now Tim's here. I don't know what to do. Heather is his daughter; shouldn't he get a chance?"

Sunny grasped Windy's hand. "I don't know the answer. I really like Kris and it touches me how he takes care of you and Heather. I think he'd be a great husband and father for you two. But you're right. Tim hasn't had the opportunity to step up yet and he is Heather's father. I've no idea what to tell you. Have you prayed about it?"

Windy shook her head. "Not really. God's been kinda on the back shelf. I doubt He wants to hear from me, especially with how I messed up."

"Sweetie, I'm not going to argue about the messed-up part. But you took responsibility. And a baby is a gift. Do you think He'd trust that precious little one to you as a punishment? You are so loved. You need to love Him back. Trust Him to let you know what's right." Sunny pulled a paper napkin from the holder on the table and handed it to her. "I'd be happy to pray with you if you want. Or I can watch Heather so you can have some alone time."

Windy blotted her eyes, sure now they were akin to puff pastries. "The alone time would be good. You don't mind?"

Sunny pulled Heather from her carrier and sat her on her lap. "Why would I mind? Not with this sweet cutie. You go have your talk with Jesus. We'll be hanging out down here."

Windy hugged her sister and set off for upstairs, moving fast at first but slowing as she neared her room. It'd been a long while since she'd had a heart to heart with God. Not since before she left for college. Without her grandmother's daily example, it was easier to procrastinate. Soon, a lot of time passed. She wasn't sure how to start.

She closed her bedroom door and struggled for an opening. Then she spotted Sunny's Bible on her nightstand. Maybe that would help with inspiration. The book fell open to Romans chapter three. Windy scanned the verses until something familiar jumped out:

> *For all have sinned, and come short of*
> *the glory of God; being justified freely by*
> *his grace through the redemption that is*
> *in Christ Jesus:*

That reminded her of something else and she kept reading for five more chapters until she found the verse her heart craved.

> *There is therefore now no condemnation*
> *to them which are in Christ Jesus, who*
> *walk not after the flesh, but after the*
> *Spirit.*

No condemnation. She could talk to God. He'd provided a way knowing she'd mess up. Windy slipped to her knees next to her bed. "Father, I am sorry. I should have waited for You to bring Kris into my life. Done things by Your rules. But You still gave me Heather. She's the most beautiful gift ever. How do I thank You for turning my sin into a miracle? But I do thank You. I'm so blessed. I'm also confused and don't want to mess up again. I know how I feel, but I can't act on feelings alone. What should I do, God? What do I say? Please help me. In Jesus's name, Amen."

She still had no answers, but now she was ready to discover them. After getting off her knees, she splashed cold water on her face, hoping to take care of the puffy eye problem. She fixed her makeup and headed downstairs to the kitchen. Sunny's office was just off from there, but she wasn't in it. So, Windy moved toward the front and heard voices coming from the living room. She peeked around the door frame to find Sunny and Heather with Tim.

"Do you want to hold her?" Sunny held Heather out to him.

He shook his head, his eyes enormous behind his lenses. "I don't think so. I've never held a baby. What if I drop her?"

"You won't. Sit down and I'll put her on your lap." Sunny practically pushed him into the rocker.

Windy covered her mouth to keep from giving herself away. She'd never seen Tim look so terrified. Almost made her feel sorry for him.

"Are you sure?" He held Heather, stiff-armed, not allowing her to cuddle in.

Her little face turned to his and she started her staring contest.

"She's watching me." Tim stared back.

"She does that. We call her the Queen of the Stare. Relax."

He turned to Sunny and Windy couldn't miss the fear in his gaze. "What do I do?"

"You rock her and talk to her. Let her get to know your voice."

"Um, I don't ..."

Heather's little face scrunched, and she released a yell.

Tim jumped up and shoved Heather into Sunny's arms. "I don't think this is a good idea. I don't know what I'm doing. Did I hurt her?"

Sunny cuddled Heather, who stopped crying right away. "It was probably a gas bubble. You didn't hurt her. You just need more practice."

Windy decided it was time and stepped into the room. "Morning, Tim. You're still here."

"Yeah." He put space between him and Sunny, getting closer to Windy in the process. "We didn't get a chance to talk last night. So, I thought I'd come back. Besides, I need to give Kris his key when he comes home."

"His key?" What did he mean?

"Yeah, he's letting me crash at his place. But him and some chick have to run an errand. He's supposed to be back tomorrow evening."

"Some chick?" What was he talking about?

"Yeah, she got there late last night. Said her name was Marsha? His old man sent her and they're doing something for him."

Marsha? As in Marsha Myers, his old flame? That would be too weird. As was the feeling creeping up from her gut. She didn't like it, not one bit. Even if she wasn't his old girlfriend, what was she doing spending the night there at his house? If Tim hadn't followed him home, it would've just been the two of them.

No, she didn't like this. At all.

"Tell me about this *chick*." His choice of words fit her feelings at the moment.

Tim shrugged. "She's nice? A professional type with a briefcase and heels, suit, that sort. A pretty brunette. We didn't talk, other than to say hi. Kris took her upstairs and gave me the couch."

Her head was about to bust. Still, a little voice reminded her *Kris is a nice guy. Trust him.*

There was a limit though. It was possible to be too nice. She might be able to trust him, but should she trust that bimbo?

Bimbo? Okay, so could be it's all innocent. Maybe Marsha isn't his old girlfriend. *And* it's exactly what Kris explained before he left.

She'd just have to count on him. There was little else at this point.

But she didn't have to like it.

"So, you are staying until Kris is back?"

Tim nodded. "That's the plan, I guess. What I'd like is for us to talk. Is there anywhere private?"

"Get your jacket and follow me." An idea occurred and she would run with it. Could be God's way of telling her what to do.

She swiped a kitchen towel and led him out through the garden to the sycamore tree, now bare of its leaves with branches appearing as great black fractures against the sky. A quick wipe off of the wrought iron seat Kris designed gave them somewhere dry to sit.

Tim blew into his hands. "I've missed you, Windy. I think about you every day. It's nice up there but it's not home yet."

"You had other choices."

"Not really. My grades bottomed out. My number was right there. I'm terrified. I don't believe this is a good war. Is any war good? And making me fight for big corporations, that's not right. If I stand up for myself, I land in prison. Yeah, that sounds fun, ya know?"

"So, what is your plan?" She glanced at the branches over his head. No sign of red in sight. Not even the fake bird they used. Kris must have brought it in.

"I want you. Windy, will you please come back to Canada with me?"

Thursday, December 24, 1970

KRIS TWISTED ONCE MORE, hoping for just five minutes of sleep. The door handle poked his ribs and he wanted to strangle his father. Oh, it had been a wonderful twenty-four hours.

First Marsha talks him into taking her car so the three of them didn't have to sit on one seat in his truck. Fine.

She wouldn't let him drive though, since she'd signed out the Chevy. Something about insurance coverage in case of an accident. He could put up with that.

But then she openly flirted with him the whole way. What had he ever seen in her? Plus, nothing discouraged her.

They got to the Canadian lawyer's office and the two of them talked while Kris did his best to hang back. The lawyer explained he should be able to push all the paperwork through. They'd pick Ralph up at eight. This morning.

But the evening wasn't over yet. Marsha suggested dinner, which was fine. Then drove to the motel where Dad had made reservations. Make that *a* reservation. One room. What was that old man doing?

When Kris wouldn't agree to stay, Marsha turned red and slammed the door on him. Fortunately, she threw the keys at him since she knew there were no more rooms. Besides, it was questionable that Kris had enough cash with him. All U.S. currency to boot. So, the amount didn't matter. Who knew where it'd be accepted?

Therefore, on the eve before Christmas Eve, there was no room for him in the inn.

Instead of a stable with hay, he chattered his teeth in a freezing car, trying to wrap up and running the heater for short bursts to raise the temperature before turning off the engine so they wouldn't run out of gas.

He pounded his makeshift pillow, fashioned from his spare pair of jeans, and groaned as the sun began to rise, sending fingers of light his way.

Mom always complained he was grumpy in the morning when he didn't get enough sleep. She should have warned Marsha.

A part of him wanted to grab breakfast. Another was positive if he wasn't in the car, Marsha would leave him stranded. She was not amused by his response last night.

Twenty minutes later there was a tap on the glass. Marsha.

He rolled down the window. "Morning."

"Sleep well?" Her tone didn't match her words.

"Slept fine. Are you ready?"

"Sure. Scoot over. I'm driving."

He obeyed. She didn't sound flirtatious today. Hopefully, she got the message.

They arrived where Ralph was being detained and checked in. The lawyer met them there. All paperwork was reviewed, certified, and approved before they brought Ralph out to them, still all smiles. Did anything faze that kid?

"Dude, you came. Who's this pretty mama? Man, for a guy who don't know any foxy ladies, you've sure got your pick. How's your sweet chickee back in Ko-ko-mo?"

Marsha glanced up at him and understanding flashed in her eyes. Well, at least he didn't have to explain.

"She's fine."

"Yea, dude. So fine." His cousin waggled his eyebrows and giggled.

"Shut up, Ralph. Let's go."

They marched to the car where Ralph slid into the rear seat. Kris took his place on the passenger side and Marsha climbed into the driver's seat.

"You lettin' this pretty little thing drive, dude? Where're your manners?"

Marsha glared in the rearview mirror. "Ralph, my name is Ms. Myers to you. Not pretty mama, or foxy lady, or chickee, or anything else you want to try. I am driving because I signed for the car. He's not on the insurance policy. Now if you'll sit back, I'll return you to the land of the free, the home of your birth, and maybe we can get breakfast."

"Oh, right, Ms. Myers, I can dig it. You do your thing and I'll do mine." He leaned against the seat and pulled out a harmonica. Before anyone stopped him, he started "Home on the Range."

Marsha skidded to a halt on the shoulder, turned, and held out her hand. "Give. Now."

Ralph looked like a kicked puppy but placed his harmonica in her hand. "Gee, Ms. Myers, you're no fun."

Kris did his best not to laugh out loud, but Marsha glared at him anyway. Oh well, it was still funny. Especially since Ralph needled someone else for a change.

They crossed the bridge connecting Windsor, Ontario, Canada, and Ralph was finally on United States soil.

"So, are you ready to eat? I have an old classmate from Ohio State who lives in Allen Park. We're going to meet her for breakfast at her favorite restaurant." She smiled. Kris had seen his mother smile like that when she attempted to convince him that what she desired, the polar opposite of what he wanted, would be so fun.

"I need back home as soon as possible. We're not staying long, are we?"

She turned her glare on him, a phaser set to stun. "I haven't seen Liz in a while and I'm not about to drive this close and not say hello. You'll get home, I promise." The glare became a sneer, but he figured she was trying to smile. Guess it's not easy when you're that angry.

"Fine."

She continued driving until she passed a sign and pointed it out. "Allen Park, here we are." Without taking her eyes from the road, she reached in her purse and pulled out a piece of paper and handed it to him. "Read the directions to me, Kris."

Chills froze his body. All that moved were his eyes. They merely blinked. His chest wouldn't let air in to form a word. What was he to do?

"I'm waiting. There're lots of turns getting to the place." She glanced his way, and something registered on her face. "What's the matter? Just read me the directions."

Kris stared at the paper covered in loopy cursive. Could be a Spirograph design for all he could tell. It was going to come out. His secret was about to expose him. He'd rather streak buck naked through downtown Detroit at rush hour than let that be uncovered.

She pulled to the side of the road, shoving the gearshift into park. "Kris, talk to me. What's the matter?"

He swallowed hard. "I...I can't." His head wanted to explode.

"You can't what?" She crossed her arms over her chest.

"I...can't read the words."

"What do you mean?"

"I can't read it." There. He'd said it. Could he simply disappear now?

"Wait, dude. You can't read? My five-year-old next-door neighbor can read. What's wrong with you?"

Kris tossed the paper back to Ralph. "Then you do it." He leaned his face against the cold window glass and closed his eyes.

Marsha started the car moving. "You heard him, Ralph. Read the directions to me."

Ralph did and they were soon at the restaurant. The guys went to the table while Marsha used the pay phone to let her friend know they'd arrived.

Kris debated on saying anything but decided he'd better. "I'd appreciate it if you didn't talk about that anymore."

"About what? That you're an idiot?"

"Fine, I'm an idiot. Just don't talk about it, 'kay?" Kris would agree to almost anything if Ralph would keep his trap shut.

"You've treated me like some disease for as long as I can remember, and I finally see the big guy isn't perfect? Your poor daddy, what's he gonna do for an heir? Man, you are so lame."

"Not so lame that I won't leave and hitch-hike home right now."

"No!" Marsha arrived to hear the last. "No, you can't. No hitchhiking. It's freezing out. Ralph will keep his mouth shut. Got it?"

"You're the boss lady, Ms. Myers."

Breakfast was mercifully short. Turned out Marsha's friend had to work so couldn't stay long, allowing them back on the road in less than an hour.

Kris curled up on the passenger side and closed his eyes. The rhythm of the driving and his lack of sleep last night blurred with the mellow radio station Marsha played, caused him to drift. He'd be home in about four hours. He could hang in there that long.

A bump caused him to bang his head against the window. He opened his eyes. Nothing looked familiar. He checked his watch. It was a little after two. Guess he caught up on his sleep. Some. "You can grab lunch at my house before you start for Dad's."

"No need." Marsha kept her eyes glued to the road and Ralph giggled from the back seat.

"You two aren't hungry?" He glanced at them both. It was like they shared a secret.

"I've got apples and peanut-butter sandwiches in that box on the floor back there, Ralph. Want to pass one of each up to Kris?"

"Sure, Ms. Myers." He giggled again.

"I can eat at my house. We should be getting close to Kokomo."

Now Ralph was rolling on his seat.

"Sorry, Kris. Your dad told me to bring you home, and he didn't care what it took."

The nerves at the back of his neck tingled, clenching the muscles. He reached up there to rub as the truth settled on him. "Where are we?"

"Nearly to the Pennsylvania border. We'll be in Pittsburgh in about half an hour."

"NO. I promised Windy I'd be back for her. Tonight. Don't do this Marsha. *Please.*"

"Who's Windy?" She glanced over at him.

"She's that foxy mama he's got stashed away in Ko-ko-mo."

"Shut up, Ralph. Please, Marsha. This is important." He'd never wanted to yank the steering wheel from anyone so much.

"Sorry, Kris. Your dad's my boss. I won't lose my job for you."

This was wrong, so wrong. He'd basically been kidnapped. And at eighty miles per hour on the highway, opening the door and jumping was out. If he wanted to live to see Kokomo again, that is. How did he get word to Windy? He'd have to call her before he did anything else.

Thirty minutes later they pulled into the drive at his parents' ranch-style house. Built for his dad who no longer could do stairs. The door opened. Jan and Suzy ran out to greet him. That removed some sting from the situation.

His mother met him just inside with a hug. She could tell he was angry. "Don't blame your father. He realized I really wanted to see you for Christmas."

"I told him it was important that I was in Kokomo. Mom, I gotta leave. I need a car. Or money for a bus. Something."

Her face crumbled and his heart twitched. "You won't stay?"

"I'm sorry, Mom. If he'd listened to me, it would've been better. I'd be bringing someone to meet you very soon. Since he's pulled this stunt, she'll think I'm a liar. I swear, if he's ruined this, I'll never step foot in this house again. Now, where is he?"

"Right behind you, Kris. You can go home after we celebrate Christmas as a family. You owe that to your mother. Any girl worth it will understand. I'll get you back, but you need to give your mother this gift."

Kris spun, heading for the nearest room with a telephone—the living room. "I'm making a long-distance call."

"Make it in my office. You'll have privacy." His father wheeled down the hall.

Kris entered the den and closed the door before dialing the mansion. Sunny picked up on the second ring. "Sunny, it's Kris. Is Windy there?"

"Yeah, Kris, I'll get her. Hold on." Like he'd do anything else.

"Kris? Where are you?" Windy sounded worried.

"I'm in Pittsburgh. I'm so sorry. It's a long story. I'll tell you when I get home. But I didn't do it on purpose. Can you believe me?" *Please believe me.*

"I do. But I need to talk to you." Was she about to cry?

"What's wrong?"

She sniffed. "Tim asked me to go to Canada with him."

That took his breath. He finally pushed out some words. "What did you say?"

"I couldn't say. What should I do, Kris?"

He squeezed his eyes closed until his heart found a beat. "I can't answer that for you, Windy. I love you, but you gotta make that decision."

"When are you coming home?"

"My plan is sometime tomorrow. Not sure when my warden's gonna release me, but I'm aiming for morning." He knew he sounded bitter, but at this moment he didn't care.

The door burst open. His dad rolled in followed by his mother.

"I need to go now. Something's up."

"I love you, Kris. Come home soon."

"I will. Bye."

He hung up the phone and stared at his father. "Thank you for the privacy."

"Thank you for the honesty. When did you plan to tell us?" Tell them what? Then he spotted Ralph's grin in the doorway. And he knew. His secret was out.

Chapter 13
Friday, December 25, 1970

Windy woke to a thin blanket of snow on the ground and a chill in her heart. She'd come to a realization last night after talking with Kris. This was not about what she wanted. She must consider what was best for her daughter.

She stretched on her bed, causing Frazier to jump off. There was no room to force her desires. Instead, she had to put her faith in God to lead her. After a lot of praying during the night, she was impressed to watch Tim. Determine if what she noticed in his character was what God would honor.

Windy needed to do the same with Kris when he returned. The God-centered man who demonstrated a father's caring, that's who would win her loyalty.

She couldn't say her heart. There was no denying Kris had that. But if Tim turned out to be the one God chose, could she then give him her heart?

If she put her trust in God and he chose Tim, He'd make a way for the rest. The man she married deserved to be number one, no second place. Therefore, God must figure it out. She had to believe that or live with a broken heart.

Heather stirred, so she pulled the baby into bed with her. "Good morning, little love. Today is your first Christmas. Maybe your big gift's gonna be to know who your daddy will be." What if God didn't choose either of those men? What if he had someone completely different in mind?

She'd never considered that possibility.

No. She was fairly sure it was a matter of Tim having a claim to honor or Kris who'd already shown he wanted this.

But where was Kris's relationship with Jesus? Now that she'd renewed that connection, she wanted her daughter to come to a saving knowledge of grace, the grace that brought her into the world despite her mother's sin. An unbelieving father would never work.

She traced a finger over her baby's eyebrows that were coming in dark like hers. "We'll do this God's way, lovey, no matter what. Let's get you some breakfast."

Her mind raced through the day's plans. Everyone would meet at her grandmother's for gifts and dinner starting at eleven. Gramma even said to bring Tim along. Not that she wanted to, but it would be rude to leave him out on Christmas. So, she'd told him yesterday before he returned to Kris's house to meet her here. He appeared grateful and scared all at once, first thanking her and then questioning about every person he'd meet. His big worry was if they knew about him and would anyone turn him in.

Guess he needed to be cautious. Her father would not be pleased, but she hoped that despite being a veteran, he'd be civil. But the way Gramma always tried to bring peace, it was no surprise that she'd do this. The bigger conundrum was how her parents would get along. They'd not experienced the same breathing space in over a decade.

She glanced at the clock. Seven thirty. How was Kris faring with his family? He'd promised to explain how he got there. He'd also promised to be with her by yesterday. Did he make promises lightly? No, she didn't think so. At least there'd been no past evidence. However, they were at a new level in their relationship. She might uncover things.

Heather had finished, looking satisfied with the world while milk dribbled from the corner of her mouth. Oh, her sweet baby girl.

She'd better get moving. Sunny, always the early riser, had slipped out. It might've been what woke Windy to begin with. But her sister enjoyed the privacy of her office to have a quiet time of prayer before starting her day. Just hope she started the coffee pot too.

Once Windy and Heather were dressed, they went downstairs. All the Christmas decorations were turned on. The latest *Goodyear Christmas* record played softly on the stereo. Normally she would've taken the landing turn to the kitchen, but the lights wrapped around the balustrade caught her attention.

Sunny was at the tree, putting something beneath. "Good, you're up. I wanted to give you your gift before we go to Gramma's. Go sit on the sofa."

Windy did as instructed. Her sister's present, along with the others, had been transported to her grandmother's yesterday to make today's travel lighter. What did she do about that? "Your gift isn't here."

"I know. You wrangled Stormy into taking them for you." Sunny winked. "Don't worry. This is more private." She pulled out a package, almost flat. "I put this together for you. I think you need to see it."

Windy removed the bow and released the tape to pull back the paper as Gramma had taught the girls—"don't rip it, we can use it again next year." Inside was a photo album. She lifted the cover to find picture after picture of their family during their Los Angeles days. Some were goofy poses of her and Stormy together. Some with Dad. Sunny wasn't in many and Windy realized it was because she'd been the photographer. There were even some with her mother.

One in particular had her mother in a chair and the three girls surrounding her. Her father must have snapped that one. Sunny and Stormy knelt on either side while Windy stood behind, wrapping her arms around the seated woman. The telling part was the looks on their faces. The woman smiled up at Windy, who returned it with a grin. They looked so...loving.

Windy wiped a tear from her face. "I remember that. It was a weekend where we drove to the beach, then as a surprise went to Disneyland. My favorite moment came on the ride home, curled up next to Daddy in the front seat. He's always been our rock."

"We have some good memories, Windy. Let's not forget that, okay? I know today will be tough for all of us. Stormy has yet to make peace, but she keeps showing up. Dad and Mom'll be at the same table. I can't even guess what to expect. But if we concentrate on the love, we'll get there. And I do love you, baby sister of mine." Sunny pulled her into a hug. Wet spots warmed her neck before turning cool.

Windy pulled back and grabbed tissues for both of them. "I hope this'll be the last of our tears." They both laughed. "Thank you for this. It's precious." She hugged her sister one more time. "How about some breakfast? Heather's eaten but I haven't even had coffee."

"It's ready in the kitchen. I left pancakes and bacon warming in the oven for you too." Sunny stood and kissed the top of her head. "I've got a few more gifts to wrap. Pat is joining us after opening gifts with his family. I expect him here just before we need to leave." She disappeared into her office.

Windy carried Heather to the kitchen and got breakfast together. Sunny was right. There was a lot of love in this family. God had seen to that. She finished and cleaned the kitchen before choosing to spend time reading her Bible and perusing the photo album more carefully. About ten, she stopped to feed Heather. Then they needed to get ready. She came downstairs as Pat and Tim arrived.

Sunny suggested Windy and Tim ride together and retrieved Heather's car seat to fit into Tim's Beetle. Then they caravanned to Gramma's.

The whole way Windy's stomach clenched. Between anxiousness about her parents being together, missing Kris, and wondering about the reception Tim would get, it was enough to make her consider jumping from the car and hiding in her room. But she'd not leave her baby. Heather instilled determination to see things through.

Tim smiled, though she could see his nerves were about as frayed as hers. "Merry Christmas."

"Merry Christmas, Tim."

"Have you thought more about coming to Canada with me? I don't think I should stay here much longer." His gaze sought hers and she tried to avoid it. but he deserved her honesty.

"I'm still reflecting. If it were only me, it'd be easy. But I've got Heather to consider. What's best for her? But I am thinking hard, Tim, and praying."

Little furrows sprouted between his eyes. "You can bring Heather. That's not a problem."

"Did you think I would leave her?" Didn't he want to know his daughter?

"Um, no, I figured you'd bring her. Just saying I'm good with that." He paused. "Can I ask you something?"

"Okay."

"When did you get religion?"

She breathed a sigh. Guess she'd kept her faith so far back on that shelf that he never had a clue. "I was raised in church. I've been a believer for a long time, since I asked Jesus into my heart when I was twelve. But I got away from it while in college. I can't do this parent thing without my spiritual roots getting stronger. That's an important part of this decision."

He chewed his lip. "I see."

They pulled up at Gramma's and Windy got Heather out of the car.

Dad greeted her at the door. "Give me a hug so I can capture this little beauty." He was already reaching for Heather.

Windy didn't mind. "Merry Christmas, Dad." She handed Heather over and hugged her father. "Say Merry Christmas to your grandpa, sweetie."

The baby cooed and grabbed for Dad's hair.

Laughing, he kissed the baby's cheek. "Let's get you in here."

Windy touched his arm, stopping him a moment. "Dad, this is Tim. He's here for Christmas."

Tim stepped from in back of Windy and offered his hand.

Dad glanced between the two of them before receiving the handshake. "Good to meet you. Come on in."

Windy slipped off to the kitchen to see if she could help. "How's it going in here?"

Gramma and her mother looked up. Sunny was tying on an apron.

"We're right on schedule, Windy girl. I think we can stop and open gifts." Her grandmother wiped her hands on a towel. "Ready, ladies?"

Her mother wiped her hands as well. Windy noticed they trembled. Was she afraid?

Sunny smoothed her apron skirt. "Let's go." She winked at Windy.

When she sent her gifts with Stormy yesterday, she decided to include something for her mother and Tim, sweet photos of Heather she'd taken and developed, and hoped they would appreciate. It was last minute in Tim's case and a struggle in her mother's. But this was Christmas. It's what Jesus would do. She didn't want to hang on to the hard feelings. Even though she didn't hate her mother anymore, things weren't simple. However, she would be courteous, maybe even show kindness. It could lead to a new relationship.

When she entered the living room, all the seats were taken. So, she sank to the floor like she had as a kid. She flicked a glance and realized her father had scooted over to make room for her mother to sit with him while he held Heather. She caught the look they exchanged before her mother sat. It felt strange yet familiar to see them together playing with her baby.

Gene wore a Santa hat and began passing out the gifts. The pile around Windy grew enormous since all of Heather's were stacked there too. Everyone had gotten something special for the newest member of the family.

She'd just started to unwrap a box from her father for her daughter when the phone rang.

Gramma hopped up, answering it with "Merry Christmas!" She listened a moment, then covered the receiver. "Windy, it's for you."

She climbed over the packages and raced to take the call.

"Windy, I'm on my way. I'll be there in about six hours. Where will you be?" Kris. And she knew he wasn't just meaning Gramma's or the mansion. He wanted to know if she'd be in Kokomo or on her way to Canada.

"I'll be here, waiting for you. Drive carefully, Kris. The roads can be crazy."

"I will. The sooner I say goodbye, the faster I'll arrive."

She let her heart do the talking. "Then bye, Kris. I love you."

⁂

THE KINKS IN HIS NECK crackled and popped as Kris moved his head, twisting from side to side. He needed to stay alert. But he must get to Kokomo as fast as possible. While there was still time.

He didn't doubt Windy's love. What concerned him, crazed him really, was that she'd sacrifice herself and what they'd built for what she figured was the right thing. A right thing that excluded him. He pressed harder on the accelerator while the needle crept up to eighty.

At least things were better with his parents and sisters. Ralph thought he was giving him the business, but it ended up good. Turns out Mom had an uncle who had trouble reading. Uncle Charlie shared experiences with her when she was a little girl. She'd wanted this kept a secret from his dad because she blamed herself, thinking it was something she passed on to him. His mother apologized for asking him to keep it from his father. His parents would have to work that one out now.

Kris and his dad talked privately. He explained that it was being on the basketball team that kept teachers from flunking him out in high school—the old whatever it takes to win the game mentality—but he couldn't carry that over to a university. Finally, his father saw things from Kris's perspective, why he couldn't go to college. And he admitted that he was proud of Kris's talent as an artist. Apparently, Gramps had kept him informed of the commissioned work and how he was building a business. To hear his father say those words meant more than any Christmas present.

There were still some questions about his tactics in getting Kris to Pittsburgh. Turned out Marsha begged Dad for the job. She wasn't who was supposed to come originally. Dad had reserved two rooms, plus she was to spend the night with Gramps and Hazel, he'd changed that when she became the official liaison. All points she conveniently forgot. Marsha had an agenda all right. When Dad called her in and questioned her, her complexion changed colors like a chameleon. First, she ran pale, then her cheeks pinked, and by the time she was fired, her face flamed. So did her temper. Dad and he shared a moment after she stormed from the office.

They came to an agreement. Not what Kris wanted, but he could work with it. As long as Windy waited for him. He'd have dinner with the family, go to Christmas Eve services, and then stay in the morning until after they'd opened their gifts. All his presents for his family had been mailed so his mother placed them under the tree with the rest.

They'd been generous with him and appreciated the items he'd crafted especially for each of them—jewelry boxes for his sisters, a spice rack for his mother, and pipe for his father. That he'd made each piece seemed to cause amazement. He brought home cologne, a new wallet, a pair of mother-of-pearl cuff links, a new argyle sweater vest, socks, and the title to this car. He'd mentioned that he'd hoped to earn enough to get Windy a vehicle, and his father signed it over to him so he could present it to her.

Now to arrive without an accident, before she decided to go to Canada.

He was nearly to the Ohio and Indiana border. Another two hours and he'd be charging the porch steps.

Maybe he oughta go home first. All his gifts for Windy's family were there, including Windy's. He blew out a breath and pushed the accelerator harder. *Please don't let me get a ticket.*

Windy's smile scrolled through his mind, reminding him of her laugh, her touch, her understanding. He needed to see her. He needed to be with her. He needed her.

Two excruciating hours later, he pulled up in front of Gramps and Hazel's place after changing vehicles at his place and loading up the back end with his gifts. The six-hour drive, all the mental bombardments, the anxiousness, the anticipation of this moment washed over him as he sat at the curb. If he didn't go in, all this was for nothing.

But what waited for him inside? Did she remain just to say goodbye? What was going to happen?

He drew in air and held it, gathering all the what ifs into that one inhale, and then he blew it out, ridding himself of everything but what was important. Windy and Heather. His family was in there. Okay, so maybe they weren't his family. Yet. Still, if he had any choice in the matter, they would be.

Windy met him at the door. At first greeting him warmly, then shying away. Had she made her decision?

He carried his gifts into the house and set them by the tree.

Aaron stepped from the den. "Hey, Kris. You made it. There's plenty of food left. You know Mom, she'll make sure you're fed." He glanced toward the tree. "Looks like more presents to open. I like how you're spreading this day out." He tossed a little salute and returned to the den. Kris imagined all the men were watching the game in there.

Windy looped arms with him. "I've waited as long as I can."

He froze.

She must have caught the fear in his eyes. "No, I mean, about your gift. I can't wait to give it to you. Sit on the couch." She pushed him back and grinned as he flailed.

He grabbed for her, pulling her onto his lap as he landed. "You are one violent woman."

"Big baby." She punched his shoulder, a lot more playfully than she'd hit Tim, which made him grin. "Let me up so I can get your gift."

He released her and she popped up, stooping beneath the branches to bring him a package about the size of a piece of paper, only thicker.

As he ripped the paper, she grabbed his hand. "What are you doing?"

"I'm unwrapping this."

"By tearing? Be careful. Gramma will want to use the paper next year."

He stared at her. Was this one of their traditions? Bet opening gifts Christmas morning took quite a while. Fine, he'd adapt. He slipped his finger between the tape and paper, popping it free. "That better?"

She nodded as he uncovered a frame turned upside down.

He flipped it around and caught his breath. Somehow, she'd managed to get a photo of him holding Heather. But it wasn't merely that. It was how they captured each other's gaze. His heart swelled and his eyes leaked. He didn't care about biology; this little girl was his daughter. Now and always. He cleared his throat. "Thanks, Windy. You couldn't have given me a better gift."

She kissed his cheek. "So, where's mine?"

That brought a laugh as he set the frame aside to reach under the branches to pull out the largest gift under the tree.

"Ooh! I like it already!"

"Crazy girl, you don't even know what it is."

"But it's big. That means it's good." She grinned.

"Not always, but hopefully in this case." He watched as she methodically unwrapped the paper, wanting to reach past her and rip it away. But he controlled himself.

Once the wrappings were free, she picked up the frame, turning it so she could see the front. "I love it, Kris! This is perfect to put that collage of Heather's photos on display." She trailed a finger down the carved edges and over the wrought iron designs he'd added at the corners. "You did beautiful work on this." The paper slipped to the floor, and she trampled it trying to hug his neck.

"Guess we were both thinking along similar lines."

She pulled back and nodded while running a knuckle under her eyes. "Guess we were. I like how we're sort of in tune with each other."

"Me too." He put his arm around her, pulling her close.

She rested her head on his chest.

"Have you made your decision?" He'd waited as long as he could for her to tell him.

"Not exactly. I've been praying about it. I know what I'm to look for."

A thought crossed his mind and he had to say it. "Has he asked you to marry him? What is his plan for you once you're in Canada?"

She became still. He wasn't sure she even breathed. Then she slowly backed from his arms and sat. "He hasn't said. That's important to me, Kris. You know that, right?" She raised her head, locking gazes with him.

"I do. Maybe you need to ask him about it." Like he wanted to give the guy more opportunity. But if it uncovered answers, and that helped his cause, then *goforit*. "Where's Heather?"

"My mother, sisters, and grandmother are spoiling her. Why don't you check on getting a bite to eat while I drag Tim from the den and get some clarification."

That made him smile. If he were a betting man, he'd guess she wouldn't like the responses. But he'd wait. In the meantime, he had a gift for Heather. He swiped it before heading for the dining room.

"Kris, I thought I heard you. Have you eaten? Stop, don't answer that. I know you haven't. Besides, even if you had, you're ready to eat again, right?"

Hazel knew him too well.

He sat at the table where she indicated and set the gift for Heather next to the placemat before holding out his hands for her.

Cheryl passed the baby to him, and he pulled her close. If there's a God, He had to realize that Windy, Heather, and him belonged together.

"Hey, sweet thing, I brought you something."

She made a raspberry at him.

"So that's how it is. Fine. I'll help you unwrap it. It's to hang on the outside of your bed or your wall." He helped the baby pull at the paper to reveal a wooden chain, all carved from one piece of wood. From the links, that had no splits in them, he'd hung the letters of Heather's name.

The women all oohed and ahhed making him feel accepted. He sure hoped they all thought he was the better choice.

Hazel brought in his food.

Gramps peeked in from the den. "Glad you're here, son. I need to talk with you. Thought I'd let you get your hellos in first. Ladies, could we have a few minutes?"

Stormy took Heather from him, and they all filed out, leaving Gramps and Kris alone in the dining room.

"You sure can clear a room, Gramps." He forked another bite of Hazel's turkey. This was the first he'd eaten since he left home. He was hungry.

His grandfather sat at the table across from him. "Guess I can, huh? Well, I wanted to tell you I spoke with your father today after you left. He filled me in on a few things."

Kris felt the heat prickle up to his hairline. "So, you know too."

"Well, honestly, I'd been wondering for some time. Just hoped you'd come to me first. He also said you are serious about Windy."

"I am. She has to make her decision though. I understand, I guess, in theory. But I can't lose her, Gramps." There was no more eating. This roller coaster in his gut had kicked up speed.

"Have you prayed about it?"

He shrugged. "I'm not much of a praying person. Don't know how to, really. It's about as foreign as reading."

"Not a problem. I might not be able to teach you to read, but I sure can help you pray. Have you asked Jesus to be your Lord and Savior?"

Kris shook his head. "See, that's what I'm talking about. I don't even understand what that means."

Gramps smiled. "Sorry, I get churchy sometimes. What it means is that you have to reach the point of understanding there's something bigger than you out there. Then you gotta understand that 'something' is God, the Creator of the universe. And that He loves us, you, so much He wants a relationship with you. But because of sin, everyone has messed up at some point. God is holy, we're not, so that relationship has some flaws. That's why He sent His son. Jesus cleared the way for us to have that relationship. Jesus's death on the cross and His rising three days later defeats the sin that keeps us from God. Now there is a way—Jesus. He tells us in the Bible He's the Way, the Truth, and the Life. No one can come to the Father except through Him. But if we believe in Jesus, that He is the Son of God Who takes away the sin of the world, if we give Him our heart and put our trust in Him, He will never leave us or forsake us. He'll see us through whatever life throws at us. Does that make sense?"

"Then asking Jesus into my heart is saying I believe in Him?" Kris hadn't had it explained like that before.

"Yes, but more. You accept Him and His gift of salvation and believe what He says in the Bible. You confess that you need Him and trust what He says. Do you want to do that?"

Kris couldn't explain it, but he did. He wanted to ask Jesus into his heart.

His grandfather prayed with him, giving him the words to repeat. When they finished, Kris discovered newness to the day. To the room. Like the light had brightened. He breathed in feeling cleaner.

"So, Gramps, what happens next?"

"That's up to God and you. He'll guide you, but you have to decide to follow what He says."

Hazel burst in. "Kris, do you know where Windy is? It's Heather. Something's wrong." A baby's cry split the air.

"No, but I'll find her." Kris pushed from the table. He'd spotted her slipping out the back way with Tim.

He raced for the door, praying his first solo prayer. "God let me find her fast."

Chapter 14

Windy shoved her hands into her jacket pockets and led Tim to the swing out under the arbor in Gramma's backyard. She'd done a lot of thinking on that swing when she was a girl. Maybe it would help Tim to figure things out too.

"We need to talk before I can make a decision." She wiped off the seat of the swing and sat, motioning for him to join her.

"What about?"

"You're asking me to leave my family, my country, everything I know to be with you. But you haven't shared what it'll be like up there." Hopefully, if she didn't spell it all out, it would come from him. That would mean more.

He shrugged. "Windsor is just over the border. It's very much like here. No language change, which makes it easy. It gets a little colder than here but it's not a big deal. Of course, I've never lived through a Canadian winter. Only moved last February, like you didn't already know that part. What things worry you?"

"Our living arrangements, for one thing."

Tim leaned back, his hands in his pockets, and gave the swing a push off with his toe. "I have a small apartment. It'll be tight at first. Maybe I'll find a job, so we'll have something bigger. My folks have been sending me money, but I'm not so sure they want to support both of us." He chuckled.

"The three of us, you mean?"

"Yeah. Is that what you wanted?"

She shook her head. "What about marriage, Tim? Where will we get married?"

"You want to get married? Guess you would. But is it really necessary? What if we find we don't get along? Or after a while it all fizzles? We'd be stuck with each other."

"It will fizzle and we will fight. That happens in relationships. But how we handle it, how we reignite the spark, that is what counts. Don't you think marriage is part of God's plan?" She had to give him one more chance, to be fair.

"I'm not even sure there is a God. If there is, He's not interested in what's happening. He hasn't stopped the war or saved any lives over there."

She stared as though just now seeing him. Could he really be so blind? Well, maybe she'd been blinded too. For a while. She really couldn't point fingers. Neither could she build a life for her daughter with a man who devalued marriage or distrusted God.

"Tim, I'm—"

"Windy! Come quick!" Kris dashed her way. "It's Heather."

Her heart froze mid-beat. But her feet knew what to do. She raced past Kris into the house. "Where's Heather?" She began calling from the back door, hearing Heather's loud cries, and racing toward the sound until Gramma caught her.

"We don't know what's happening. Your mom was feeding her, and her little lips started to swell. Her face is flushed, and hives are popping out on her arms, legs, and abdomen. I don't think we should wait. Let's get her to the ER now."

Windy pushed past her, searching until she found her mother holding a screaming Heather in the living room. The commotion drew out the men. The women had gathered around Mom.

"Let me have her." She snatched Heather from her mother.

Her baby's face was twisted with pain and her lips and mouth area showed signs of swelling. Heather's stomach was hard and covered with red blotches that traveled down her legs and over her arms. "What did you do?"

Gramma tried to calm her. "Windy, your mom was feeding her a bottle. But I think it's my fault. I saw that the soy formula was a little cheaper, so I bought it. She might be allergic to soy. We'll never know, though, if we don't get to the hospital."

She looked up from Heather. "Her car seat is in Tim's Beetle."

"Forget the car seat. Let's go." Dad grabbed her arm and pulled her toward the door.

"Wait. Hand me the blankets there." She pointed to Heather's carrier. At least the baby would be bundled and warm.

Gramma snatched them and helped get Heather wrapped, then pushed her forward.

Dad grabbed her elbow again and got her to his rental.

Once she was inside, she tried to soothe Heather, cuddling her, singing to her, kissing her little head. Nothing worked. Heather seemed to be running out of steam with her cries.

Dad headed for St. Joe's Hospital and pulled in at the emergency entrance.

Windy hopped out as soon as he stopped and raced for the sliding doors. "Please help my baby. We think she's having an allergic reaction."

The duty nurse took one look at Heather and sent them to the front of the line, calling for the doctor right away and directing them into a cubical. Windy placed her daughter on the bed and unwrapped her.

The doctor arrived and examined Heather, listening with his stethoscope, while Windy continued to try to calm her. He peeked at her eyes, checked her neck and breathing, and made note of the swelling and hives before ordering a syringe of Epinephrine. "This will help. Give it a few minutes. Do you know what was going on when this happened?"

"My mother was feeding her a bottle. I just learned my grandmother used soy formula for the first time with her. Could she be allergic to soy?"

The doctor nodded. "That's highly likely. This was pretty intense, so I'd say watch her diet for a while. Often children grow out of this. Since the reaction was more severe, though, that might not happen. Just to be safe, I want to admit her. She's still awfully young. Just over two months you said?"

Windy nodded. "Born October ninth. Can I stay with her?"

The doctor leaned closer. "We're not that busy on the children's wing so I think it should be fine."

For the first time since Kris called to her, Windy's heart began to beat normally. She heard noises in the hall, a voice she loved, and pulled the curtain aside allowing Dad to find them.

He did, coming in and standing with her at the bed. "Doctor, is she going to be all right?"

"We're going to keep an eye on her tonight, but I expect you to be able to take her home tomorrow. The nurse'll come for you once the room is ready." The doctor, whose name Windy never remembered to get, patted her arm and left.

Heather had stopped crying and her mouth looked more normal.

Windy wiped away the last of her baby's tears and settled in a chair with her to hold her until the nurse showed up. The truth was, she craved to feel the closeness of this precious girl more than the baby needed comforting. It was good for them both. That was the bottom line.

Dad stood guard over them, squeezing her shoulder, then checking the machines, then peeking into the hall before starting it over again.

"Once we know the room number, should we call Gramma to tell the others?" Windy followed him with her gaze, knowing he was trying to hide his concern.

"Good idea. These places haven't changed that much since I took you in for your leg. Some stuff looks newer, maybe more compact. But it's the same tightness in your chest when your baby's in pain and you are helpless to do anything." He glanced her way, and she knew he'd experienced those feelings when she fell from the block fence.

"Do you ever stop worrying about us, Daddy?"

"Nope, baby girl, I don't." He walked over and stroked his hand down her hair.

She leaned her head against his side. "I'm glad. I don't want you to stop."

He kissed her forehead. "Your little Heather just gave me one more to worry about. Got a feeling she's an awful lot like her mother." He winked. "It's a good thing."

That made her smile.

The charge nurse arrived. "We've got a room up on the third floor. If you'll follow me, I'll take you there."

Windy carried Heather while Dad brought all the blankets and stuff that had been dropped in the cubicle. They took the elevator up two floors, then down a wing to double doors. When they entered, it was obvious they'd moved into a place designed with children in mind.

Nurse Jessie led them to room 354. It had one baby bed and a rocker, plus one more chair.

Windy thought of something and tagged Jessie before she left. "May I nurse her if she gets hungry?"

"I'll check with the doctor, though I'm quite sure it's fine. I'll be right back." She left for a few minutes.

It gave Windy time to settle into the rocker with Heather. The baby still had her eyes wide, but kept her gaze on her mother and no longer cried. Her face grew red and Windy figured she was trying to fill her diaper. Maybe she could pass what had caused the ruckus.

When the RN returned, she said the doctor approved the nursing and had Windy put Heather in the baby bed so she could take her vitals.

Heather made another straining face, turning her cheeks pink, and this time it was obvious she'd filled her pants.

"Want me to change her?" Windy figured it was her child, she ought to.

"Let me finish the exam and I'll let you." She checked Heather's pulse and listened with her stethoscope. "All yours." Nurse Jessie winked, setting a clean diaper and a wet washcloth within reach.

When Windy pulled back the diaper, her baby had diarrhea.

Jessie noted it and exited.

After Heather was clean again, Windy took her to the rocker and settled in.

Two minutes later, the children's ward doctor arrived. "I hear we've got a little one with an upset tummy."

"I don't think she likes soy." Windy tried to match his lightness.

"So, let me understand, you nurse and supplement?"

She nodded. "When she is with other family members who need to feed her, they give her formula."

"She's never had a problem with formula before?"

Windy shook her head. "No, but this was the first experience with soy."

"Won't do that again, I'll bet." He patted her arm. "I have two concerns right now. Neither is pressing. Just want to make sure they are addressed and won't develop into problems. The first is her diarrhea. If it continues, she can become dehydrated, which for a baby her age is serious. The other is the nurse thought she heard a little wheezing in her chest when she listened. I better check for that. Want to bring her to the bed?"

Windy laid Heather back on the tiny mattress before stepping to the side. Her insides shook like a leaf in a breeze while her arms ached with emptiness.

The doctor smiled at Heather and tickled her tummy. "Here we are, princess. Let me listen to you." As he set the stethoscope on her chest, her bitty fist reached for the black tubes that ran to his ears and pulled. "Hey there little one, you need to let me hear."

Windy held her hands while he listened. What was he hearing? Was there a problem with her baby? What was going to happen now?

She closed her eyes and sent up another prayer.

⚘

KRIS FOLLOWED WINDY TOWARD the house only to notice Tim held back. "Are you coming?"

"I guess." Tim shuffled to the porch and Kris held the door for him.

Inside Heather's wails mingled with Windy's shouts.

Tim froze.

"What's with you, man? Aren't you going to see what's wrong?" Kris wanted to shake some sense into him.

"I don't know. She really loves that baby."

Kris stared at him. "Of course, she does. It's her baby. It's your baby. Aren't you going to do what fathers are supposed to?"

Tim flicked a glance at him, then took a step toward the commotion, staying on the periphery.

Hazel had Windy's attention and was speaking with calm and focus. "...She might be allergic to soy. We'll never know, though, if we don't get to the hospital."

The hospital? Could it be that bad?

Windy responded finally. "Her car seat is in Tim's Beetle."

Tim backed up into the dining room.

Kris followed him. "Where are you going? Won't you drive them?"

"No, no, I can't. What if someone asks my name? I could get caught."

"You could lose your daughter. If she doesn't get help, that baby could die." Kris's patience wore thin with this guy. "You really don't get it, do you?"

"Do you? I took a big risk sneaking back to the states. A friend loaned me cash to get me here. I've put everything on the line to see her. She's so into this baby and gone establishment square. It's the Twilight Zone man." Tim's eyes darted around the room.

"You are a coward."

"I just told you I risked everything to come here. I'm not a coward."

Kris poked him in the chest. "Yes, you are. I know guys who don't like the war. But they stand up and say so. If that means filing for Conscientious Objector status, then they do that. If it means enlisting into the Coast Guard because they still love their country despite the war, fine. Or they protest. Or go to prison. Yeah, some even left for Canada. But not out of fear of getting hurt. They disagreed with their country's policies and decided to become a citizen elsewhere.

"But not you. You're hiding like a panicky little punk. Putting yourself ahead of your daughter. That, my friend, is a coward."

Tim stared at the floor. "What if I am scared? Wouldn't you be?"

"Scared isn't the problem. Anyone who says they aren't is lying. The problem's letting your fears rule. Do something about this. Go to your kid." Kris needed to give the guy a chance, but caught himself hoping Tim wouldn't take it.

"Think what you want to think. I can't." Tim shook his head. "I've been here too long anyway. I better scram."

"Running again? Fine. I'll meet you at my house while you get your stuff and drop off the car seat. I've got something for you there."

Tim's eyes grew wide, and the fear gleamed like a Star Trek phaser beam.

"I'm not setting you up, you idiot. I have something for you. Not gonna stop you from leaving or call the authorities. You really have trust issues, man."

"Fine. We'll meet at your pad. Can we go out the back way? Not sure I want to see anyone."

Kris blew out a sigh and nodded. This guy had more problems that he'd ever be able to solve. However, he'd found one thing. If the guy accepted it, several problems would get fixed. He followed Tim out the rear door and around the house to where he'd parked his truck. One more reason he was glad he'd gone home first, so he could change vehicles.

Five minutes later, he pulled in his drive. Tim was already unlocking the front door.

Once inside, Kris searched the stuff he'd saved from the trip, finding what he needed. A business card.

"Tim, if you're gonna be up there, you should have a good lawyer. I've got the name of one who knows about guys who've relocated from the US. Here's what I need you to do."

Tim's fingers had just touched the card when they drew back. "I knew there'd be a catch."

"It's not what you think." Kris cleared his throat. "I've kept my mouth shut because I figured you deserved a shot. I won't be Windy's consolation prize. If she chooses me, then it was right. But I don't want her pining over you when she's with me."

"What are you getting at?"

"She never put your name on the birth certificate, but if I adopt Heather, you could come back to claim your rights. That'd mess up that sweet little girl's head. What I want is for you to have this lawyer send documentation that you give up all parental rights to Heather." There, he'd said it. The ball was in Tim's court. Fighting for his daughter didn't seem to be his choice.

Tim fingered the business card. "Just put it in writing that I won't contest anything?"

"Yep."

"I don't know."

Kris didn't want to push and end up screwing up the whole deal. But he needed to say something. "Do you have a better plan?"

Time froze like the icicles hanging from the gutter. Like Kris's heart with fear that he'd gone too far.

"Will you tell her about me?" Tim glanced up.

"That's up to Windy. I think she should. Honesty is better. But I want to be that little girl's dad. I love her like my own. I love her mother more than I can say."

"Enough to marry her?"

"In a heartbeat." No doubt about it.

He picked up his backpack and fit the strap over one shoulder. "You'll take care of them?"

"Yeah. I will."

Kris watched as Tim shuffled to his car, set the car seat on the curb, and drove away. Now he had to find a way to tell Windy he sent Tim packing.

He put Heather's car seat in the house and hopped in his truck to head for St. Joe's.

It took some convincing, but finally he was directed to the Children's Ward, Room 354. A guy in a white coat exited just before Kris tapped on the jamb.

Windy glanced up. Scooping Heather in her arms first, she ran to him, burying her face in his chest. "You're here."

"Where else would I be?"

Aaron stood. "Here, take my chair. I need to walk off some of my energy." He left.

Kris snagged Aaron's seat and Windy plopped in the rocker. Heather slept.

"What have they said?" He needed that information, more than he'd realized.

"They think she had a bad reaction to the soy formula. The worst is over, but she's in danger of becoming dehydrated. The doctor is getting something ready."

Two nurses arrived with a rolling pole and some bags of clear fluid. The first one caught his elbow. "Take Mom for a walk. We need to do an IV."

Windy's eyes rounded as did her mouth but no sound escaped.

"C'mon. Let's go wander a few minutes." He took Heather from her arms and handed her to the nurse before drawing Windy to him.

She didn't fight, but terror etched her face.

He laced his fingers with hers and gently tugged her out of the room. "It's going to be okay. They realize that it's hard for a mother to watch, is all." He led her to a nearby alcove with a couple chairs. "Let's sit here a few minutes. Tell me about what you got for Christmas." If he could distract her, it would help.

"Um, I don't know."

"What did Hazel and Gramps get you?"

"Uh, a couple pretty sweaters."

"Stormy?"

She ran her free hand through her bangs. "She got me some new sheet music. 'Bridge Over Troubled Water,' 'Walking in the Rain,' 'Leaving on a Jet Plane.'

"I enjoy hearing you play piano. What else?" He had to keep her talking.

"Sunny gave me a photo album. It was filled with pictures from when we were kids in Los Angeles."

He could feel her start to relax as she talked about the album.

"She took most of the photos with a camera she got for her ninth birthday. But there were some that brought back a remembrance." She paused and looked at him. "There was this weekend we went to the beach and stayed in a hotel. Then the next morning we all went to Disneyland. It was...it's my favorite childhood memory. We saw all the characters, posed for pictures, rode all the rides—I was finally tall enough to enjoy an E ticket. And then we drove home. I remember curling up next to Daddy and falling asleep."

"That's not what happened, sweetie." Aaron stood listening to her share.

"Sure it was. I've got the photos now to prove it."

Her father shook his head. "We did all those things, yes, but you fell asleep against your mother. She had her arm around you and brushed your hair from your face. You'd snuggle against her, and she held on to you. That wasn't me. I had to drive."

"But..." Her face paled. "I can't recall her being in the car."

"Oh, Windy, I know she hurt us, but there were good times too. Don't change your memories to hide the pain." Aaron knelt in front of her.

"She really did that? I don't remember, Daddy. I can't remember her touch. She loved me?" Tears trembled at her lashes.

Kris squeezed her fingers but remained silent. She needed this with her dad.

"Yes, sweetie. Your mother loved you. She still does. She's just fighting her own guilt."

Windy leaned into her father's embrace, releasing from Kris's grasp. He wanted to snatch her hand again but fought to restrain himself. She needed her father more than him now.

Aaron rubbed her back. "It's going to be okay. There's a lot of healing to be done. I know. Trust me. It will never be what it was. But you girls can have your mother in your lives if you want her."

Windy pulled back and wiped her eyes. "I do. If she ever loved me like I love Heather, then I want to give her a chance."

"Oh, she did." He cupped her cheeks, drawing her face forward, pasting a kiss between her brows.

The nurse stepped into the alcove. "You can go back now."

"Thank you." Kris stood, offering his hand to Windy.

She took it and linked her other arm with her father's.

Together they entered Heather's room. The sweet thing had an IV attached to her leg, but she lay in the bed sleeping.

Aaron pulled Windy into a hug. "I'm going to head home now since you have Kris here. He's a good man."

Windy gazed at him, making his neck feel warm. "Yes, he is, Dad."

Then an idea hit. "Sir, could I speak with you a moment? I'll be right back, Windy."

She was bent over the baby bed, peering at Heather. "Okay."

Once in the hall, Kris summoned his courage. "Sir, I love your daughter. I'd like your permission to ask her to marry me."

"She's sort of in a vulnerable state right now, Kris."

"I realize that. I'll pick the right time. I just need to know if I have your approval." He shoved his hands in his pocket for fear they'd flop away.

Aaron patted his shoulder. "You have my blessing. Thank you for asking. I'll see you later." Kris watched him head for the elevator.

Once again in Heather's room, Kris returned to the chair. He'd watch over his girls as long as the nurses let him. Now with Aaron's blessing, they were his girls.

He just needed to convince Windy of that fact.

Chapter 15
Sunday, February 14, 1971

Windy slipped among the guests snapping candid shots. This wedding, up in the ballroom, wasn't that large. Still, the bride pulled out all the stops, celebrating with red heart motifs. Her groom arrived from Viet Nam two days ago and they made a cute couple.

Since they couldn't have the engagement photos under the sycamore back before Christmas, they'd planned for special snapshots after the ceremony. Now it was time.

She drew up next to Sally Ann Riley, whispering at her ear. "If you and Steve meet me outside, we'll get those photos before we lose the light."

Sally Ann tugged on her groom's sleeve. He was telling Hien's husband a story and the two were cracking up.

"Honey, time for some special photos."

He excused himself and followed his new bride and Windy out to the back yard.

It was chilly. Another reason to snap these pictures before the temperature dropped even lower. Out of sympathy, Windy left her coat inside, but that inspired one shot of Steve draping his tux jacket around Sally Ann's shoulders. Turned out sweet. And when they kissed, a real cardinal landed on the branch. Windy made sure to capture that. "Go on back guys before you freeze. I think I've got some great stuff. I'll get these developed and call you later next week."

The Rileys hustled back to their party.

That left Windy, staring in wonder at the cardinal that remained watching the couple return to the house. Would she and Kris ever get that kiss beneath the branches? He seemed so busy lately and she missed him.

It had been seven weeks since they'd raced Heather to the hospital. She ended up spending two nights there but showed no aftereffects. In fact, she learned new skills faster than Windy could handle. This watching her child grow up before her eyes was as hard as it was magical.

Plus, she and her mother were finding their footing. That hole in her life was filling. There were still bumps to overcome. But it was better since Dad talked to her at the hospital.

She shivered, bringing herself back to the present. It was time to get inside before she froze to death.

Sunny met her at the door. "How did it go?"

"They had a live cardinal. I didn't tell them. I'll let them discover it in the photos." Sometimes it was better that way.

"You and Kris still have plans after this?"

Windy smiled in anticipation. "Kris is bringing Heather back. He says we need to have a talk."

"Oh?"

"Yeah. He's been funny ever since Heather came home from the hospital. Like in some sort of protective mode. Yet, with our schedules, we haven't had any real time with just us. We'd better be making some money finally, because none of us have had a private moment since before Christmas. How many weddings has it been?"

Sunny nodded. "Twelve. And yes, I think we've found some breathing room financially. I want to make sure we have built some savings. Then maybe we'll modernize that fifties-style kitchen. By the way, I have an idea. Remember how Hien's sister-in-law, Thea, came through on the alterations? I learned she's got a degree in Home Economics from Valparaiso. What if we hired her part time to help cater these events? It would take some of the weight off Gramma's shoulders."

"I like it. She seemed really nice. You've got my vote. What does Stormy say?"

Sunny squeezed her arm. "I still need to ask her. Since she and Mom started talking, she's over there all the time."

"Over where?" Stormy peeked her head around the corner. "Who are you talking about?"

"You, goose. I said you've been spending a lot of time at Gramma's house." Sunny raised her eyebrows.

Stormy glanced between them, then pulled them into a huddle. "I needed to know some things. I had questions because...we're going to have a baby." She put her finger to her lips. "Don't tell. It's still early and with my track record, we don't know what will happen. But Rob and I are too excited."

Sunny and Windy pulled their sister into a hug and the three of them bounced on their toes, trying to keep their excitement contained.

Windy pulled back. "How far along are you?"

"We figure eleven weeks. We're one fourth of the way there." Stormy's grin made her eyes twinkle. "It was a really great Thanksgiving getaway."

"Are you sure you are okay with this?" Sunny stared at Stormy's eyes for the truth.

"I'm positive. That's one of the reasons I've been talking so much with Mom. I needed to make sure."

"You told her first?" That said a lot about how their relationship was developing. Windy didn't know whether to be happy or a tad jealous.

"No, I told Rob first. But with mom, I was asking things. Then she sort of guessed. This morning at church." Stormy grinned. "I'm going to have a baby. We'd given up and decided to just relax."

"Sounds like it worked. I'm so happy for you. And Heather will have a playmate." Windy glanced at Sunny. "Sure you still want to wait for your June wedding? We can move up the date you know, if you want to start working on your cousin contribution sooner."

Sunny blushed. "We're sticking to our plan. And speaking of plans, we'd better let the couple know they've only got another hour."

The girls started for the stairs, but Windy held back, glancing around the mansion where her existence had changed. She'd started putting pieces of her life together. There was a grounding now to her. A safety net. She had freedom to sail with her creativity. Still, the responsibility of being a mother and businessperson meant that she moored in a safe harbor. She didn't need to let any old breeze blow her from one idea to the next.

However, she couldn't imagine this new life as a solo journey. Before she knew that Heather needed emergency help, she'd been about to tell Tim she'd decided to stay in Kokomo. But he left without giving her that chance. She would've shared photos and information on Heather's milestones, but he never said where he could be reached. She still didn't know how to contact him. Or even which of the three couples she'd written were his parents.

However, she had informed him he was a father. Whatever he did with that information was up to him.

The front door opened, and Kris came in carrying Heather in her car seat. "Hey. So, we're still on for tonight?"

Windy nodded and hugged him before taking Heather out of her straps. "Absolutely. I've been looking forward to our own Valentine's Day celebration." She turned to the rosy cheeked beauty in her arms. "Haven't I, sweet girl."

He checked his watch. "How long until their party is over?"

"About another hour. Then I have to help with clean up."

"No worries. Is Sunny going to babysit for us?" She loved how he said "us."

Windy nodded again. "Yes. She and Pat want to celebrate tomorrow. Something about the Monday after being their special day. Sometimes I wonder about those two." She handed Heather back to Kris. "I'd better go take a few more photos. But when you see everyone coming downstairs, that's your cue. It's only a matter of cleaning the worst of it. The deep cleaning we'll do in the morning."

"Gotcha. See you in a bit." He winked and headed for the kitchen.

Windy climbed the stairs to the third floor, wishing again this event was over so she'd finally be with Kris. He'd been so insistent that they needed their own Valentine's Day celebration that he was willing to wait until late just to do it. The wedding started at two. The party was scheduled through seven—one hour for ceremony and four for the celebrating. That meant by eight she and Kris should hopefully get time together.

The wedding celebration wound down. People began slipping to the porch for the sendoff. Finally, only the bride, the groom, and a handful of guests remained. Windy watched Stormy play the diplomat and whisper to Sally Ann, who nodded and hugged her.

Little gauzy bags sat on the table near the front door. Windy positioned herself to get shots of the couple exiting while being pelted with rice. Once over, clean up could start. She chose the job of sweeping the porch and dumping the grains into the trash before heading back upstairs to clear out the leftover glasses and plates and food bits.

She glanced at her watch. It was five minutes until eight. Funny how she was getting the timing down at this point. Sunny nudged her. "Finish that and call it quits for tonight. I'm on my way to get Heather. Meet you downstairs."

Once Windy carted the last load to the kitchen, she began her search for Sunny, Heather, and Kris. The first two were easy. They were on the floor in the living room. Sunny was tickling Heather and the baby giggled. Such beautiful music. It was hard to interrupt and stop the joy. But she needed to find Kris.

"He said to get your jacket and meet him out back." Sunny lowered her head and blew a raspberry on Heather's belly.

Which gave Heather a free shot at Sunny's hair. She grabbed handfuls with both tiny fists.

"Ow! Let me go, you little stink pot." Sunny laughed but Windy was sure the pulling hurt.

She helped release her sister from her daughter's clutches. "You're on your own after this. You know what she can do."

"I do. I was having too much fun and forgot. You'd better hurry." Sunny winked before returning her attention to the baby.

Windy didn't stop to reply but hustled out the back door while shoving her arms in her sleeves.

Kris stood beneath the sycamore, his hands in his pockets, gazing at the sky through the branches.

Windy stepped back inside a moment and flipped the switch bathing the backyard and the tree in white light.

Kris looked over when she did, his grin making him the most handsome man she'd ever met.

She crossed the yard to him, and he drew her in, wrapping her in warmth and security. With her ear resting against his heart, she counted the beats in her head, like the measures in a song playing just for her. "I'm so glad you insisted on this. I've been trying to survive to the next day with everything going on. But you are what I've been missing. Just being with you."

He pulled her closer and rested his chin on her crown. "Me too. I've so much to tell you. We've got important things to discuss. And, well, ...it'll have to wait."

She drew back and captured his gaze. "Wait? Why?"

He tipped her chin up. "Because I need to do this first."

As he lowered his head toward her, she suddenly understood. And agreed. Her fingers feathered through his hair, and she pulled him to her, meeting his lips with hers as electrical impulses tingled over her skin and shot straight to her heart making it skip beats. This man's kiss could restore the dead. It had to. She'd never felt more alive than when their lips met.

His hands held her face and his kiss deepened before he drew away. "That might not've been my best idea."

She could feel his heart thumping in duet with hers. "I disagree. That was brilliant."

"Yeah, but I'm not sure I can pull my thoughts together now." His lopsided grin made her pulse race.

"Then should we kiss some more while you figure them out?" She winked at him, but she was only half kidding. This man she could kiss all day. All night too.

"We'd better wait until after we talk." He chuckled.

"More waiting?"

"Just for the kissing. And only for a few minutes." He blew out a breath. "I'm ready. How about you?"

⁂

Kris watched her eyes. He'd waited until he was sure. Now all the pieces were in place. Well, most of them. Enough of them.

He took her hands. "Windy, first I want to explain. I needed any downtime we had these last few weeks because I've been doing something. When Heather had her reaction, I was in the dining room with Gramps. He'd just helped me pray to become a believer. This had to be a lifelong decision before I spoke to you. Gramps is helping me study. Since I can't read the Bible too well, he's been reading it to me, and we've been discussing it. He calls it discipling. Anyway, I talked with the pastor this morning and scheduled a meeting with him this next week. I'm getting baptized."

Windy threw her arms around him. "I needed to hear that so much. I'm happy for you, Kris, but for Heather and me, this is huge. And wonderful."

"I had a feeling." He'd decided for himself, but that it was important to Windy was the finial on top. "But there's more." She might not be as thrilled about this part. Still, he had to get it off his chest. "You haven't spoken of Tim since he left."

"No, I was about to send him away when you got me. I figured he understood that." She shrugged.

"I'm the one to blame for him leaving. I called him a coward for not helping you get to the hospital. Sort of pushed him into a corner and he chose to run north again." He waited for her to get upset.

"Funny. I didn't miss him. You were there, Dad, Mom, Sunny, Stormy, Gramma. We were surrounded in love. It's fine." Windy patted his hand.

He grasped hers again, pulling her fingers to his lips before continuing. There was much more to tell. "Before he left, I gave him the business card of the Canadian lawyer who helped us with Ralph. I told him I love you and that one day I hope to adopt Heather. Even though you didn't add his name to the birth certificate, he could still make trouble, so I asked him to send documentation from this lawyer stating that he was giving up all parental rights. That he'd make sure I could become Heather's father."

She pulled her hands back, covering her mouth, and her eyes grew round. "Oh! Kris, I don't know what to say."

"Did I overstep?" More than the cold made him shiver.

She shook her head. "No, no you didn't overstep. You did the perfect thing." She threw herself into his arms and her tears ran down inside his collar.

"I heard from him this week." He undid her grasp and helped her sit back before he reached inside his jacket and pulled out the paperwork from the lawyer. "Here's the documentation I asked for."

Her hands trembled as he set the fat envelope in them.

"Windy, I want to ask you to marry me. But we've gotta have our time. Plus, I need to be ready financially to be the husband and father you and Heather deserve. So, I'm asking you to give me that time. Let's let Sunny and Pat have their day without any shadow from us. It's only a few more months. Then we should be able to make a plan for you, me, and Heather. Will you agree?"

She sniffed and stroked the envelope. "You're right. Yes, as much as I hate waiting, I will. Besides, you brought me this. You've no idea how this lifts a worry off my shoulders."

Yeah, he had an inkling. But he wouldn't argue. "I should also explain why it's so thick. The paperwork for your car is also in there."

Her head snapped up. "Car?"

"Yeah, I needed a way to Kokomo and my dad felt bad for what had happened. He told me to keep the car as a gift. So once the title transferred, I signed it over to you. Now you have your own vehicle."

She jumped up. "What kind? Where is it? Oh, I want to kiss you again!" She threw her arms around his neck and froze. "No way."

"What?"

"There's a cardinal watching us."

He started to look but she pulled him back.

"I've no idea if the tradition is for real. Still, I love the notion of a long life together. So, kiss me, Kris Norman. See if the cardinal agrees."

Any excuse was fine by him. He ran his finger down her jaw to her chin, drawing it closer before lowering his mouth to hers. Could his heart handle the erratic beats that her kiss imposed? If not, he'd still die a happy man. His fingers wove parts through her hair, and he kissed her nose, her eyes, her forehead before returning to the sweetest lips he'd ever tasted. "Windy, I love you."

A door slammed and suddenly they were not alone.

He pulled back to find Stormy and Sunny, who carried a bundled-up Heather, grinning from ear to ear.

"You got a cardinal. And at night. I tell you, I think that legend is pretty strong. Anything you guys want to share?" Stormy snickered while she wrapped her sweater tighter.

Windy glanced up at him and winked. "Nothing yet. You two might have broken the legend. You know, rushing out here like that? Just saying."

Stormy's mouth dropped open and she shook her head. "No, don't say that. Look, we'll go back inside. Continue what you were doing." She grabbed Sunny's arm and headed for the house.

Sunny glanced over her shoulder and mouthed, "Sorry."

Windy gaze up at him. "Now, where were we?"

"I think I was about to show you your new vehicle. Besides, it has a heater. It'll be much warmer while we sit in it." His feet were turning to blocks of ice.

Her face lit. "Right, the car. Lead on, Macduff."

"Who's Macduff?"

"Just go." She punched his arm.

"Ow!"

"Big baby."

He stopped. "I could take the car back you know."

She bumped into him. "Oh no. Sorry. What if you pretend I'm Ronnie Specter, and I'm singing 'Be My Baby'?" Is that better?"

He gathered her in his arms. "Baby, you're the greatest." With Jackie Gleason flare, he bent her back and kissed her again. When he righted her, he wrapped an arm about her waist. "Now let's get in the car before my feet fall off."

"Let's."

In the back parking lot, she zeroed in on the one car she didn't recognize. A yellow 1969 Chevy Impala. "Kris?"

"Yeah?"

"This is my car?" Her voice rose in pitch.

"Yeah, Windy, this is your car. Want to test drive it?"

Her eyes twinkled. "Oh, yeah."

He unlocked the driver's side, held the door for her and handed her the keys.

She reached across to unlock his side so he could slide in. Then she slipped the key in the ignition and started it.

The engine purred and so did she.

He rubbed his hands together, laughing. "Turn the heater on. Let's warm up."

She winked at him and obeyed.

He suddenly realized what he said, and his face didn't need the heater. "I shouldn't have teased like that Windy. You need to know something. Waiting is going to be hard. But you will never have to worry about me pressuring you. You are worth the wait. You got that?"

She wrapped her arms around his neck. "I'm sorry, I should have waited for you, Kris. You are worth waiting for too." Windy dropped a peck on his cheek then straightened in front of the steering wheel. "Where are we going?"

"Wherever you want. But one thing, you will have to drop me off at my house tonight since this was my ride." It would help to not have to walk home in the cold.

"You've got it." She put the car into reverse and backed out of the spot. Then, shifting to drive, she pulled out of the lot, heading for the street. "Hold on to your hat, Kris. This is gonna be fun."

Kris had no doubt she was right.

Epilogue
Saturday, June 26, 1971

"**I** now pronounce you husband and wife; you may kiss your bride."

Windy swiped a tear as her sister Sunny wrapped her arms about her new spouse, Patrick Grey Whitcomb, and received a kiss that almost made her jealous. But a glance from her bridesmaid position toward the groomsmen, and Kris's handsome face wiped out any such emotions. This simply meant their day was closer.

Kris's gaze didn't follow the happy couple, only focused on her, adding to the anticipation of being in his arms for whatever reason she could conjure.

The air was filled with the heady fragrance of Sunny's garden, in full bloom, and her stunning gown, designed and crafted by Thea Carpenter, all melded together to accentuate her sister's beauty. It was a day worth waiting for. Windy was happy for Sunny and Pat.

She glanced over at the attendees, spotting her mother holding Heather on her lap. The baby fidgeted but Sunny wanted her here. No babysitter today. This was a whole family affair. Dad sat next to Mom and...did her eyes deceive her? He had his arm around her. Holy cow! Windy nudged Stormy who stood next to her in a pale peach organza off the shoulder creation that mirrored her own. The gowns were empire-waisted to accommodate her sister's growing figure.

Stormy peered where Windy indicated with her glance and her eyes enlarged. She spotted it too.

Windy turned to the main show, Sunny and Pat. The pastor was introducing them as Mr. and Mrs. Patrick and Sunny Whitcomb. The guests applauded, the music cued, and they headed out between the rows of white chairs to the back of the garden. Stormy and Rob linked arms and he escorted her out to join the wedding couple before Kris offered his arm to Windy.

She gazed up at him, wanting to wrap her arms about him. Instead, she threaded her hand through to rest on his forearm and walked out according to plan. Just like a normal person would.

Dad escorted Mom, Gene walked with Gramma, and then the Whitcomb clan followed. Sunny put a moratorium on the invitations since the backyard held only so many. The compromise was that Mrs. Whitcomb could host a ginormous party at the Murat as soon as they returned from their honeymoon in Bermuda.

Several people were hired for this day. All the business owners were busy being participants. Thea Carpenter took charge of the food and Hien Salem, who'd been a professional photojournalist, stepped in as photographer.

Sunny hired a group of teens from the church to help reset the stage from wedding to reception. She'd made them practice numerous times until they could take down and set up in under ten minutes. Boys did the grunt work with tables and chairs, while girls placed the table settings and décor. Windy watched from the back. They swarmed in as the last guest filed out.

Thea took charge of seeing that every place card was correct. It couldn't have gone smoother. The wedding party enjoyed time to chat with those invited during the transformation.

Luncheon with a savory chicken cordon bleu was served by the same teens all dressed in white shirts and black trousers. The wedding party table seated Stormy and Rob to the left of the bridal couple, Windy with Kris to the right.

It almost was Pat's friends, Trey and Eric, sitting as the groomsmen, but Eric the lawyer was in the middle of his biggest court case ever in Arizona, and Trey's sister-in-law decided to plan her wedding for the same day. He apologized, but his wife's baby sister's wedding won. And so did Windy, with Kris sitting next to her at the bridal table.

Mom, Dad, Gramma, and Gene had one of the two tables up front while Mr. and Mrs. Whitcomb and their daughter, Venita, with her new boyfriend, Sam, occupied the other front table. Sunny confided that Pat's sister made a much better choice this time. There might be another wedding in the not-so-distant future.

After the meal, music started and the dance floor opened. Funny how with all the weddings she'd helped to produce over the last year, she'd never danced once with Kris. She'd been too busy doing her job and he had taken on the responsibility of caring for Heather during the events. He and Heather were forging a bond that brought tears of joy when she watched them. That sweet girl would have a wonderful daddy. Guess she already did, unofficially.

Karen Carpenter's voice filled the garden with "We've Only Just Begun." Kris stood and offered his hand. He remembered. It was perfect for the wedding. It was more perfect for them. As he spun her onto the dance floor, he leaned toward her ear. "I'm not a great dancer but couldn't pass up our song."

Her arms slipped up around his neck and she smiled into that face she loved so much. "It is our song." She leaned her head to hear his heartbeat as they moved in rhythm. He was the best dancer as far as she was concerned.

The rest of the party was fun with more dancing and laughs.

Pat, ever the gentleman, offered Sunny cake without making a mess on her face. Sunny, though, had to put frosting on his nose before letting him have his bite. Stormy must have inspired her.

When the bouquet was tossed, Stormy took charge again. Windy not only caught the flowers, but also the glance between her sisters. Yeah, seconds before the toss she got pushed to the front to make the catch. She didn't object.

Finally, after the new bride and groom climbed into the rented limo to take them to the Crowne Plaza in Indianapolis (they'd leave for Bermuda in the morning) Kris laced his fingers with hers and led her to the carriage house.

During the wedding it served as the station for the help to organize things, store what wasn't needed. He guided her past the mess as a teen exited to start cleanup.

"Maybe this isn't the best place. I just wanted to be alone with you for a few minutes. And we've spent a lot of time working together in here."

She nodded. "We've got special memories in this room, don't we?"

"Yeah."

Another teen ran in rolling a table to the storage room.

He squeezed her hand. "I have a better idea."

She followed him back to the mansion and up the stairs. As they passed the second floor, two thoughts collided: No one else was in the house, and this was her living quarters until tomorrow when she moved into Gramma's giving the newlywed couple their privacy. But his promise that he'd wait reassured her and she let him lead her up to the third floor and the ballroom.

He guided her inside. "This is our other place. We did a lot up here too. But my favorite spot is out here. Let's watch the sunset."

Windy stepped out onto the balcony with him and memories flooded from Stormy's vow renewal party. They'd stood in this exact spot, and she'd wondered what life had in store for this year. He'd pointed out the first star of the evening and she'd made a wish. It came true, just not the way she imagined. For Heather to have a father.

Tim showed up, met his daughter, and rejected her. But the rejection didn't hurt like she'd imagined it would. Instead, it was like chains dropping. Kris had confided Tim's request that he take care of Heather and her. When she examined her heart, she had no hatred for Tim. She only wished him well.

In fact, God had dealt with her hidden hatred, softening her heart to love even her mother. They'd grown a little closer with each passing day and though no one would say they were stereotypically American, she knew they were family.

There was no shivering tonight. The warm spring air lay about her shoulders like a soft shawl.

"I've got a confession. The last time we were here, I almost kissed you." Kris's lopsided grin drew her closer.

"I might have let you. But since my sisters were just outside the door, probably spying, it's a good thing you didn't." She winked.

"We've been through a lot already. I think we've gotten to know each other's hearts. There's tons I want to say." He dragged his fingers through his hair, a sure sign he was nervous. "You know I'm not good with words. But you've brought out a strength in me to feel deeper, try harder. I can't imagine where I'd be if I never met you, Windy June Day. Your laughter blows away the fear inside, your belief in me raises up courage. We've waited for our time, and I think it's here." He dropped to one knee. "Will you marry me, Windy, and allow me to be Heather's father?"

He said the words.

She'd waited so long and now he said them. Joy sent off fireworks in her heart and her knees turned to jelly. Then she glanced at his hand. A simple solitaire diamond ring blinked through her tears, which turned her vision into prisms.

"Yes, Kristopher Jakob Norman, I will marry you and yes, you are Heather's father." She looped her arms about his neck as he rose, their lips meeting, her body rising, her feet dangling in the air.

He twirled her in a circle before standing her back on the floor.

She melted into his embrace, never wanting to leave the shelter of his arms.

Finally, he drew away. "Let me put this on you."

Windy held out her left hand and shivered with delight as the ring slipped onto her finger, the diamond continuing to sparkle in the fading light.

A bird chirped from a nearby branch.

She turned to spot a cardinal in another sycamore. "I think he's trying to tell us something."

Kris followed with his gaze where she pointed. "Could be." Then he pointed to the sky. "Look over there. The first star of the evening. Make a wish, baby."

She wrapped her arms about his waist and leaned into his hug. "Don't need to, Big Baby. They've all come true."

And in case he didn't understand, she kissed him again.

Acknowledgements:

Abba Father, thank you for the dream to write, the stories You whisper, and the amazing people you bring across my path. You know exactly what I need even before I do and no one tells a story the way You do—I hope I have shared it faithfully.

To my wonderful P.I.T. crew who prays me through each story keeping me accountable—Annie, Deb, Lori D., Julie, and Dorothy —you ladies must have callouses on your knees! Thank you! I love you all!

Thank you to my cover artist, London Montgomery. Another winner!

My Beta Readers and Street Team, you are such a huge support. Thank you! And extra thanks to Lisa Canton and Trudy Cordle who bent over backwards to help on this series.

Thank you to my Pencildancer friends—Jennifer Crosswhite, Diana Brandmeyer, Liz Tolsma, and Angela Breidenbach. You are all such amazing authors but even better friends. Thank you and I love you!

And speaking of Jennifer Crosswhite, my editor and friend. We've done it again! I get nuts before each launch but you talk me down and give me support. Plus our brainstorming sessions are the best! Couldn't do this without you, dear friend. Hugs!

My extraordinary family has stepped up their encouragement and support in this insane season—Phil, Jaime, Jonathan, Alyssa, Juan, Natalia, Meg, Mat, Owen, Kami, Mom, Amy, Rick, Rusty, Sandi, and all my extended loved ones. I couldn't do this without you all.

And, as always, E.B. I still miss you.

Author's Note

HERE WE ARE AGAIN, dear Reader, at the end of another series. I hope you've enjoyed getting to know the Day family and my hometown of Kokomo (from my faulty memories and not necessarily fact). It's so sweet to remember the good things about that amazing place.

A new location I dropped into this third story is Coney Island, a downtown restaurant back in the day, run by the Volikas family. Dino Volikas was a childhood friend from kindergarten through fourth grade. Later, we ended up at KHS where he was known as the Mad Greek on the football field, and a good-looking guy anywhere. Dino and his sisters were able to take the family business to a new location on the east end of town, renaming it after their father, Louie's Coney Island. I recently got word that our KHS class lost Dino. He'll be missed, and my deepest condolences go out to his family, especially his sisters, Maria and Tula.

If you are ever in the neighborhood, try a bake. It is delicious.

I also learned while writing this that my memory is terribly faulty. I remembered two movie theaters downtown and that one had burned. Turns out there were five or more theaters at one time, and the one that burned wasn't called the Oasis but the Sipe. The Oasis was a bar! Good grief! Fortunately, I chose to use the other name—the Isis. Soon after 1970, the Isis changed the type of films they showed so I didn't see a lot of movies downtown in my high school years.

By the way, if you were thinking "why use diaper pins on Pampers diapers?" there's a good reason. Up until 1970, there were no sticky tabs on the diapers. That was the year they introduced that concept. You could buy with the tabs for more money or without for less until they phased them out.

One last thing, if you've read *Relentless Heart*, you would have recognized some characters who dropped into this story. If you haven't read it, keep going to find the first chapter of my retelling of the book of Ruth, set in 1968 Viet Nam and a little made-up town just north of Kokomo—Breadville, Indiana.

Following that, I've included the first chapter of the first book in my newest series that I hope to release sometime in the spring of 2022—*Cheryl's Going Home*. The series title is *The Weather Girls Wedding Shoppe and Venue* and will feature Ferguson House (and the sycamore and the cardinal), but each book will be a stand-alone and titled from a 1960s- early 1970s song with a girl's name. *Cheryl's Going Home* is probably the least familiar title as it was supposed to be the A side of the release, but the B side is what became popular—"Elusive Butterfly" by Bob Lind. The song has been covered by many, including Sonny and Cher, but never gained much popularity. However, it's the perfect title for this next book which is Cheryl and Aaron's story. Other titles I plan to use are *Judy in Disguise*, *Sylvia's Mother*, and *Runaround Sue*, to name just a few. Hope you are as excited to read them as I am to write them.

Feel free to check out my website for the latest information. jenniferlynncary.com

Or scan here.

Abundant blessings,

Jenny

PS Keep reading to get sneak peeks of *Relentless Heart* and *Cheryl's Going Home.*

About the Author

Historical Christian romance author Jennifer Lynn Cary likes to say you can take the girl out of Indiana, but you can't take the Hoosier out of the girl. She is also a direct descendant of Davy Crockett, which along with her Indy upbringing, adds fodder to her sweet/clean books. She and her husband make their home in Arizona where she shares her tales of heritage and small-town life memories with her grandchildren.

You can contact Jennifer via her website www.jenniferlynncary.com

Sneak Peak of Relentless Heart

Prologue

The Oval Office, May 24, 2068

"HE'S READY FOR YOU."

Natalia Alaniz stood. Her heart pounded as she brushed a wrinkle from her skirt. After all the strides of this twenty-first century, why had no one invented a method to keep clothes from wrinkling? Did she look professional? She brushed the thought away with one more swipe and followed the secretary.

Breathless, Natalia pinched herself. Since childhood, she'd dreamed of this room. Old and new media often used this setting for broadcasts and photos. Yet standing in this place bathed her in surreal almost as much as the sunlight filtering through the floor-to ceiling windows. Her eyes roved from the ornate desk to the curved walls, landing on the Seal of the United States, emblazoned on the carpet at her feet.

"Your first time, I see."

Startled, she spun as another voice, the one in her ear, spoke, "Don't be too much the fan. Remember, you're the professional."

She held out her hand. "Mr. President. Thank you for seeing me."

Mr. David Joshua Salem, President of the United States, shook her hand, and guided her to the chairs set up, all in one motion. Natalia's mind screamed like a teenage groupie—*I'll never wash this hand again!* —while the voice in her ear brought her back to earth. "Breathe, smile, and make nice."

"You're correct, sir. This is my first assigned interview on-site outside of the Press Corps room. I'm sure it shows all over my face."

"Not at all. You are doing fine. You'd never believe how I behaved the first alone moment I had in here."

"Would you like to tell me about it?" She'd have an exclusive.

He shook his head and chuckled. "You are good. Almost let that secret out of the bag." He winked, taking the other chair.

"Well perhaps we can get started." She double checked her right earring. Her producer's voice came through loud and clear. Next, she touched the statement necklace that held the camera, waiting a second to hear the "looks good."

Last, she handed the tie clip to President Salem. He put it on. She gave him a thumbs-up as her producer expressed approval for the wireless reception.

"We're set." She paused, ignored her thumping heart, and began. "This is Natalia Alaniz, correspondent with CBS *Sunday Morning*, streaming live from the Oval Office. My guest today is President Salem. Good morning, Mr. President."

He leaned back, ever so slightly. "Good morning, Ms. Alaniz." Open, friendly.

One last glance at her bracelet of notes. For months she dreamed of and prepped for this moment. Now here it was. She took a breath. "You are concluding your first term in office and gearing up for a second. Overall, the American people seem to think they know you. Is that accurate?"

"Pretty much, yes, that is accurate. In this day and age, not much is hidden. The opposition has tried to expose my sins or faults. But what you see is what you get. I'd say I'm fairly transparent."

"Your military career is of public record, along with the heroic actions for which you received the Medal of Honor while serving in the Sudan War. I understand you come from a long line of warriors."

President Salem crossed his legs. "I guess you might say that. My father, grandfather, and great-grandfather all served in the military."

"How did their service impact you and your new program, Plows of Peace? How does it impact you as Commander-in-Chief?"

He chuckled. "I am who I am because of their choices as much as my own. The nucleus of Plows of Peace started many years ago in my family, eventually growing to include others from my hometown. We believed the time was ripe to present it on a bigger stage."

"Do you view Plows of Peace to be the Peace Corps of the twenty-first century? In some ways that might put you on level with President John Kennedy, wouldn't it?"

He sat straighter. "I don't see that. I just know POP, as we affectionately call it, has served many. By championing it with a national platform, the number of people helped grows exponentially."

"So, what was the nucleus for POP? How did this get started?"

He smiled. Memories twinkled in his eyes. "There was another warrior. She inspired the idea."

"Another? Who was she?"

He nodded and held out his hand. "Come, I'll show you." He led Natalia to a table behind his desk, picking up an old-fashioned double frame from a group of digital photos, two five-by-sevens hinged together. The left held a shot of an elderly Asian woman. Her smile tired, but gentle, nearly closed her eyes to thin lines. Strands of silver hair wisped about her face while the rest was pulled to the back. She appeared to be... Natalia couldn't guess. Her only thought was ancient.

The one in the other frame included the woman, though one could see she sat in a rolling chair—what they used to call a wheelchair. Now her smile was wide. A small child, perhaps preschool age, pushed the chair from behind. "This is my *Bà*." He rubbed his thumb over the rolling chair picture. "My great-grandmother." Pointing to the boy, he added, "That's my son, David Junior."

"He met his great, great-grandmother?" How could that be?

"Yes." He sighed. "She passed away not long after this. Bà lived to be 104 years old. I remember when it was taken. DJ says he remembers, too, though I'm not sure that it's her or the photo he recalls, but yes, they were great buddies."

This was something new. Excitement bubbled from her toes. And he seemed to want to talk. So, she nudged. "She's lovely, very sage like."

"She was. And she was more than determined. Not ruthless or anything negative, but her faith, the way she loved, it was strong, tenacious. You could say relentless." He replaced the frames.

"How do you mean?"

Mr. Salem motioned to the chairs. "To understand, you must go back one hundred years to a city once called Saigon."

PART ONE
Viet Nam

Chapter 1: How Can I Be Sure

Saigon, Viet Nam January 1, 1968

Hien gazed square into the eyes of the man whose hands held hers, the man whose eyes captured her heart. The heart that was about to pound out of her chest if his eyes didn't hold her captive. If she blinked, it would all fall apart.

And so would she.

"Michael Ryan Wheaten, do you take this woman to be your lawfully wedded wife? To have and to hold from this day forth, for richer or for poorer, in sickness and in health, 'til death do you part?"

"I do."

He said I do! *Heart, calm down!*

"Nguyen Han Hien, do you take this man to be your lawfully wedded husband? To have and to hold from this day forth, for richer or for poorer, in sickness and in health, 'til death do you part?"

Michael squeezed her hand.

She squeezed back. "I do." A tear etched its way down her cheek, plopping in a warm, wet blob on her new red *ao dai*, the traditional Vietnamese dress she bought for today.

Tears welled in his blue eyes too. He looked so handsome in his Air Force dress uniform.

"By the power vested in me by the United States of America, I now pronounce you man and wife. You may kiss your bride."

Michael's lips were on hers before she caught a breath. But how sweet to faint in those arms. More than a peck but not so much as to be embarrassing, they broke off the kiss together. He swept her off her feet.

"Oh! Michael."

He spun her around before planting her feet back on the ground.

Heat flooded her cheeks. Hien glanced at the man who performed the ceremony. The officer grinned. So did Michael's parents. Apparently, it was not too embarrassing.

His father, Minister Ernest Wheaten, a retired colonel, pulled her into an embrace. "Welcome to the family, Hien. You are now Hien Wheaten. Think you might get used to being a Wheaten?"

Hien nodded, whispering her new name in her brain. Yes, she could get used to anything with Michael by her side.

His mother, Melanie, hugged her, not as effusively as his father, but still warmly. "We're so happy for you two."

Then she was back in his arms.

With a new name.

And a new home.

So much new. But she could figure it all out with Michael.

⚓

That evening she lay curled in her husband's arms. He tucked a few wayward strands of long hair behind her ear. "We can't tell my mom yet. Dad plans this big surprise once we get out. Brother Charlie's enlistment won't be up for a while. He's already told me he wants to reenlist. He and Lai might settle down here, with her teaching and all. They're not sure." He sighed. "I'm rattling on."

"No, Michael. I love the sound of your voice. I want to just listen. Tell me more plans." Her finger made lazy circles on his sternum.

"You sure?"

She nodded, nuzzling next to his neck. His words flowed softer than the moonlight, filtered by the cherry tree leaves, through their balcony window. Their bed in the room he kept at his parents' in the embassy villa was only a single, but she had no complaints about sharing it tonight. Or any night.

"Okay, so the farm is near a little town called Breadville in Indiana. It's a few miles from Bunker Hill Air Force Base. Kokomo would be the nearest bigger town, I suppose. Peru's not far either. Mom and Dad came for a visit one time while I was stationed there, and we got talking about the future. Dad has wanted to retire to a farm like where he grew up, and I suppose I've always listened to his stories, because he's got me thinking that way too. We found this place close to some of Mom's family. The farmhouse is in good shape. It has all sorts of possibilities. My cousin is caring for it until we can get there. He lives close by, so he said he didn't mind. It will still need work, though."

Hien nodded into Michael's shoulder. She could do anything if they did it together.

"But here's the part you can't tell Mom." His finger made a slow trace from her temple to the base of her throat. "Dad is signing the farmhouse over to you and me as a wedding gift. He plans to build her a new house on another part of the property, but this way we won't have to inherit the farm. It'll be ours when we move back. Think you might enjoy being an Indiana farmer's wife?"

She nodded and nibbled his ear. As much as she loved his voice, it was time to stop talking.

※

"Morning, Hien! Glad you're back. Where've you been?" Nick Jones, a correspondent for a small newspaper in upstate New York, threw out the soliloquy as he dashed past. Hien figured out awhile back that he did not want answers unless he was sure it led to a story. If he wanted answers, he would pause to give you the opportunity. No pause, no real interest.

Today he didn't slow down. "Morning!" She plunged herself into the atmosphere of stale coffee and keyboard clacks and headed for her desk.

To call it a desk was a kind misnomer. Rather it was a disintegrating school desk with the attached seat removed. A metal pipe protruded where it once had been. However, it was perfect to stow any immediate work and a few belongings—a box of Kleenex tissues, two Bic pens, a stenographers pad, an extra tube of Slickers lip gloss (the only makeup she allowed herself because Michael liked how it tasted).

Hien did not mind. Her camera always stayed with her. Two or three spare rolls of film lay hidden in the Kleenex box, and that, as well as the rest of her treasures, remained stashed beneath the lift-up plywood board which served as a desktop, though it barely held on by the grace of one tiny hinge.

Unused film disappeared faster than they could replace it, unless you had the backing of a big media outlet. Hien's photos were for the independent market. There was no telling who might buy them. Film was a precious commodity not to be wasted. Out of habit, she felt inside the tissue box. The canisters were where she'd hid them.

She started with the Corps as a translator. Her English was fluent. In truth, it was extremely fluent, thanks to the Catholic school nuns who drilled the language into her and her brother. She gained a reputation for accuracy and an awareness of semantic subtleties.

One day, she brought her camera to an interview and snapped a shot. No other cameras were available. The correspondent she assisted grew excited for the photo. He did not care how amateurish it turned out.

It turned out better than amateurish. Hien's life changed.

Tony Bennett crooned from someone's radio, extolling that for once in his life he had love and hope. Hein understood. He sang her story.

Had it only been a year since she left her family in Hué? One year. She went from a daughter to a working woman, from translator to photographer, from single to married. Her two-week-old ring glittered like the candle in the little paper boat she sent sailing down the Houng River last Tet, filled with wishes for the new life she would start the following week in Saigon. The river gleamed that night with all the tiny New Year boats sailing off into the future.

Funny, in two weeks it again would be the New Year—Tet. What would this New Year bring? Perhaps she would become a mother. She and Michael might start their family. Four more weeks and he would be done flying sorties over jungles. They could leave Viet Nam. She would say goodbye to everything familiar, more than when she left Hué for Saigon. But the excitement tantalized. Her destiny lay on the other side of the ocean. She was sure.

Indiana, what a strange name! She shook her head.

Hien checked the schedule for the darkroom. Someone got there before her. Too much daydreaming. She knocked, inquiring how long the wait.

Of course, she could fly to Hué. When she lived there, she built her own darkroom in the bathroom of her parents' apartment building. People knocked on the door there too. But it was a four-hour flight.

She missed that world—her family, the city, her home. Never did she expect to return to it. Yet, her family was there.

Her family.

She sighed. Her family had not attended her wedding. They sent word that it was too dangerous to travel.

At least, that is the reason they gave.

Hien shrugged and knocked again.

"Almost done. Five minutes."

"Okay." What could she do but wait? She leaned against a table cluttered with dirty paper coffee cups, crumbs, and dried smeared something.

Mat Morrissey shouldered past to grab the schedule clipboard, grunted as he perused, and tossed it back onto the file cabinet. "Hien, you gotta let me in ahead of you. I think I've got something. Something big."

"Like what?"

"I'm not sure. You know that niggle when you know something, but you're unsure what it is?"

Hien nodded. She did not know, but she knew Mat. He could not let go of this any more than her brother's dog could let go of a bone. "Fine, you may come in with me. I will share my time, but you must tell me what you learned."

Mat hesitated. "Deal. But I've got the scoop. Right?"

"Deal."

Mat checked his watch, then pounded on the door. "C'mon, Riley! You're holding up the show!"

The voice behind the door called back. "Gimme a sec, Morrissey! Geez Louise!" Usually the language was saltier, but Hien was sure Steve Riley realized she was there and controlled himself.

Finally, the lock clicked, and the door opened.

"About time, man!" Mat pushed through.

"Hey, you can't rush perfection!" Steve waved a sheaf of photos. "And, you're welcome."

"You coming, Hien?"

"Coming, Mat." She smiled at Steve as she hurried past and shut the door fixing the lock which would keep others from coming in and destroying their work. Steve left the safe light on. "Where were you shooting?"

Mat opened the small film canisters. "I was over by Hué last evening. Just got back. There's this feel in the air. Something's not right. That city used to be so beautiful, even the atmosphere. The one place the war overlooked. Now it's like walking into the opening of a suspense movie."

"What do you mean?"

He shrugged, the red glow casting eerie shadows on his face. "Like nothing is out of place, yet something is. It's a sensation I can't shake. I swear, if Alfred Hitchcock stepped out from behind a tree, I wouldn't have been surprised. Terrified, yeah, but surprised, no."

Hien's heart climbed its way up her throat. "My family is there."

"Oh, sorry." Mat's gaze met hers and then returned to his work. He was reconsidering his bargain.

"I remember the area well. Perhaps I can see something."

"Perhaps." He didn't raise his head.

They worked in silence until Mat had his second roll developed. "Man, I thought for sure there was something. I'm just not seeing it."

"Let me look." Hien started with the first photo hanging from the drying line. A teenage girl on a bicycle. She studied the next. Then the next. Bicycle girl was not the only human photographed, but the manner in which she showed in different places... and she was only in maybe eight shots? But Hien could see it, rather sense whatever it was Mat meant. But she could not put a name to it either. "The city looks weird, different." The fear she had pushed away reared.

"Yeah. There's a curfew in effect for the locals. They don't get far from home that late in the evening. This isn't even inside the

Citadel. I took these in the Triangle district, just south of the river. Still, I can't shake the eeriness. What does it mean? Have they gone underground or are they following orders? And why was that girl in those places?

Hien shook her head, reviewing each shot. It was where she grew up. It was where her mother lived. Mat developed sixty photos altogether and only eight of the girl—a girl she had never seen—but in a different locale each time. Who was she? What happened to her beautiful city? "What is this?"

Mat searched where she showed.

The girl did something near a doorway. What? "Hand me a magnifying glass, please."

He grabbed one from the table.

She peered closer, pointing to a shadow in the doorway next to the girl. Was she talking with someone? Was it supposed to be secret? It made no sense. Huế was beloved by both the north and the south. Battles raged near it, but neither side wanted to desecrate the Imperial City. Plus, the cease fire for Tet was just around the corner.

She must see for herself. "Can you get me there?"

"Not a good idea."

"I must go. I need to see this."

Mat shook his head. "I can't take you there. Not without some kind of security team. Your new husband would kill me deader than dead."

"If you will not take me, I will go on my own." New husband or not, she almost added. Michael was on call for a flight today, anyway. He would not learn of this before she returned tonight.

Mat paused. His eyes gave him away before he spoke. "This is against my better judgment, but there's a guy who owes me. Let's go."

Hien returned her film canisters to her purse for another time and grabbed her camera before Mat changed his mind.

"C'mon, Hien, the sooner we leave, the sooner we can get back to Saigon."

⚿

The immense cargo hold of the C-130 Hercules allowed no room for conversation. The plane's four engines roared loud enough to silence the most talkative. That left Hien running scenarios in her mind and asking herself questions she had no information with which to answer. Mat appeared calm, from the waist up. The rhythm of his right knee bouncing the entire flight belied him.

The second they rolled to a stop, he was out of his seat, heading for the cockpit.

"When do you need to take off?"

The pilot, Capt. Juan Andrade, shrugged. "This is a turnaround flight. Just long enough to unload."

"Can you give us an hour?"

"An hour, yeah, I'll stretch it that far. But, if you're not back, I'm not waiting."

Hien grabbed Mat's arm, speaking in his ear. "Tell him not to leave us!"

"She says don't leave us."

Juan shrugged again. "Then be back in an hour." He returned his attention to the controls.

"We'd better move. I'll get a vehicle." Mat climbed out and ran for the operations shack, leaving Hien to dismount the plane on her own.

She followed, only to have him return, running with keys in hand.

"Let's go." He grabbed her elbow, steering her toward a jeep on the edge of the runway. They both jumped in, he started it up, and they were on their way into the city. Hien gave him directions to her parents' apartment building. That was the easiest place to start.

Fifteen minutes later, they pulled in front. Everything looked the same, though different. The tree outside her old bedroom window appeared taller. The flowers in the pot beside the door bore a different color. A neighbor she did not recognize swept the stoop of the adjacent building. Her heart did a little twist. This must be the definition of bittersweet.

Clambering out, she motioned for Mat to follow, and ran to her parents' door, what used to be her door. She tried her old key, but it did not work. She reinserted it, trying again. It would not turn. Hien left the key in the lock and knocked. "*Mẹ, chính là con.*" She called to her mother. Now she heard her brother's dog, Bao, barking from the back of the apartment. Surely someone was there. Bao grew quiet. She knocked again. "I do not understand, Mat. Mother should be here."

Mat tapped her shoulder, put his finger to his lips, and pointed down.

A small piece of paper stuck from the threshold. The folded sheet moved, sliding further out. She stooped to retrieve and opened it. Only three scrawled words.

Rời khỏi, Ngụy

Get your copy of *Relentless Heart* here:

https://www.amazon.com/dp/B085X2GZ67

Or scan here.

Sneak Preview of Cheryl's Going Home

Book One of The Weather Girls Wedding Shoppe and Venue Series

Chapter 1

Saturday, October 9, 1971

Kokomo, Indiana

THE MUSIC ABRUPTLY CHANGED. Cheryl Day glanced up to see her youngest daughter headed her direction.

Windy beamed with her long white-blond hair crowned in a wreath of baby's breath as she floated toward her. Cheryl's grown-up little girl was dressed in a soft ivory gown of antique lace while the autumn-colored decorations of the carriage house cast a by-gone-era feel to the lovely wedding reception.

The last of her daughters to marry, it meant another span of Cheryl's life drew to a close. She'd missed far too much. Thank God she didn't miss this.

It was then she realized Windy wasn't looking at her but past her. Over Cheryl's shoulder. She turned to spot her ex-husband, Aaron.

He raised his head and caught Windy's grin, returning one of his own.

The song, the look, the outstretched hand. Now it made sense. Time for the father-daughter dance.

Cheryl blinked her eyes to abate the tears. She wasn't a father. Dancing with her daughter at this wedding was a right belonging to Windy's dad. It had nothing to do with Cheryl. No need to get all weepy. She pulled a hankie from her clutch and stuffed half a stick of Juicy Fruit in her mouth.

"The Way You Look Tonight" drifted from the speakers while Aaron twirled their youngest onto the dance floor, holding her with practiced skill and guiding her through the four-four time. He always was a great dancer.

There was a time they'd danced great together. Drat, not where her thoughts needed to meander.

The tears returned but this time for the beauty, the poignancy of what she viewed. She'd watched the same thing unfold a few months ago when their eldest, Sunny, married. Back then Cheryl had just started making inroads toward healing with their relationships. By now, she'd hoped she wouldn't be so much the outsider. Yet, still she watched, almost like an audience member while the play unfolded on stage. Always the voyeur, never a part. It had been too much to hope.

If she could only get through this test, maybe she'd finally believe she'd quit smoking for good. She chewed harder on the gum.

"Looks like they've done this before."

Cheryl startled at the speaker who had rolled up next to her in a motorized wheelchair. His oxygen hose was hooked over his ears and snugged beneath his chin. Windy's new father-in-law. She masked her surprise and nodded. "Yes, Aaron always did like to dance with his girls. When they were little, he had them stand on his feet." The words sparked a memory and it made her wince.

"I guess you and I were meant to watch. Kris will dance with Ellen next." His voice sounded melancholy despite his smile.

"The kids are excited that you were able to make it to the wedding." Cheryl decided to attempt conversation, for the sake of her daughter and to steer things toward a cheerier topic. "How long do you get to stay?"

"We leave for home in the morning. The girls need to get back to school on Monday." He sighed. "I'm just glad to see Kris is doing well. Dad had told me, but I needed to see for myself. And I think he chose well with your Windy. She's a lovely girl."

"Thank you." The compliment warmed her cheeks and neck. There was nothing she could lay claim to that had any bearing on Windy or her sisters turning out as wonderful as they did. Still why unlock the family's skeleton closet, especially on this beautiful Indian Summer evening?

The song ended and the dancers embraced while Aaron dropped a kiss on Windy forehead. So sweet it squeezed her heart. They looked like they could be centered in a musical snow globe, waiting for someone to wind it up and start the dancing all over again. Just so Cheryl could watch.

The next song, "Try to Remember" brought her new son-in-law, Kris, out to the dance floor with his mother. He wasn't as adept as Aaron, she noted, but she doubted Kris's mom cared about that. Ellen gazed up at her tall handsome son and chuckled at something he'd whispered at her ear.

A short while later the new Mr. and Mrs. Norman cut their cake followed by Windy tossing her bouquet. Sunny's sister-in-law caught it. Cheryl had a feeling it was planned, especially when she spotted her middle daughter, Stormy, next to the girl with her hand at her back.

Everyone one returned to their tables for the toasts. The best man, Sunny's new husband Pat, and the matron of honor, Sunny, started them off. Then Aaron made a toast followed by Kris's father...What was his name again? Too much to remember and she had enough on her mind with the champagne so close. But her water glass would have to do.

Soon the event drew to a close. Thank heavens. Not that it wasn't wonderful—it was—but between the pinching shoes and the flood of memories that drenched her in shame, Cheryl was ready to get home and be by herself. As if anyone would miss her if she headed over now.

No, one of the girls might look for her. So she'd stick around to the bitter end. Her bitter end. Everyone else was having a blast. The way it should be.

Sunny wandered over carrying eleven-month-old Heather. She and Pat were babysitting while Windy and Kris went on their honeymoon. Heather was getting squirmy and looking about for her mother.

Stormy followed holding her six-week-old baby boy, Bobby, who slept with a milky look of satisfaction on his sweet face. "These cutie pies sure hung in there today. Not bad for as little as they are."

"Ah, my angels." Cheryl reached for Bobby as Heather made a grab for her. "Hang on, lovey. I can hold you both." She tucked Bobby in with her left arm and scooped Heather up with her right. Then she buried her nose in the little girl's white-blond hair, so like her mother's.

"They sure love their me-maw." Aaron startled her from behind, putting a hand on her shoulder while he made silly faces with Heather.

Did he really mean that? Well, they were babies. They had no clue about her shattered past, the mental illness she'd worked so hard to overcome.

Or how his touch sent shock waves up her spine.

Sunny cleared her throat. "We're all going to head to Gramma and Gene's after this. Our crew can get the important stuff done. Stormy and I will finish up the rest after church tomorrow."

Her daughter's look told her she was expected to make an appearance. For her girls, she would. Whatever it took to rebuild the relationships. "Are you sure I can't help you put things away?" Keeping busy always helped.

"No but thank you. We've got the kids well trained." Sunny hired the youth group from church as wait staff and clean-up crew to help fund activities. "They'll have the tables and chairs put up fast. Then it's a matter of sweeping and hauling the dishes to the kitchen. I made an extra key for Thea. She's going to supervise and lock up. The rest can wait for tomorrow." Thea Carpenter was the newest addition to the staff and a godsend considering the rest of the employees were part of the wedding party.

"Then, if you don't mind, I think I'll run next door and change clothes before heading for Hazel and Gene's." She ended with an unspoken question.

"Sure, great idea. I might get out of these shoes while I can too." Sunny smiled and headed out of the carriage house toward her home—Ferguson House. She and Pat lived above the business, The Weather Girls Wedding Shoppe and Venue, in the beautiful Victorian.

"Then, if you'll excuse me." She handed Bobby back to Stormy.

Heather struggled reaching out to Aaron. Yup, he's the favorite again. And she hadn't even screwed up with this baby. Yet. Drat his magic touch.

She shook her head to loosen the clinging thought and trudged next door. Her apartment was actually the top floor of the small neighboring Victorian that Pat purchased when he left his corporate law practice in Indianapolis to open his own defense firm on the bottom floor. He'd lived upstairs until he and Sunny married but once the space was vacant, it was the perfect place for Cheryl so she no longer had to live in her former mother-in-law's home. Not that Hazel wanted her to move out, but living alone was a way of life anymore. And she valued her privacy.

Getting into something presentable yet comfortable wasn't nearly the battle as was convincing herself to go meet with her family. Sometimes it was simply overwhelming. They'd call her Sarah Bernhardt if they knew what raced through her mind.

But for her girls, she'd make an appearance.

Charged with that determination, Cheryl headed out to what served has her car—a 1957 Renault. Scraping together the cash for it had been a challenge. Keeping it running proved to be another —all she could afford was chewing gum, duct tape, and prayer.

She slipped behind the wheel and turned the key. At first there was a click-click. "C'mon, Pierre. You can do it." But after a few more tries, even the clicks grew silent. She sunk her forehead onto the steering wheel. Now what? She could walk, but the walk home would be dark and chilly. It wouldn't be the first time she'd walked alone after dark but that was supposed to be in her past.

She heaved another breath and tried again. Tapping on driver-side frame caused her heart to skip. "Oh!"

Aaron stood there, motioning for her to crank down her window.

She did. "You scared ten years off me."

"You can fight with it, or I can give you a ride." He peeked in as if seeing the inside of her car for the first time. In all likelihood, it was his first glimpse.

"I don't want to impose."

He opened his mouth to say something and closed it just as fast. Paused, then tried again. "No imposition. We're going to the same place."

"That's where you're staying. I still have to come back here." She didn't want to be alone with him any more than he must want to be alone with her. Truth was he made her nervous.

"It's not as if you live across town. Come on, Cheryl. We can do this."

Even though his words propelled her to give in and try it his way, she doubted either of them believed what he said.

⚓

AARON ALMOST CHUCKLED to himself but knew Cheryl would catch him. Offering her a ride to his mother's house was no biggie. Besides, talking with Cheryl used to be fun.

Only now there wasn't a lot of talking. She practically hugged her door for the five-minute drive. Did he really make her that uncomfortable? Did he really need to ask himself that question?

He turned into the driveway, just barely keeping his backend from hanging out onto the sidewalk. The one-lane driveway was long, and everyone had pulled in ahead of him. Apparently, they were the last to arrive. Guess it was a good thing he needed to drive Cheryl back home so the other cars could get out.

Aaron rounded his rental to open her door.

She looked stunned.

"What?" He'd always opened her door for her. It was how he was raised. Why was that so shocking?

She shrugged and looked away as she climbed out.

Now he was nervous. Dare he guide her with his hand at the small of her back? *Be yourself, Day. You don't need to second guess every move.*

Though the old house had a big porch, it also had several steps leading up to it. Not a big deal normally, but Gene's son—Kris's dad—was in a wheelchair. Kris built a ramp giving a new look to the old house.

They found everyone in the dining room. Mom was pouring coffee and plates of cookies were being passed around.

His mother glanced up after topping off Rob's mug. "Hey, you made it. Wondered where you were."

Aaron kept his hand at Cheryl's back. Somehow, he had the impression she'd turn and bolt if he didn't. Well, there was precedent.

They slipped into chairs, the only two left at a very full table.

Frank, Gene's son—who was now his Windy's father-in-law—had his wheelchair wedged in at the table. It was a tad strange that Mom's new husband—okay, so they've been married a little over a year—was the grandfather of Aaron's newest son-in-law. Talk about a close-knit family. But that was how Windy and Kris met, through Gene. And he'd been very good for Mom, so Aaron wasn't about to complain.

Kris's sisters seemed excited to have been part of the wedding party, chatting with Sunny and Stormy like long lost friends. They'd been junior bride's maids and lit the candles before the ceremony.

Rob held Bobby and Gene bounced little Heather on his knee. Took all of Aaron's reserve to not reach for her. That little princess had wound herself around his heart the moment he met her. So like Windy at that age. Did Cheryl remember?

"Oh no!"

All talk ceased and gazes turned toward Sunny.

"What's the matter?" Stormy voiced for all of them.

"The microphones. We borrowed some from the church because we thought ours had died at the last minute, remember? Pastor said we could use them if we returned them right after because they're needed tomorrow for the service. But Rob got ours working and I forgot to get them back."

Her eyes scanned the group until she got to him.

And he knew his little girl hoped he'd help. "Where are they?"

"They're in the back of the car. We've got to run. Gramma, can you call to let someone know to meet us at the church so we can return them?"

"Sure, honey."

Aaron stopped her. "Hang on a second. You're blocked in. Just give them to me and I'll..." He glanced at Cheryl. "We'll drop them off."

Cheryl peeked up, her forehead furrowing while her eyes grew large.

He winked at her. "We'll do it. Mom, make the call. Sunny, let's get them out of your trunk. Cheryl, you don't mind, do you?" He'd put her on the spot, but an idea was forming.

"Ah, no. I, um..." She stood.

They'd avoided being alone for the past year, always making nice. Easy to do when he lived in LA and only visited on occasion.

As much as he'd tried to help ease Cheryl's path toward getting back with the girls, there's only so much he could do. Holding onto the bitterness got him nowhere—and yes, he still had moments. But his girls needed their mom. He knew it. It wasn't a matter of picking out a replacement. For better or worse, Cheryl was their mother. They needed to accept and move forward.

He held out his hand. "Ready?"

She glanced about before allowing him to assist her through the obstacle course of chairs. "As I'll ever be." Her Texan twang still colored her speech after all these years.

They followed Sunny out to Pat's Mustang where she popped the trunk and handed over the microphones.

Then they climbed in his rental and were off to Wabash Community Church.

"Why did you need me to come along?" Cheryl's question broke the silence of the first mile.

He shrugged. "I'm your ride."

"I know better than that. Besides, with Sunny and Pat living next door, I could've asked them."

"But you wouldn't. Your pride wouldn't let you." Yeah, he knew her well enough to figure that.

"Oh."

They pulled into the parking lot and the pastor waited at his car. He got out as Aaron shut off his engine.

"Thank you for returning the mics this evening. I guess I could have taken them when I left the party, but it looked like things were still going strong, and I had to get home to put the finishing touches on tomorrow's message." Pastor Mussing smiled as he bridged the distance between the cars.

Aaron retrieved the box and handed it over. "We appreciate you letting us borrow them. It all went off the way Windy hoped. Thanks again."

"Good, good. So, I'll be seeing you tomorrow, right Aaron?" He bent and peeked in the window. "You, too, Cheryl."

Aaron nodded and glanced at his passenger. She'd pasted a smile on her face and mimicked his nod. "Good night, Pastor. And thanks again."

"Goodnight."

After Pastor Mussing headed inside the church, Aaron put his car into drive and pulled out, sneaking a peek at Cheryl. "Guess we got told. I'm not leaving until Monday afternoon anyway, and you know Mom."

She chuckled. "Yeah, I do. I'll need to figure out a ride until I get my car fixed."

"I'll come get you."

"No need. Sunny is next door and Stormy across the street."

Aaron glanced her way. "Didn't we just establish that you most likely won't ask? It's no imposition and will make my mom happy." He took a left onto Sycamore and headed west. "And when Hazel Day is happy, life is sweeter."

"Where are we going?" She stared his way, her voice growing tense.

"Thought we might grab some coffee."

"There's coffee at your mother's house."

Aaron kept driving. "Probably all gone by now. Besides, the dining room was stuffed to capacity."

He saw her jaw working something—he'd bet money it was Juicy Fruit—and figured her nerves were taut enough to pluck like a guitar. He knew better than to push her. "There's a restaurant I discovered a few years back on one of my trips home. I like to take the girls out, one at a time to give them undivided attention. They each got a turn per trip. This place was one of Windy's favorites. It's called *Krieg's Sycamore Village Inn*." He braved another glance before pulling into the parking lot. "Have you checked out many of the places around town?"

She shook her head. "No, not so much. Watching the babies keeps me busy enough."

He didn't really believe her. Not Cheryl Ann Webb, the starlet he once knew. She was head-over-heels in love with life. Or was when they married. But then, she'd spiraled into that hole and trapped herself in their bedroom for days on end. Was she heading for another fall through the depression looking glass? One more reason not to push too hard.

"Are you doing okay?" If there was going to be a problem, he'd better be prepared.

She glanced over, her eyes unreadable. "I'm fine. Taking it one day at a time." Her jaw worked harder on the gum.

That put an end to that line of questioning. He braked into the parking spot.

The hostess showed them to a table leaving menus while she filled water glasses.

"The sugar cream pie is wonderful." He peeked over the top of his menu to catch her reaction.

"Oh, Aaron, you still have a sweet tooth? I can't imagine what with all we had at the wedding. How do you do it, staying so lean and eating all those calories?" She chuckled and it was like music. At least she'd relaxed a little.

Her voice had deepened with maturity, but he was betting her cigarettes also contributed. Speaking of which, he hadn't seen her light up once since she replopped in their lives. Back in the day she thought it made her look more sophisticated. He wasn't fond of it. Maybe she had quit.

"No idea where it goes, just grateful for not having to buy all new threads." He winked. "What looks good to you?"

Cheryl sighed and set the menu on the table. "I know better. But you talked me into the pie."

"We could split a piece. Then you wouldn't have to worry so much."

There was a startling in her eyes, for the briefest of moments, before she nodded. "Sure. Okay. Good idea." Was she afraid sharing a dessert would cross some line? Oh, the questions he wanted to ask her.

The waitress arrived to take their order. She acted miffed at first that they weren't ordering more. Poor kid. Probably lived on her tips. But she did end with a smile and brought the pie with two forks and two cups of black coffee.

Aaron added a spoonful of sugar to his and then another—because he could—and allowed Cheryl the first bite, after she'd wrapped her gum in a piece of napkin.

"Oh, you're right. This is really good. Glad I didn't get my own or I'd have eaten the whole thing." Her eyes closed as she slowly pulled the fork from her lips of her second bite.

"You will save some for me, right?"

"Don't count on it. You should've warned me." She winked.

"If I remember correctly, I'm the one who told you it was wonderful." *In fact, I've told you a lot of things you didn't seem to believe.* Aaron cut a forkful for himself and enjoyed it almost as much as he enjoyed watching Cheryl's pleasure with the treat.

Stop. This would only open old wounds. "So, tell me what you've been up to."

She paused, eying him as if for motive. "I'm watching the babies while the girls run their business. Heather is getting active and will be walking any time soon. Makes me nervous about the stairs but I've got a gate at the top, so we pretty much stay on the second floor. Besides, during business hours, I never know when Pat will have a client, so I need to keep away from that part of the house."

"That's not what I was asking. What about the eleven years before this one?" It was out before he stopped himself. He was pushing again, but he couldn't help it.

Even though she'd been in town now for nearly a year, they'd never had an alone moment. Too many questions remained bottled inside and he'd waited as long as he could.

"You don't want to hear about all that."

"Yeah, I do." He reached for her hand.

She pulled back so fast she knocked her spoon to the floor, and she slipped beneath the table to retrieve it.

And to be away from him.

He shouldn't have tried. But it was important. And if he were honest with himself, she still had some power over him. He wasn't out to judge, just get some answers. Finally.

"Hey, Aaron, good to see you. What brings you to town?" Marshall North stood at their table.

"Oh, Marshal, hi. Our daughter Windy got married this afternoon. Have you met my wife?" She popped up like a Jack-in-the-box, eyes big and round. "Cheryl, this is Marshall North, who among other things directs productions for the Kokomo Civic Theatre."

Cheryl's face blanched the moment she straightened from fetching the utensil. But she didn't let that hold her back and extended her hand. "It's lovely to meet you, Marshall."

"Same here. You look familiar. Cheryl...You aren't Cheryl Ann Webb, are you? Aaron, you never said you were married to a movie star." Marshall covered her hand with both of his. "You know I'm always recruiting for our group. Are you staying in town a while?"

"She is, I'm not. Gotta fly back tomorrow." Did no good to tell the man that. His back was turned to Aaron while he stared into Cheryl's eyes, still holding her hand.

"Well then Cheryl, come check us out. We've just cast our current production, but we'll be having tryouts again soon. Oh!" Marshall snapped his fingers and posed as if he'd just discovered method acting. "Our spring musical is *Applause*. You'd be perfect for Margo Channing."

Cheryl shook her head. "Thank you for offering. I look forward to seeing your shows, but I think for now I belong in the house rather than on the stage." She slipped her hand from his.

"Think about it. I'd better get going. The family's waiting in the car. Nice meeting you, Cheryl. Take care, Aaron." He headed out the front door.

"You really don't want to do any acting?" That was a shocker. He thought she lived for the spotlight.

She shook her head again, keeping her hands in her lap. "I've worked hard at my..." Her eyes grew wide again, and he could tell she'd almost shared something private. But she recovered and met his gaze. "And I'm not your wife."

* * *

Look for *Cheryl's Going Home* to release in 2022.

Made in United States
Orlando, FL
12 November 2021

10375983R00163